The Talent

The Talent

A Novel

Daniel D'Addario

SCOUT PRESS

New York Amsterdam/Antwerp London Toronto Sydney New Delhi

Scout Press
An Imprint of Simon & Schuster, LLC
1230 Avenue of the Americas
New York, NY 10020

First Scout Press hardcover edition February 2025

Interior design by Kathryn A. Kenney-Peterson

Manufactured in the United States of America

10 9 8 7 6 5 4 3 2 1

Library of Congress Cataloging-in-Publication Data is available.

ISBN 978-1-6680-7547-0
ISBN 978-1-6680-7549-4 (ebook)

To Jacob

The Talent

"I want to be seen; to be understood—deeply; and to be not so very lonely."

—Jodie Foster

"AND THE AWARD GOES TO . . ."

Adria Benedict sat upright in her seat, squared her shoulders, lowered her brow so that the camera wouldn't quite be able to read her gaze. Instinctively clasped her hands, then after a moment unclasped them. She worried that they might look too much like a prayer, or a balled fist. Smiled gently as she could, but was sure not to show her teeth. She'd been here before. Won three times. She could get through tonight. She could win again.

Bitty Harbor was certain she'd sweated through the dress that the fashion brand had picked out for her, but a surreptitious glance down—the kind of ducking her chin that would read as a gesture of humility, so that was good—revealed that it was all in her head. The gown looked pristine. What felt like fabric grabbing greedily at her skin would read on-camera like the way a dress was supposed to fit her body. She found her publicist's hand without looking, willed herself not to start crying until the presenter said her name.

Contessa Lyle grinned. People would pick apart her reaction if she didn't. Lately, things had been going so well for her—as far as everyone knew. Nothing worth looking stressed about. She willed herself not to look at her costars. Not now. She could thank them from the stage. And for one of them, she'd actually mean it.

Davina Schwartz suppressed the urge to roll her eyes. A few more seconds, and this would all be over. Either way. And she would get the chance to walk away from this place she'd thought, for a foolish moment, might be hers to keep.

Jenny Van Meer looked into the middle distance. She'd realized something, something she didn't want to admit. Her eyes grew unfocused before she shook her head, brought herself back. She looked back at the presenter to see if her sense of what was coming was correct.

The envelope tore.

From "The Power of Partnership," cover story
in a fashion magazine's September issue

IT'S HARD TO BELIEVE THAT THERE'S ANYTHING ADRIA BENEDICT STILL HAS LEFT ON HER CAREER TO-DO LIST.

She's the first to admit—with the trademark self-effacement fans have come to love—that, from an unending string of iconic leading roles to an awards shelf groaning under the weight of trophies, she's had a blessed career. "I can't deny that I've been fortunate," she says over tea service on a recent sun-dappled Friday afternoon in Los Angeles. "But it's all about the work, of course."

Spoken like—well, like Adria Benedict. But now, the woman whom countless movie lovers have grown up watching is extending a bridge to the next generation of actresses. In the new film *Who Is Lisa Farmer?*, to be released this fall after a festival run, she stars as the therapist to a young woman with schizophrenia, played by rising star Delle Deane. Benedict is classically enigmatic about her process (she's never been one to explain how she arrives at her remarkable performances). But watching the film, one feels Benedict's deep connection to the material.

Nurturing comes as easily to her onscreen as it does at teatime with Deane, her colleague—and her new friend. "Please, Delle, don't let me talk about myself anymore," she says, gently touching the cowl neck of her sweater. "And tell me which of these pastries you'd like to split." She looks up, guileless eyes revealing admiration, even love. "Listen to me. In mother mode. Could it be clearer that Delle became . . ." She pauses. Like moviegoers the world over, I find myself hanging on Adria Benedict's next word.

". . . became," she continues, her voice suddenly thick

with appreciation, "like another daughter to me?"

Deane, clad in her trademark punky ripped jeans and leather jacket, picks a cream puff, and can't wait to take a bite before effusing about her colleague. "Adria isn't like any actor I've ever met!" Deane says, slugging Benedict lightly in the arm before reaching for her cup of oolong to wash down the pastry. "Every day I learned from watching how Adria works. Just the mood she creates on a set—it's like nothing else."

And Benedict returns the compliment. "You asked me earlier what I still want," she says, with a familiar chuckle. "Well, to see all three of my children happy, of course. My real children." At this, she laughs again, then gathers herself. "And to maintain my health, and keep getting these opportunities."

She pauses, and a faraway look enters her eyes—thinking, perhaps, of all she's surmounted in her rise from the New York City stage, and all that there's still left to do as she nears her seventies. "But I do also want to be sure that I do a good job helping this younger generation. As best I can, I want to support Delle, because—well, we taught each other. She was such a terrific support." She smiles, clearly relishing memories of their time together.

"Yes," she goes on, reaching for the half of the cream puff Delle has left on the plate for her, then hesitating, grabbing an untouched eclair instead. She holds it neatly in her hand, contemplating its weight, before finishing her thought. "Yes. That's it. Delle Deane is the kind of supporting actress one dreams of."

Adria Benedict, *Who Is Lisa Farmer?*

EVERYONE CRIES UPON DESCENT.

Well, *almost* everyone. That was what Adria Benedict's agent had told her about the plunge she would take the Friday before Labor Day as she landed at her destination, a small mountain-town airport whose single runway was carved into the side of one of the Rockies. Moving safely from the clouds to this perch required a steep angle, a dexterous pilot, and passengers more afraid of missing the film festival than of death upon impact.

Adria had no real complaints about the mechanics of the flight so far. Indeed, it had been effortless, even the car trip out to the airport in Van Nuys. That journey, familiar enough by now, she tried to bear with grace, lending the driver a smile about which he might tell his wife, assuming she, like most women, had seen Adria's movies. The supposed fearsomeness of the journey's end had only entered Adria's considerations as a sort of spur for her to do it. Adria knew she was getting too easy to goad, but there was still a simple, desserty pleasure to the conversation she'd had with Howard, her long-suffering agent, about how frightening the flight was, a preemptive sense that this was yet another challenge she'd surmount.

"They all do. *Weeping*, I tell you," he'd continued, in their debrief over the phone a couple of days prior, running through the obligations she'd have to fulfill on her trip to the mountains.

Adria had made a tell-me-more pout into the phone receiver. She had come to believe, on some level, that her facial expressions carried with them a sort of crackling electricity that could be communicated over great distances through the wires, or through the air. Plus, Bill was in the next room, solving crosswords with cable news on mute, just as he did most evenings, and Adria didn't like him to overhear her being competitive.

"You shouldn't take me down this road," Howard went on, continuing a game he'd honed over decades with Adria. "But a couple of years ago? Remember that terrible movie Jenny was in?"

"Jenny Van Meer?" Adria asked, glimmering with incredulity.

"The very one. She went to the festival for that film about a sheep... lady—a, you know, a shepherdess."

(Adria did know; Jenny Van Meer had, surprisingly, failed even to get a nomination for *Judith of the Ewes*, which she'd told the press had been a special passion project of hers. But then, they all were for Jenny, weren't they.) "I really shouldn't say this, but she screamed as the wheels touched the tarmac. We're talking full-on, blood-curdling *acting*."

"A shame the voters couldn't have seen that." Adria chuckled into the phone. Before Howard could respond, she blurted, "Oh no, now, I never said that." She tried to allow herself one open cruelty only in a very great while, and only in close company; flaunting her own good fortune was not what Adria Benedict did. She had already triumphed over Jenny so many times. And she would once more, as she greeted the runway with crystalline stillness. She wondered if they'd let her keep the cup of tea she planned to order, so that she might sip it as the plane plunged. It would be a performance only she'd know she'd given, but there was a secret joy to that.

♦ ♦ ♦

SHE KNEW SHE OUGHT TO BE A LITTLE LESS, WELL, PRIVATE ON this private jet. This flight was, after all, her big opportunity to get what she wanted out of Delle and the director. And that awful man from the studio too—no, the *streamer*. But she could work him easily enough. Delle, her costar (her supporting actress, assuming they all came to agree that Adria was in fact the star of their shared film), had been sitting near her, on a couch directly opposite, and Adria had given her a nod and a half-smile, reserving the full arsenal of her charm for some hypothetical other traveler who hadn't held up the flight by being twenty minutes late to the tarmac.

After some brief conversation, during which Adria flipped through her phone—no word from Bill, who'd already headed to the office before Adria woke up, and no word from Lindy about Thanksgiving—they mutually decided to enjoy their reading material. Adria had kept herself from being caught looking at Delle. She had the A section of the paper (never the Arts section, too easy to look like one was reading about oneself). Delle spent takeoff flipping through a magazine. When they were told they could take off their seatbelts and move about the cabin, Delle was the first to do so, heading to the front of the jet, toward the two men, without Adria detecting a glance thrown her way. Adria could wait twenty minutes. It would make the fact of her following Delle less obvious. She called over an attendant and ordered an Earl Grey.

Delle Deane's empty seat still bore the signs of her: an overflowing Birkin bag—messy as Lindy kept her own handbag, though of course Adria would never dream of buying her daughter such an ostentatious thing. (Nothing worse than a blatant show of wealth. Except, perhaps, a lack of care.) Delle had been reading, or pretending to read, a women's magazine that featured the two of them in awards-season-ready gowns on the front, under the headline "The Power of Partnership." There it remained, splayed with its cover glaring back at the more powerful of the partners. Adria was half-tempted to flip through it, to remember what it was she'd said in the forty-minute conversation with some nice young man. Of course she didn't read her own press, but Howard had sent her the image on the cover: She thought she looked appropriately dignified, but there was something unfair about standing next to a woman half her age, in this context. On a magazine that, no matter how lofty the language around the photos, turned their beauty into the explicit topic of discussion. She supposed she looked good enough.

Adria got up, making sure the lid on her paper cup of tea was secure, and began moving through the plane. She hoped that her presence might come as, if not a pleasant surprise, then at least a visitation that might make them straighten up. The two men sat on adjacent chaises, a bottle of champagne in a sweating ice bucket placed on the table before them. Delle sat on the floor opposite, lotus-position. She seemed almost astoundingly casual. But then, Adria too had always been struck by how much she herself had gotten by acting as if she needed nothing at all. Adria squinted into the side of the director's skull, bobbing up and down in laughter at the studio man's inaudible joke, drowned out by the engine's din. They could make these planes comfortable, but they sure couldn't make them quiet.

Delle looked up at Adria, shifted her weight, and smirked—no, smiled. *Be fair,* Adria chided herself. What a relief: it was the studio man who spoke first.

"So, our thrice and future winner. Sit down!" He laughed, not unkindly. "Preferably not on the floor."

Adria took the unoccupied loveseat perpendicular to the couch; it was as though Delle had ceded it to her.

"You happy with the movie?" he asked, once Adria had arranged herself.

What *had* Adria thought of the movie? She thought it was nice that she'd gotten the final shot, which was, of course, a matter of wrangling. Delle, as Lisa, spent so much time dissociating while her therapist watched and tried to help. The film ending on Adria's Dr. Lydia wistfully nodding as Lisa completes a 10K run, striding offscreen as this miracle worker of a mental-health professional ponders what she achieved with her patient, brought things back to equilibrium. (Of course, that ending had been negotiated—thank you, Howard.) But Delle had been somewhat . . . was "destabilizing" too strong a word? At the very least, Delle had confounded her on set. When they weren't rolling, her face remained knit with a shocking tension, one that thankfully resolved as soon as the day wrapped. Adria was never concerned, exactly, but she wanted Delle to be able to get through the shoot, and she wasn't a *monster*.

"It's so . . . it's just so dynamic," Adria settled on. "Muscular. Delle, you practically stole the show. You're a powerhouse."

"We loved that story in the September issue," the studio man said.

He'd been assigned to accompany them; the film had been bought after it was made by this company that promised to put it in everyone's home at the same time. That was Howard's business, and not something that Adria cared to delve into.

"That part you said," the funder went on, "about how she was like another daughter. That's the power of making movies. You become family."

"Thanks, *Mommy*!" Delle said, her voice creaky with sarcasm, or with exhaustion. Adria noticed the long black roots in her bleached hair as she gazed down at Delle, attempting a smile and to find within herself something like love. Say this much: Delle's unmaintained hair had a certain rocker's sexiness to it. It *did* look something like Lindy's when she had surprised her mother with a new hairstyle after her first year at Princeton. But, of course, Delle's delicate features suited the look better than did Adria's actual daughter's heavier ones.

A silence fell. The director still hadn't spoken.

"I mean it!" Delle finally trilled, in an unreadably jocular voice. "It's not just the champagne talking, which . . ." She whistled, spun a finger in the air. "Any more? Mama had a late night." She sighed. "Anyway. When someone plays your therapist . . . well, what's closer than that?"

For a tilty second, Adria considered pressing the case that she should be nominated as lead, saying something about how wonderful it was that there was finally a film that placed a therapist right at its center, because therapy is so important—but then there was a bump, as if the plane had been punched. Adria had a primal, violent feeling of losing her place, falling away from the course. She heard some sort of deep grunt, but couldn't tell where it had come from.

Her first thought was of her composure—she'd kept it. What a relief. She glanced at her tea, still in her right hand. Not a drop had emerged from the lid. Her hands were always so steady. She glanced quickly at Delle, who seemed barely to have noticed the disturbance.

"Hopefully not too much more of that," the studio man boomed.

The director, who'd been gazing forward since Adria arrived, finally spoke. "Maybe we should all go back to our seats."

"It's fine, it's fine," the studio man said. "They'd tell us."

The director continued staring forward.

"You and Delle—you both—are just terrific," he went on. "But now we wait and see how the crowd likes it."

"And it's"—Adria didn't know if she was truly feigning ignorance; the bump had rattled her focus—"it's critics in this crowd?"

"Not entirely," said Mr. Money. "It's critics, yes, but also industry, and also this crowd of really, really wealthy people who just love film. Tastemakers. And they're the ones who kick up word of mouth."

"Those are the people I'll be speaking to at—"

"Tonight at dinner, Adria, yes! We're so glad you agreed to do that." (Adria had been fine with introducing her film onstage, but getting her to attend a ninety-minute "dinner" her very first night, in the open air, with film festival donors, had made for an especially long Howard call.)

"Oh, anything for the movie, really," Adria sang, in a light, affectedly unaffected voice. Maybe it was better to play Mother Bountiful, dispensing favors upon her subjects. "I was just, well, *surprised*."

"It's strange you haven't been to this before," Delle said. "It's really not that bad. We get to mingle with the common people. There's a fun bar by the hotel lobby." She downed her second glass of champagne. She too hadn't spilled a drop.

Adria could not recall having been to Colorado before at all. Strange. Was there not a single local television affiliate in Denver that had wanted to hear from her in those early, rushed days? She'd learned to rope in Montana for *Lovelorn Ridge*, the movie that had gotten her the second of her three prizes, but those mountains, in memory, had seemed less jagged than the ones Adria saw when Googling the festival's name. She had recalled the peaks, but not the saw-toothed way that their edges seemed to injure the sky.

Things like this came up for Adria very rarely now. She'd had dozens of nominations and—up until very recently—her "campaigns" (that word! like some horrible politician) had consisted of a couple of interviews in which she would remind her public that Adria Benedict was quick-witted and willing to reveal just enough of that wit to charm them, all before she receded once more. Once she did, she could do whatever she liked: She lately received invitations to speak at college commencements, or to accept lifetime achievement awards—she accepted for UCLA, so she wouldn't have to go far, and for a humanitarian gala in Shanghai, so she would. If this accretion of celebrations of her Adria-ness seemed, individually, like nattering reminders of her time running short, the sheer mass of want for her presence pleased her. It made each way she spent her time seem of consequence. Brewing a bag of herbal tea before bed, reading a script, trying to call her daughter: She could be in Cannes, or at Juilliard, or (as long as the Democrats were in office) at the White House. And she was choosing instead to be where she was.

But she hadn't won since her third time. Then twenty years had passed—a drought. So here she was, fulfilling obligations.

"Well, let's hope we get a standing ovation too," said the director.

"We so will," Delle said. "It's not that the film isn't good, because, Scott, you know it is. But also, they're total applause sluts. They're just excited to meet stars."

The director—*Scott*, a name Adria had known, of course, but had better start actually using, since she couldn't issue orders through Howard at the moment—laughed.

"Honestly," he said, "I'll take it."

Delle grinned. Those two had . . . something. This little connection, one that had, from the first, made Adria nervous. It was just like the way Delle was never the same twice from shot to shot—it made Adria feel like she was losing control. Adria had worked hard to assemble her character, to build Dr. Lydia Mason. She'd mixed together the barely controlled wince of Dr. Golden, the marriage counselor, and Bill's way of running his left hand down his cheekbone when concentrating, and Lindy's sudden sharpness when asked a question that might, somehow, be seen in the most ungenerous of lights as undermining her. And these all had to fall away, or to blend into something elemental. But Delle hadn't prepared, hadn't done the work. Adria had earned the right to be the one determining the climate of the scene. Scott had never been strong enough to stand up to Delle. Which was his job.

"We'll take it too—right, Adria?" Delle grinned, seemed to let her eyes narrow. "Your two leading ladies."

♦ ♦ ♦

ANOTHER SILENCE. DELLE WAS MAKING IT TOO OBVIOUS, MAKing the game feel too apparent. Maybe that was smart. Adria took a sip of tea, her first since sitting down. As she removed the cup from her lips, the plane seemed to rumble from below, and for a crazy moment, she wondered if she should let the liquid fall out of her mouth and burn her chin. At least that way, she'd likely be excused from the dinner, or at least the donors' brunch.

"I'm sorry," the flight attendant murmured, emerging from whatever dollhouse he was kept in when not in use. "We really have to ask . . ."

"I know, I know, I'm sorry," said Delle. "Look, I already finished my drink." She waved the empty glass at the attendant. "I just—five minutes. I want to tell Adria something."

The flight attendant sighed, took a step back without leaving the scene, busied himself with brushing invisible crumbs off his uniform.

"Adria," Delle began, "I mean this. I want to thank you for picking me to be the lead of this movie."

And there it was. Adria's smile sat fixed there, rigid. She stared hard at Delle, who was twirling the stem of her glass between her fingers, seemingly transfixed by the last drops wending their way across the crystal. Probably trying to find a way to get every last bit into her bloodstream.

It had been Adria's contractual right to pick her costar—her supporting actress, damn Delle—and now she could barely remember why she'd done it. After a cull of names on the list and watching some tapes she'd been sent, it had come down to Delle or Bitty Harbor (terrible name, couldn't be real), who'd employed every wrong strategy in their meeting.

Adria had some ambient sense of Bitty as a figure of scandal, though she only really picked up gossip when it was about women of her own generation. How disappointing that Bitty had simply been an extra-pumped-up version of normal, an even more energetic version of the girls Willy and Jamey used to bring home from school. These girls had all been so *eager* to pay homage, when the greatest homage of all would have been to follow Adria's lead, to react with calm and—if she could use such a word without sounding ridiculous—a touch of decorum. It had hardly helped matters that Bitty's nerves had clearly expressed themselves in a smoking jag just before the meeting. Adria prided herself on a sensitive palate—that wine-tasting class she'd done with Bill and the Thomases a couple of years ago in Tuscany had confirmed it!—and she preferred Delle's perfume-over-tar scent to the unfiltered stale smoke of Bitty. Delle was at least willing to put in the effort. Adria could respect that.

Bitty had laughed in a you-probably-don't-want-to-hear-this way as she said that her mother had shown her Adria's early movies when she was in grade school. A more intelligent and sensitive performer might have actually recognized that, no irony here, Adria really *didn't* want to hear that. The girl was very "on," shimmeringly "on," so "on" that Adria suspected Bitty didn't notice her retreating within her own mind to contemplate, first, whether this movie was worth meeting the young go-getters of American acting, and then, for a while, whether Lindy would really be coming with her and Bill to the Montecito place in a few weeks or whether she'd cancel again. (Better to just check with Bill, once Bitty was through talking.)

So it was Delle that she'd chosen. Adria could acknowledge that each of them had made the other better. But the process had taken too much from her, ripped away her steady sense of herself and how she worked. It had made her an actor again, and she was too established—too old—to play theater games anymore.

"Well, Delle," she said, "I was so lucky to get the choice."

There was some slight shifting in the seats across the aisle. But Delle stayed put. Ignoring the increasingly sharp looks from the flight attendant, she looked comfortable enough to stay on the floor through landing. Delle had set the glass on the floor, and was now occupying her hands by picking at her inky black manicure.

"I feel really lucky," Delle said, "that I got to be the Lisa Farmer in *Who Is Lisa Farmer?* And really, Adria, that's because you supported me every step of the way."

She was too good at this.

"Well, we probably ought to be making some decisions soon," the studio man said. "There's certainly a way that you could both win. But the worst thing that could happen would be you two canceling each other out."

"I'm not worried," Delle said. "No one cancels me!" At just that moment, the steward had taken a step forward, casting a slight glare toward a broad radius of the floor that included Delle. "Except myself. And maybe the flight attendant." She looked up. "I know this is so insanely unsafe, but we're talking about some important stuff, I swear. Five more minutes?"

"You really ought to take a seat, Ms. Deane," the attendant said. "There'll be turbulence ahead."

"Pretty please?"

"I really have to insist."

"Wait," Scott said. "We actually do need to finish a conversation. Adria, could you . . . ?"

He made a motion with his hands in the air, as if he were shifting Adria, or pushing her aside.

The steward stood over Delle's crouched body, waiting for a resolution. The air started to shift, ripples forming.

"Okay," Adria sighed. There was, technically, room on this loveseat for two. And so she scooted over. It was becoming a bit too familiar, accommodating Delle.

"So, Adria." The producer clapped his hands and leaned toward her. Adria felt faintly nauseated—she could suddenly and all at once smell him, flat champagne and the wrong sort of aftershave. "There's time to formalize this later, and we've all been drinking—"

"Not all," Adria said. "I try never to drink on the clock."

"Are we on the clock?" Scott said. "Oops!" He smiled, seemed abashed, then put his hands to his cheeks and pulled them down over his mouth, following the path of his dark cropped beard. "Look, Adria, it's a decision we're all going to make together, but—the movie's about Lisa Farmer. We start on her."

"And we end on Dr. Lydia Mason," Adria said. "I fought for that ending."

"Yeah," Scott muttered quietly. "Yeah, you did."

"Adria," Delle said, leaning toward her. "You know, working with you was a master class. Really. And if we didn't connect as much as we should have, it's because I was so deep in Lisa. It's this crazy role, and I do think the movie is about her journey."

A pause. The things Adria didn't say, couldn't say, about the journey that Lydia went on too—the way that a woman trying to find the person within someone unrecognizable, just like Lydia had, was the story of a life. The story of her life. The memories Adria had drawn upon to make this part work—not just memories of a gesture or a look but of the moments when Lisa, when Lindy, just hated her. Just *hated* her. Finding a way to forgive, to keep trying. The strength that took. She was the star of her own story. She had to be. Or else what was any of this for?

"Look," Delle said, "I didn't mean to upset you."

"I'm hardly upset." Adria tensed up at how horribly physically close she suddenly felt to Delle. She realized the flight attendant was stalking through the cabin, racing toward a seat in the back. After he left her line of sight, she heard a seatbelt click shut.

She shut out the world, continued with what she had to say. "I do think that—well, I don't know if any of you have dealt with Jenny Van Meer. And I'm reluctant to bring this up, but I think she'll use whatever she can to win. So I'd like us to put our best foot forward."

The director shook his head slightly, bit his lip, said nothing. It was the studio man who spoke.

"I think whatever we choose will be the best choice. This film is our very top priority this year, and we want both of you to win, in lead and in supporting. However it works out."

Delle touched Adria on the leg; Adria forced herself not to recoil.

"Adria," she practically whispered. "This is my one big shot. My chance. To do what you've done so many times. So well."

"Don't you think, Adria, that it makes sense," the producer said, "given everything. Given that it's her first shot. Shouldn't we say that Delle is the lead?"

Suddenly, the plane seemed to fall through space, before being slammed by a gust of wind and reeling back skyward. A voice on the loudspeaker was saying words that Adria couldn't hear, all in a monotone surely meant to be reassuring. She knew that it would happen before it did—she bobbled the cup of tea, watched helplessly as its little opening gushed forth onto her right hand, and then, as the weight of two teabags collided with the plastic lid, opened into a torrent. Needles, hot needles, and then numbness. Nothing.

The producer reached across the distance between their seats, as if to grab Adria's burnt hand. She thrust it high into the air, so that nobody could touch it, and then threw her body as far into the side of the loveseat as it could get, making herself unreachable to Delle. And then Adria cried. Within seconds, she knew that it was a performance that would retain a kind of infamy in the minds of all who saw it; it was one that she'd replay for far longer than she even recalled the specifics of shooting days with Delle, of trying to find a rhythm opposite a young woman who wanted to define herself against Adria. With rising agony, with panic, with a lusty sense of just how overdue she was to be recognized for her capacity for greatness and for monstrosity, she cried.

Bitty Harbor,
Lyndon and Claudia

"CAN WE TRY A DIFFERENT pose?"

It was just getting to the hour mark, and Bitty was growing frustrated with the photographer. He seemed to have no idea of what he wanted, because Bitty knew that, if given a clear direction, she could deliver. She did her best work with a strong director! But up to this point, it had just been vague, impressionistic commands to look "powerful" or "brave." It was as if he were relying solely on the pop soundtrack he'd had an assistant cue up, all thumping songs with lyrics about, well, being powerful and brave, to inspire her in a way he couldn't. And she was someone who didn't feel very powerful and brave right now. She furrowed her brow and tried to push past the vise grip of a headache building inside of her skull. It had been a wasted hour.

She was frustrated with herself too. This was supposed to be a big moment—her second shot at a Movies Issue cover! At redemption! And with a headache pounding in time to the music and a tidal feeling in her bowels, she sought, at least, to grasp on to one fortunate thing.

Well, it was fortunate that only she could make herself feel this way.

It had been her nerves about the shoot, everything that it made her remember, that made her text Josh, her costar, to get a few drinks last night, and her joy at how easy it was to banish the nerves for a while that made her have a few nightcaps when she got home. It was fortunate, too, that only she could get herself through it. She always did. There was no harm in putting yourself in a precarious position when you trusted yourself to endure it.

"Sure," she monotoned. "Another pose. What were you thinking?"

The photographer said that he thought it would show strength if Bitty put her hands on the table before her and leaned forward, "kind of like a strong businesswoman. You know, like in a boardroom." It sounded strange and contradictory—the look Bitty and her team had chosen, from the three options they had negotiated with the magazine, was a high-necked eggplant-colored dress with delicate embroidered floral detailing, like something a Victorian doll might wear to a wake. It was not exactly boardroom attire, she thought—not that she'd know firsthand—as the latest song about how she was a superwoman thumped on insistently, making her feel still queasier.

But Bitty would try anything once!

"Okay," the photographer said, "let's do it. Show us how tough you are! Come on, show me some strength!"

Bitty tried to summon toughness—strength shouldn't have been a reach. She was getting through today, wasn't she? And before that, she'd gotten herself to this point in her career. Her second Movies Issue cover—let's do this! She arranged her features into a grimace. Tough!

"Bitty?" Leanna, her publicist, said from across the set, breaking through the photographer's shouted commands. "I'm sorry," she addressed the man now. "These photos aren't usable either. There's tough and then there's constipated."

Leanna clip-clopped toward Bitty, phone in hand as always, in the middle of a text message to unseen forces, elsewhere in the world.

"Bitty," she hissed as she got closer. "What do you need to make this work?"

"Maybe five minutes?" Bitty said. "I'm getting a little nauseous—it's, I don't know, these lights or something."

"Can we please take five?" Leanna didn't wait for an answer before she took Bitty's hand, began to usher her away from the set.

"We're on the clock," the photographer spat. "We've got ten other girls to shoot today. Contessa Lyle's coming in thirty minutes. Then Davina Schwartz. Big day."

"So that'll give you twenty-five minutes to shoot her," Leanna said. "We have the studio reserved exclusively for Bitty all morning. That was the agreement."

The photographer threw up his hands. Bitty felt a rush of gratitude, a temporary abatement of nausea that she'd try to make last as long as she could. She wasn't doing this totally alone.

♦ ♦ ♦

"HOW WE DOING?" ASKED LEANNA AS THEY STOOD OUTSIDE THE bathroom.

Her general demeanor suggested that Bitty would not have time to converse with her and to use the facilities in the five minutes provided. But Bitty supposed she was happy to be speaking with Leanna at all. In the car over, after Leanna had stood outside Bitty's little bungalow for twenty minutes banging on the door and on the windows, she'd wordlessly passed her Evian, Advil, and Visine, all while barely looking up from her phone. That had been good of her, Bitty knew, to wait outside in the heat; it was one of those scorching early-autumn days in Los Angeles that felt like the deferred dog days of summer, like doing penance for the fun you'd had all year by going through hell toward the end.

The eerie unresponsiveness continued as Bitty was trundled into the studio, late, of course: the makeup artist had gone about transforming her subject with a solemn, duty-bound silence, as if she needed the sort of focus that it'd take to put on prosthetics to make Bitty play an alien. Or a human.

"I'm not so bad," Bitty said. "I just didn't think it'd take this long."

She could feel herself focusing on speaking as plainly as she could, so as not to blurt out something wrong, something that would reveal just how bad she had it. Somehow she'd manage the interview later; she'd go on autopilot.

"Well," Leanna said, "you're definitely getting the most time of any of the girls. Like I told you, the agreement was that we had all morning and that no one else would be on set during the shoot. That was what we got out of them after last time."

"Yeah," Bitty said. "I think we've come a long way since then . . . ?"

Fuck. She hadn't meant this to sound like a question.

"Bitty." The actress could feel her publicist trying not to be stern. She could sense, in that way that a hangover could nuke all social pretenses and make her vulnerable to vibrations in the air, that Leanna knew that yelling wouldn't solve anything right now.

"Just to get it out in the open. And then I think you'll feel like you can go the next twenty minutes without holding anything back." Leanna paused. "What did you get up to last night?"

"I just got drinks with Josh," Bitty said. This had been totally innocent. All she needed to do was to make it sound that way. "We tried to invite Contessa, but she had a thing. It was just drinks. A couple drinks! Between costars!" She tried to make this last part sound jovial, heard it thud, took a long pause. "He was mainly complaining about his girlfriend. She's off filming right now, but comes back soon."

Leanna sighed. She feinted toward looking at her phone, then chucked it into the capacious purse slung over her left arm. Uh-oh. Leanna's undivided attention.

"Look," Leanna said. "I'm glad you two are still close after shooting—especially since we want people focused on *your* movie and not the one he did with Contessa. But come on. Rein it in. You're clearly miserable. It shows all over your face."

Bitty considered describing what she was going through physically—prickling skin, churning stomach, itchy . . . eyeballs? Somehow? But that would make it real, something she couldn't try to push away for the twenty-five minutes left of shooting. She had to find something else to tell Leanna.

"I guess it's frustrating that . . . I know you said that this would turn the page, or whatever, on what happened last time, but it feels like this is just going to make everyone talk about me and Delle again." She felt the vertigo of accidentally saying something honest, decided to keep going. "Her movie coming out the same time as mine. It's like we can't escape each other."

"I know," said Leanna, softening. "I see why that'd make you nervous. After the whole *Lisa Farmer* thing."

Just this year, Delle had gotten to do Adria's movie. Even after Bitty had worked hard to make her idol see what made her special, what made Bitty the kind of girl who'd be perfect to support Adria. To learn from her, to absorb and reflect her light.

"I know you think playing Lady Bird was a consolation prize. But it brought you here," Leanna said. (*It brought me to Josh,* Bitty thought, but she didn't outwardly react. Let Leanna think she was under control.) "You're going to get nominated, as a lead actress. And then everyone will be talking about that. And you'll always have that. It can't get taken away."

"I mean, I hope so," Bitty said. She felt herself relax into her dress, at a strange sort of ease with the idea that for all her skin seemed to be crawling with fire ants, painfully fevered, it was her pain alone to feel and keep close; no one else would see it. Getting to wear a high-necked, frilly dress, one that looked like what a star of the stage might have worn on an opening night before movies were invented, was a small victory.

Last time, a couple of years back, Bitty had shot her first Movies Issue cover with Delle, both wearing only stilettos and posing in contorted ways to make sure that it was just prurient enough to stop short of pornography. They'd been paired with two actors in tuxes. It had been a terrible month, more than a month, one in which Bitty saw her own nude body every one of the rare occasions she left the house, and every time she closed her eyes for a good while after that.

Since then, the magazine had hired a new editor, though, one Ceridwen Darby, the sort of woman who appeared on ideas panels, the sort who made Bitty nervous. Placing only women on this year's cover, giving them a bit of control over their wardrobe, was, according to Leanna, an attempt to correct what the publicist had called "past issues of tone . . . as you well know." That was what had convinced Bitty to do it—that, and that Leanna had asked her twice more, after the first time Bitty said no. Leanna only repeated herself when something was really important.

"If you pull this off," Leanna said, "they might end up putting you on the front cover when they composite it all together." Like paper dolls, the girls the photographer shot were going to be arranged into formation later, a system Bitty had never understood. When she'd been with Delle last time, they'd shot together, splitting a bottle of vodka beforehand to torch their nerves, each one laughing at how exposed the other was, too giddy to understand she was naked too.

"Let's focus on the positive. Do you like what you're wearing?"

"Yeah," Bitty said. "Yeah, I do."

In fact, she loved it. One of the great annoyances of today was that she was so focused on holding herself together that she felt blunted, held back from appreciating that, for once, she looked like herself. Or like the self that she wanted to be. For premieres or talk shows, she wore whatever the stylist the studio had hired gave her, and these clothes, tailored denim with a crop top and an oversized blazer or gowns with strategic cutouts, felt too hip by half. They were costumes for the character she was playing, the Contemporary Actress. This was the kind of dress that she had imagined blankets and towels into, when she played dress-up as a kid.

She allowed herself, in a great, rushing moment of giving in, to feel, all at once, how much she loved this dress, loved the nostalgia and the whimsy and the drama of it, loved the chance it gave her to play make-believe. If only she could go back!

"Well . . ." Leanna said. "That's good. I'm glad." She handed Bitty a tissue. "Camera-ready, remember?"

"Sorry." Bitty dabbed at her eye, pulled a huge, implausible grin. "All better!"

Leanna had the good grace to laugh a little.

"Look," Leanna said. "This guy is an idiot, we all know it. I don't know why Ceridwen hired him, other than that—well, he's trying to be respectful. So just do your own thing for the rest of the shoot, and he'll find something usable. I officially empower you to ignore him. I trust you to figure it out. You're a good actress. Then we get through the interview. And then we go home."

"Okay," Bitty said. "I think I can do that."

"Listen, Bitty," Leanna said. *"And then we go home."*

"S-sure," Bitty stammered. "I mean—yes."

She'd need something to come down, just a little after the day she'd had. She probably still had something in the cabinet. Or maybe Josh could come over, if he was free. His girlfriend was still on her shoot.

"Do you really think I might be on the front cover?" she asked.

"I think you might."

"And—this is so stupid." Bitty considered cutting herself off, but she had to hear it. "But just . . . I just need to . . ." She breathed deep, tried not to sniffle. "Do you think I'll win?"

Leanna was, Bitty realized in the moment after she finished her question, a really good publicist. Because Bitty knew exactly what Leanna was going to say, and it still felt bolstering when she said it.

"I do," she said. "If you can get through today, I think you're going to win."

♦ ♦ ♦

"WE READY?" THE PHOTOGRAPHER ASKED AS BITTY AND LEANNA reemerged into the silent studio. "We're down to twenty minutes—more like fifteen."

"Twenty." Leanna didn't look up from her phone.

Bitty walked back onto the spare set, a pink backdrop with various pieces of antique furniture that she'd spent the morning being powerful and brave against.

"Okay," he said. "Bitty, I want you to show me how fierce you are."

Bitty looked down at her dress. All she had to do, she realized, was play pretend. She could do that. She raced through associations in her mind. Leanna—honestly, all things considered, she was being really nice today, given how she could have acted. Not a match. Her mom—nope! Let's deal with that one later! Josh—God, it was crazy how even months after their shoot in Albuquerque, he made her feel so protected. . . .

"Fierce!" the photographer shouted. "That's a little too sweet. Show me your teeth!"

Right! So not Josh. Josh's girlfriend, though. Bitty knew Josh couldn't stand her. Could he? She'd been so unsupportive of him during the shoot. They'd fought so much on her one visit to the set. That would all make it easy for Bitty, in the end.

She felt something hard and diamantine enter her eyes. Felt her lips curl.

"Yes!" the photographer bellowed.

There was a succession of clicks that sounded like gunfire. No—that sounded like the pounding of footsteps running from the press, the ones who'd be pursuing Josh and Bitty on their first real date. Maybe they could give them one picture, though, just to appease them, and to show off their love for the world to see. . . .

"Turn the music back on?" Bitty asked. Then she repeated herself, without making it a question. "Turn the music back on. Thanks!"

She grinned as she heard the first computer-generated beat. It would be the soundtrack to her and Josh's first date. That would be something she had on Delle. Delle! What if Bitty got to go to the awards with Josh as her date, and Delle went alone? Then, after all this, what if Bitty beat her when they were nominated together? People at home would watch as Delle had to clap for Bitty, as Josh kissed her right before she went up onstage and thanked everyone. Thanked her mom, because her mom would be watching too. Maybe she would call Bitty afterward! Contessa would be right on the other side of Josh—those two had been in a movie together too. She'd give Bitty a high five, because they'd be real friends by the time all of this was over. Bitty, Josh, and Contessa—the talent of their generation. Contessa would clutch her hands to her heart as Bitty thanked Adria Benedict for inspiring her to act. Adria would mouth, *You inspire me too.*

It was all so clear. Like a channel that she never wanted to turn off.

Her pulse was pounding in her skull. But it wasn't just the hangover this time. It was a vision. One that, soon, everyone else would get to see too. It would be her. The number-one girl.

"You're doing it!" Leanna yelled.

"Yes! Great!" the photographer said. "That break did something! Now—do something different with your hands!"

He needed options, Bitty realized, for when she'd be pasted in, on the front cover. For everyone to see. Her in a pretty dress—one that she'd picked out herself. Owning it.

She trusted her instincts in this moment so completely that she simply let her body move itself. So, even as she caught herself and moved her fists back down by her sides, there was just a flickering second of realization. She only barely noticed that, when she held her right hand flat in front of her chest, and her left one cupped above it, it would look for all the world like she was holding an invisible trophy.

Contessa Lyle,
The Glass Menagerie

It was silly, but Contessa loved being in Hollywood. Not being in the industry—although she loved that too, in the way she loved the sun being warm. No, she quite literally loved being *in* Hollywood, the very uncool part of Los Angeles where tourists came to get a glimpse of magic. She had to go somewhat incognito—if all the fake Scubamen on the Walk of Fame attracted people willing to pay them for selfies, the real-life Nina in Charge might risk bodily harm if she didn't wear a hoodie, cap, sunglasses.

That was what Contessa was willing to do for a couple of hours that would feel, well—"normal" wasn't the right word. But like a kind of normal that was striving to be something better. This strip of street, she felt, was where the hopeful came. It was for people who, like Contessa, wanted to make movies. It was for people who just really loved them, loved the movies and their stars. She felt a deep well of affection (and, yes, a little sympathy, as it seemed so accidental she'd found fame so young) for all the people she saw as she walked into her spin class on the Boulevard, the costumed and the plainclothed, those in character and those taking pleasure in watching.

She couldn't slow down, though; after leaving her SUV at valet, she only had about ten minutes to get to class before the studio door closed and latecomers, even famous ones, were not admitted. (Contessa had never tested this last part—she'd be too embarrassed to try to pull celebrity rank with the front desk at Spin Culture, but she suspected that she might, just maybe, get her way if she tried.) Unfortunately, her mother was practically dragging herself through the parking garage.

"You know," Melanie groaned, "the one of these on Santa Monica is so much closer. Between this, the stylist, the shoot—today's feeling a little too full. It would have been easier if we could have just done Eleanor's thing."

"We've been over this, Mom," Contessa said. "The stuff we're doing today will do more for me than going to Colorado would. And Eleanor wants us splitting up to promote the movie. The studio does too."

Spin Culture studios were the same no matter where you went. (Contessa always sought them out, taking pleasure in the familiarity, when she was doing press in New York.) But what she meant, and what she was sure her mother understood, was that being in proximity to the heart of the dream, so close to so much pulsing need to express and to be understood, made her feel more herself, more like she was doing precisely what she needed.

"Can we hurry up, please?" Contessa said.

"I got up at five for this, Tess," her mother said. "You'll get me when you get me."

And then—a glimpse of the street, but only a glimpse, as they emerged out into the winking early brightness. The Scubamen weren't out yet, but the stars in the pavement shone. Contessa loved them, loved them for being names she knew, loved them more for being names she didn't, preserved here by some intelligence that understood we need to be put down in some ledger, to feel like we mattered. Contessa might get one someday.

No matter—she already had so much!

The reverie continued as they walked the short distance down the sidewalk and into the storefront studio. It broke as Contessa waved at the front desk girl, as she considered her own impact. She recognized this girl (she was pretty sure her name was Allie), and she hoped Allie knew that Contessa was only breezing past without stopping to say hello because it was hard for a person *in her position* to stop without creating, potentially, even a small scene, which was the last thing that Allie, *just trying to do her job*, needed.

(Maybe her name was Annie?)

Contessa was trying to remember things like this, trying to stay normal. Because she was afraid of growing jaded, afraid of becoming a person who brushed past others without seeing them. The hallway leading into the main studio was empty; all of the other exercisers presumably were finishing getting their bikes set up. Contessa had a special arrangement, which anyone could pay extra for, not just actors! Her bike was set up to her specifications before she got there, so she could arrive at the moment class began without having to fiddle with the seat height. Today she'd paid extra-extra for her mom to have the same deal, even though Melanie swore she was not particular, that she'd be just as sore wherever the seat was placed.

She checked her phone for any texts one last time—nothing. Then she extracted her spin shoes from her purple gym bag, tossed the bag and the sneakers she'd been wearing into an empty locker. She made quadruple-sure it was secured—no one wants their phone stolen, but she was an especially high-value target; she would have left it in the car, but what if someone broke in—and looked to make sure her mom had done the same. But there Melanie was, already at the studio door.

"See what happens when you're not checking your phone every fifteen seconds?" her mom said. "You get there faster. Hurry up—we'll be late." Contessa laughed, then pantomimed racing to the door, her knees high in the air and her arms pumping for the seven paces it took to get there. The two of them walked into the darkened studio, where the beats of the first song's intro had just begun playing.

Contessa always booked her seat in the front row, as near the center as she could. It wasn't a star thing, the need to be front-and-center—she didn't think so. (She was trying, *trying*, to be really rigorous with herself about this stuff!) She wanted to feel connected to the instructor, to have something pass between them.

"All right, everyone! Welcome to our last-minute arrivers!" the instructor shouted.

Contessa winced. She'd never done this guy's class, but he should have known that the instructors weren't really supposed to call attention like that. When someone paid to have their bike set up in advance, they were *probably* coming just at the start of class for a reason, like to avoid causing a hubbub. Contessa clicked her cleats into place, left foot, right foot, feeling suddenly at ease, letting the annoyance go. This class ran on mantras, which Contessa found grounding, even as she could tell her mom was always on the verge of outright laughing. One of her favorite instructors had recently shouted, in the middle of the longest hill Contessa could remember, "This class is about becoming someone different!"

The symbolism of spin class, Contessa thought, was almost too easy: the ramp-up into an attack on one long, sustained challenge, leading into the catharsis of having, each time, achieved what one set out to do, on whatever terms one was willing to accept. Because you were both competing against yourself and the one judging the competition, you could be said to have won every time.

And the banalities shouted at the exercisers: Contessa was smarter than to fall for them. She was herself a storyteller by trade, and she liked to think that she knew better than to take pleasure in the simple triumph-over-adversity storyline the instructors here sold, where each rider was taking the first step toward control over their destiny with every stroke of the pedal. And yet there was a pleasure in allowing oneself to be unguarded, or simple, or a little dumb.

Physical exertion reduced her defenses, and so did the broad sentimentality of the familiar pop music that blasted throughout. By the time, deep into a workout, that an instructor would ask the class to evaluate how much more resistance to add, Contessa would find herself actively hoping that there would be a clumsy bit of jargon attached. And it seemed, as the group moved toward the hill, that she was about to come up lucky.

"You decide how you attack this today," the man in the front of the class was bellowing. "I want you to look within and see how powerful you can be. You did not come here to be meek. I want you to make some brave choices!"

Brave choices! Contessa loved that!

She turned her dial farther to the right, amping up the resistance, making the ground beneath her feel sticky with debris pulling her back toward earth. Moving her legs through this grit felt like emerging from something, like breaking free from some other, heavier planet's gravity. Her legs burned with exhaustion, and a nourishing sort of virtue. How much, already, had Contessa committed to; how much further did she know she would go? She gazed up at the instructor with ravenous eyes, wanting an acknowledgment that she, Contessa, was doing something special—that, in the midst of this busy hive of activity, she stood out. And that acknowledgment wasn't going to come from her mother. A glance to Contessa's left confirmed that Melanie was doing her usual routine of pedaling as perfunctorily as possible, with a look of aggrievement painted on her face. (She seemed fussily committed, each time they did this, to doing as little of the arm choreography as possible, none of the little push-ups and claps that were supposed to tone your upper arms . . . and Contessa knew that was her right. They didn't always have to agree!)

Still, it would be nice to get some energy, some life, from a source beyond Contessa's own strength of will, or from the music blaring. And so she looked to the instructor, finding his eyes as she somewhat pointedly turned her dial yet farther into resistance. She could handle this, because she was in this studio several times a week, and because she was a hard worker, and because she was Contessa. She knew it: she was special. But she needed to hear someone say it back.

As if by telepathy, or deference to a celebrity, he knew.

"There you go, front-row center!" the instructor shouted. "I see you, Miss Laura Wingfield!"

Contessa knew that she ought to wince at that—as a performance of humility over her new role being mentioned in a roomful of strangers, and as an acknowledgment that her fame wasn't supposed to matter in this space, although, you know, of course it did. She deserved praise for doing her best, and not just for being a girl in a movie. (For being *the* girl in the movie—take that, Eleanor.) But maybe the braver choice was to accept the compliment on its own terms. Or maybe it just felt good to allow herself to fall for something. She grinned, and pedaled harder.

"Miss Nina is in the house, and she is rocking it!" he said. "Nina's getting a nomination, just wait and see!"

It would have hurt, it would have been impossible, for Contessa to turn her head to address the room behind her. But she could feel through some flow of energy—God, she felt just like an instructor—all the invisible heads of the people who'd gotten here earlier than she had shifting their attention, shifting their focus. It was a powerful feeling, like the one she'd have again in a few minutes, when she crested the top of the hill.

"I got something special for y'all!" the instructor said. "Listen up!"

He busied himself pressing keys on the laptop strapped to the front of his bike, and Contessa recognized it, she was sure, a beat before all those invisible heads would have. There was the plunky kids' piano knocking out a few notes before being joined by a saxophone, then her own voice: "Nina's in charge, she's the only one . . . Nina's going to make every last thing fun. . . ."

This was so hilarious! Maybe it wouldn't be if she'd peaked with Nina, if she was still only known for being on a kids' show that had ended, mercifully, three years ago. But if she couldn't laugh about this, she'd be in big trouble—as self-serious as Eleanor. She shot the instructor her most winning Nina smile, pure charm, laced with just the amount of mischief in her eye that Nina would apply when her dog-sitting business hit whatever snag it did that week, and she had to come up with a solution.

"Miss Contessa Lyle, everyone," the instructor said. "Now, why don't you bring Josh Jorgen around next time!"

Contessa blinked, careful not to lose the Nina innocence and charm. She'd misheard, she thought.

"I bet it wasn't too hard having to pretend to be in love with him!"

The instructor spread his arms wide, seeming to embrace the room as Contessa heard a few other riders titter. He was bringing them all into a conversation that was growing too specific, too inane. "I'm sorry, Contessa, I'm obsessed. For the rest of you: welcome to my entertainment minute, y'all. This is the Hollywood location, after all."

Contessa looked down at the knob and turned the resistance down a bit. She'd pedaled hard enough for today. And he'd already praised her.

"She's taking it down a notch," the instructor shouted, "but that's okay. Enjoy the Nina song and some lighter resistance. Next up, I'm going to play the *Scubaman* theme song in honor of my man, Josh Jorgen!" He laughed as Contessa felt herself flush beyond physical exertion. "Nina, girl, I'm serious—bring him around next time!"

♦ ♦ ♦

"GOOD CLASS," CONTESSA SAID AS THEY WALKED TOWARD THE lockers. "Right?" She and Melanie had bolted out of their seats when the ride ended, skipping the cooldown stretch, so as to avoid being seen when the lights came up. Graciously, none of the other riders, all of whom now knew Contessa had been among them, followed. Perhaps the instructor had used up all of the socially permissible poking at celebrities for the day.

"Whatever you say," Melanie said. "I don't like the way he talked about you and Josh."

Contessa let that sit there for a second.

"Just promise you won't complain to the manager. The instructor was just really excited, and Josh and I are . . . you know, in the movie together. It was mainly really nice." She paused. "So, like we said, I'm going to shower here before we head to the stylist's, right?"

"I don't think that's so smart," Melanie said. "Do you really want to take off your clothes in public?"

"Mom," Contessa allowed herself to whine. "It's kind of the only option."

Maybe it had been a mistake to make the day too full, but they'd been told that Bitty Harbor needed the studio all to herself all morning—typical—and that left a weird amount of time. Too easy to get antsy, better to keep busy. She saw her mother begin to open her mouth.

"And before you say it," Contessa snapped, "we don't have time to go home."

"Okay, but don't blame me when topless pictures come out and suddenly you're the next Bitty," Melanie said. "We should have gone to the one in Santa Monica."

"It'll be five minutes," Contessa said.

Of course her mom had to say something about Bitty. It wasn't like Contessa didn't think badly of her too, but Bitty was just such an easy target. She was always so breathless and anxious when they ran into each other. It was like nothing came easily for her when she wasn't on set. At least, that was what Josh had told her, back when he'd just wrapped the Lyndon Johnson movie and had come on board *The Glass Menagerie* for his few days' worth of shooting—that Bitty was, you know, *a lot*.

"Be nice," Contessa went on. "We'll be seeing a lot of Bitty over the next few months. Probably."

"Terrific," Melanie muttered. Then, a little less muffled: "Let's go over the questions before we get there."

Contessa nodded, before going to her locker and pulling out her phone—a text from Jana, her stylist:

10 still good?

She sent a thumbs-up and then, so as not to seem brusque, a heart. And then Bitty.

see you at the shoot?

Just a heart on this one. She couldn't put Bitty off forever—it wouldn't be nice, for one thing—but she just didn't feel like dealing with her right now.

Then, finally, something from Josh.

you'll kill it at the shoot. you always do.

Contessa stared at her phone for a moment, wrapped up in the self-conscious awareness that every second she stood there was a second closer to the rest of the class coming into the room. She didn't respond, but very carefully, as if she were handling a live grenade, laid her phone in her gym bag, burying it beneath the street clothes into which she'd change after she showered.

She cleaned herself off in a trance, not bothering to wash her hair: it'd get styled before the shoot this afternoon. It was her custom to use this time to replay the class in her head, thinking about the songs she'd add to a playlist if she ran the studio, feeling a sudden bit of warmth as she remembered the instructor calling her out. It hadn't really been bad getting noticed. It definitely hadn't really been bad getting linked up with Josh.

She blinked. *Contessa. What are you doing?* She felt a momentum inside, something as unstoppable as the bike's flywheel, once her strong legs got it rotating really fast. She turned off the water, wrapped a towel around herself, stuck her hand out of the shower, and scrabbled around for her gym bag, hooking it around her wrist without looking.

There her phone was. Right where she'd left it. Lower the towel. Snap.

aw thanks haha she typed, feeling the rise of anticipation that came with knowing that soon she'd be appearing, for a perfect audience, outside of her body, somewhere else.

just finished up at spin and cleaning up.

think i shld go to my stylist like this ?

That she'd known from the moment she brought the phone behind the shower curtain that she'd get a heart, and something else—oh, there it was, a little yellow face with drool coming out the corner of its mouth—didn't make it any less gratifying. She placed the phone on top of her bag at the far corner of the shower stall and quickly put back on her underwear, jeans, T-shirt, sweatshirt, hearing an occasional buzz.

fuck, c

so hot

thanks for sending, this with an image of a round little smiling face; here's me right now with a photo of another body part.

She knew his rhythms, the rhythms of this. And she hadn't, before they'd met on the set earlier this year. She'd learned. Wasn't being open to experience, to trying things about which one ought to be nervous or fearful, another way of being courageous?

Yes!

they mentioned us in class btw she wrote. Send! Wait, maybe that was too weird. But he knew that she understood his situation. He knew that she was just being silly.

the instructor shouted me out she wrote. Send!

then he said i'm going to get nominated for menagerie—send!

he said he was going to play the scubaman music for you but he didn't hahah—send!

and he didn't mention eleanor lol—send!

you would have laughed lol—send! There could be more! But it was time to head to the car. Maybe this had already been too much.

As she rejoined her mother in the hallway, keeping her face down to avoid meeting the eyes of any of the stream of passersby who might know her as the star of the screen or the star of the class, she willed herself not to glance at her phone again. She would not, for some time, see whether or not those ellipsis-like bubbles had emerged to show her if Josh Jorgen—the star of the *Scubaman* movie franchise and a likely nominee himself this year for his lead role with Bitty Harbor, even as he'd also been a brilliant supporting actor opposite Contessa Lyle—had been typing a reply. It wouldn't be until much later, after hours with her stylist when nothing seemed to look right, everything seemed itchily juvenile, too much like the little girl she'd finally graduated from playing on TV, or else far too needy and attention-begging, too colorful and desperately gaudy, until after her mother told her to just forget it and head to the shoot and figure out the campaign wardrobe some future day—it was only then, in her final not-quite-right outfit of the session, that she glanced down and saw that he'd finally replied:

haha. His text ended with a period.

Davina Schwartz, *Andronicus*

DAVINA HAD NEVER WORKED WITH a stylist before, and she had to admit—it was pretty nice to let someone else figure out who she had to be. On the two occasions she'd been previously nominated for a big award over here, TV prizes for her role on *The Screaming at Salem*, the network had found her a personal shopper who bought Davina exactly the sort of thing she'd have favored for a theater industry event in London, in her previous life: tailored, but not excessively so; black, less a concealment than a simple refusal to commit. Clothes didn't matter to Davina. Costumes helped her find a character, but offstage, or off-camera, she preferred simply to sit ready to receive inspiration, rather than to call attention to herself.

Jana had explained, with eventual success, that these months would be about creating a narrative in every possible way, and, assuming that Davina would eventually get a nomination, the stylist had planned a tactical assault. Davina had a "hard out" in an hour, in order to leave for the Movies Issue shoot—she'd been asked to show up midafternoon, because, as her new manager told her in a breathless whisper,

Bitty Harbor needed the space all to herself. A touch odd, but, Davina supposed, this was Hollywood for you. And all the better: it gave her these couple of hours to run through her public wardrobe for the next half-year or so.

"If you eventually get to do *Staying Up*, which I know your team is still working out," Jana said, "for the monologue, closing, introducing the musical guest, I'd like to amp up the British-osity. You're getting nominated for a Shakespeare film, that's great. But have some fun and play it up too."

She whipped out a double-breasted silk suit, glowing lavender under the bright lights.

"Now, check this out." Jana paused to allow Davina to take it in. "I know the matching top hat will be a bit Alice's tea party . . ."

Davina didn't know America well, even after four seasons of shooting a television show here; she had always tried to flee back to London on her hiatuses. But, in a flash, she saw this boundless, naïve nation charmed by her in a way she'd never asked them to be before. Could it really be as simple as just asking? She loved the theater of it; a role to play—how much easier than trying to clomp through this time in her life as herself! So, sight unseen, she said yes to the top hat, and put it in reserve for when she'd appear on live comedy TV some future Friday night.

Davina had instantly liked Jana for reasons precisely opposite to the origin of her love and trust for those she'd held close thus far in her career. Her publicist, agent, even Beth, all seemed of a type, down to the look—clothes that seemed expensive but worn, if decently mended, and hair contained with a simple clip or headband. They all used their physical presentation to communicate that looks were subordinate to something else, something more. They were like Adria Benedict, Davina's acting idol since heaven knew when—since she'd known she wanted to do this. And Adria—well, one could tell she spent real money on what she wore, but one never thought first of her clothes when thinking about her. Or second. It was her gift that was the subject, appropriately enough. Because her gift was disappearing into the role.

Beth's presentation was surely pricey too. (Davina looked, or used to, at the household bills. But she didn't need to, to have a sense: Oxford had taught Davina how to detect cashmere at five paces.) But Beth also swam in her clothes, so poorly did they fit. That was a theater person for you: all the time and all the money to enable one to stage oneself for the world, but head hopelessly in the clouds when it came down to it.

For all that Davina didn't care about clothes—for all that she strived to resemble Adria in all things—it was nice to be in a room where first impressions still mattered. Funny, that: a quarter-century into her career, so much of it practically killing herself to earn a laugh or a tear on the London stage, and Davina was still making her first impression.

"You're so much easier than my client earlier today," Jana whispered conspiratorially. Kyle, her assistant, had departed to get a new rack of clothes. "Ugh, don't get me started."

"Started on *what*?" Davina had always had a hard time resisting gossip.

She was sitting on a leather couch, having been given a glass of white wine and free rein to say whatever she thought of the clothes Jana presented—but wouldn't you know it? She loved everything! She trusted Jana so much: she loved the lavender silk suit, loved the unexpected lime tuxedo, loved the high-necked turquoise gown with the surprise slits on either side. (She did still have legs, even if few seemed too interested!) She trusted that what Jana had to say would fill her, somehow, with knowledge of what she needed for the months ahead.

"I shouldn't," Jana said. "But it was insane. Wasn't it?"

This last bit directed at Kyle, returning to the room with yet another shimmer of women's suiting. Ooh—sequins this time! Kyle nodded rapidly, then shouted back: "Nina was *not* in charge today!"

Jana laughed, and Davina did too, to be sporting.

"I usually do one of the girls per season," Jana said. "One likely nominee. It's a conflict otherwise. But when your studio reached out, I'd already been looking for an excuse to fire Contessa Lyle as a client. And today . . ." She whistled.

"Contessa Lyle! Really?" Davina was surprised, and didn't quite know why.

She recognized the name well, not that she'd yet seen *The Glass Menagerie*, and of course she'd never spent time with her children's TV show or whatever the thing was. Davina knew she'd see Contessa this afternoon at the Movies Issue shoot, and had frankly been looking forward to it. If she was honest with herself, she'd been avoiding *The Glass Menagerie*. It's easier to fantasize about someone you haven't seen being vulnerable, someone who lives for you only on magazine covers extolling her strength and youth and—why lie?—beauty. Art, for Davina, tended to get in the way of lust.

"She was just miserable," Jana said. "Not everyone likes clothes, and that's fine, it's my job, but she's a former child star." She practically spat out these last three words, went on. "Practically still a kid. She's not above it. Not an actor, like you."

She seemed to catch Davina's eye at the exact moment that Davina was beginning to wonder if, as thrilling as this candor was, this line of thought might be a little uncouth to observe without comment. But she let the tension last a beat longer.

"God, look at the career you had onstage over there," Jana said, "and now on TV. It's an honor to dress you. Probably as close as I'll ever get to Adria Benedict."

Davina wasn't above being flattered.

"You can't possibly mean that," she said, holding on to a vague hope that Jana—whom she'd known she liked from the first, and Davina's instincts were never wrong!—might really be serious.

"You know she has a stylist—an old colleague of mine—but has never trusted her. Just tells her, over and over, to get the same kind of things. Things that look like Adria."

Davina made a noncommittal murmur. If Adria didn't need to be reinvented—if she was committed to a particular type of clothing, those fabulously unobtrusive, tasteful clothes, an accent to her talent but never a distraction—then where had Davina's own vanity led her? She had only just begun recalling how spurious Beth had sounded on the phone yesterday, her tone as she said that she was simply surprised Davina wouldn't trust her own judgment, when Jana piped back in.

"And God knows she should start taking professional advice. The last time she was nominated . . . that big white thing? Like a bride jilted at the altar again. Better when she sticks to her usual eggshell."

"Eggshell, cream, and gray!" Kyle squealed.

The two laughed together as Jana reached for one or another scrap of clothing. Davina suddenly saw the rack, in all its showy color, as less a rainbow than the diminished iridescence of some petrol in a puddle.

"Another friend of mine is in Colorado, working with Delle Deane," Jana rambled on, "and apparently Adria just landed there? And is holding them all hostage, refusing to promote the movie!" She smirked. "We all love her work, but—oof."

What did "holding them all hostage" even mean? Why wait to find out?

"Jana," Davina said, rising from her seat, "Adria and I both began in the theater, and there, it's considered pretty poor form to criticize your peers."

She realized she was slumping slightly: the wine, perhaps, and the jangling feeling of having to confront someone whom she liked so much, someone new who was willing to do so much for her. But this was Adria Benedict they were talking about. Adria Benedict!

"Thank you, Jana, for everything you've done so far." Davina was feeling herself grow a bit grand—but maybe, just maybe, it suited her. "But I do have that hard out."

♦ ♦ ♦

"I TOLD YOU THAT YOU WEREN'T GOING TO LIKE HER."

Davina had her phone on speaker as she sat in the backseat of the car hired to take her to the shoot. They'd parted as friends, she and Jana, and they'd agreed on just the right thing for the cover. Apparently Bitty's team had already snagged a purple garment, and they had some leverage to determine everything, so everything around Bitty would be complementary, in deep jewel tones. Davina would be in maroon.

And now, after a fitting and before a photoshoot, she was back—despite the heat, which was reminding Davina that she sometimes really did miss London weather—in her black schmatte. It was just a hooded sweatshirt, and jeans that the Gap had torn on purpose, but it was a look that called as little attention to Davina as possible. To dress as she always had in her life up to this point was now, she thought, to dress as if between important engagements.

"I didn't not like her," Davina said. "Which is to say, I did like her. But the chatter, it drives me mad."

"And for good reason."

"Pardon?"

"Well, because you've largely avoided it to this point," the voice went on. "The highest-browed lady of the West End, dodging her nation's crazy tabloid culture to raise a kid with her wife, then booking a role on a horror TV show, but it's the only unsexy character, so no one really cares."

"Oh, stop."

The traffic was horrendous. Maybe Davina ought to have insisted on allowing more than an hour to get there. She hadn't figured out how to time things right, with this hideous Los Angeles traffic. In London, she took the Tube.

"I'm kidding. Kind of. Prudence Snell the witch is not sexy. Tamora, in our movie, is pretty sexy. Davina is . . . profoundly sexy. But the chattering classes haven't figured that out yet."

"Rory," Davina cut in. "Do you think I was being a prig? To Jana?"

"I think you were being a theater person," Rory said. "And that's why I cast you. Because theater people are the best kind of people. Way better than actresses."

Davina laughed.

"I should have come with you," Rory said. "I have some skin in this game. I'd like to have directed you to a nomination, or a win. And you're going to be on my arm at the awards." A long pause. "I mean, we'll be seated together. We're all there for the movie."

"Yes, it's certainly all about putting the movie in its best light." Davina began to wonder how she could wind this conversation down.

"Just," Rory said, "don't get so hung up about the things people say. It's just talk. Everybody talks about, you know, Bitty Harbor, and there she is, doing her thing. And you don't get to be Adria Benedict without a million people trying to take you down."

"Do you think . . ." Davina said, stopping herself, going on. "Do you think people will talk about me?"

"Only to say you're a beautiful genius." Rory chuckled. "But if you're asking what I think you're asking, I don't think anyone knows you're my beautiful genius. Here or back in jolly old England."

"Well," Davina said, "cheerio, I suppose."

The kooky Brit. That was something she knew how to summon, and Rory always seemed to love it. Indeed, there she was, cackling into the phone.

"Come say hi after the shoot. Only if you want. I don't have anything going on tonight."

Davina's phone beeped. A good enough excuse.

"Let's see how long it takes me," Davina said. "You're the one who once told me no magazine photoshoot is ever done before the photographer takes an extra hour or two to pull the camera out of his arse."

Punching that last word, just for fun—just to be the Brit. She'd been here long enough to know the word "ass"; Rory had been the one with whom she'd called her costar, the Titus to her Tamora in *Andronicus*, an "asshole," in pure, uninflected, aggressive lesbian-American English.

The phone beeped again. Rory began speaking about how she hoped Davina would get off early because it'd be a busy few weeks and Rory had a new film to prep—

"I'm sorry to rush you, my dear," Davina said, "but it looks like I'm getting close to the studio." She had no idea, but it certainly didn't feel as if she'd made much progress. "And I must take this before I get out of the car."

"I get it," said Rory. "Talk later, I hope."

"Ta," Davina chirped.

The waiting call had gone to voicemail; she pulled up Beth's number and called it.

"Hi," Beth said blearily.

"It's only . . . what, there?"

"It's half nine," Beth said. "I've only just gotten Jeremy down. Little demon, he can be."

"Ah." Davina wasn't sure how to proceed. "Well . . ."

"I know. How was your morning of fashion fantasy?"

"It was . . . interesting," Davina said. "Honestly, there's a chance I might get to host this series *Staying Up*, and I might get to do some very oddball things. Be the little Mad Hatter for America."

"I know what *Staying Up* is," Beth said. "And I hadn't realized the Mad Hatter was your ambition."

"Well—it's just, you know, to make people laugh. For fun. For now."

"Say." Beth suddenly sounded a bit more alert. "Will Adria Benedict be at this photoshoot today? I'd like for you to finally get to meet her."

"I think not. The biggest name, I keep hearing, is Bitty Harbor—unless it's Contessa Lyle."

"Oh, heavens," said Beth. "I'll have our divorce papers drawn up now, and I wish you and Contessa the best of luck in your lives together."

Davina laughed with Beth for the first time in a long while.

"Well, I'm told Contessa is a bit of a brat, which we might have expected. That much success, at that age. Looking like that." She considered getting further into the story, stopped herself. "But why do you ask?"

"Jeremy was asking, once again, about how we met, and I was telling him about that production our third year. Remember?"

"You were the very best director."

"You were the very best Baker's Wife. I wish you sang more these days. But there was that song you sang about having . . . I don't know,

Dav, I'm really run-down." Beth sighed. "But about moments in your life of having an experience, a really profound and unusual experience, and then knowing you did it, and returning home. And I felt like if you got to meet Adria Benedict, you could come home. You could say you really did it."

Davina paused. The flow of traffic seemed to have sped up; looking out the window, she seemed, suddenly, to be switching lanes.

"Well, I . . . that's a larger conversation. But I hear you. I do. And . . . I want . . . I want you to know that."

"Okay," Beth said. "Jeremy misses you. So do I. Enjoy these moments. And tell me how it goes."

"Bye now."

Davina kept looking out at the traffic—abated somewhat now, they were really moving—and then, for the first time in a while, up at the driver, the man who'd been listening, she hoped not too closely, to her conversations with the women in her life. Instinctively she looked up at the car's right side, so, rather than seeing the driver (surprising, still, that he wouldn't be seated there, but that's America), she saw, packed in tissue paper and hanging from the car's built-in hanger, her maroon gown. It was something that someone had chosen for her, knowing the person that she was and the person that she wanted to be. All so that she could wear it on the cover of a magazine. One that Adria Benedict might see. Before they finally got the chance to meet, later this season.

She had enough battery life in her, after two phone calls, to send a text, and so pulled up Jana's number.

sorry to leave things on a sour note.
Shall I come by next week to strategize
a few more options for "staying up"?
think it could be fun.

She hesitated over the final line, then decided to type it, why not.

it would be nice if you could help me be a little fancier dressed than adria x

She hit send, surprising herself by feeling nothing but a simple hope that she'd hear back soon. It was easy enough, too, to begin a text to Rory about later tonight. This was only going to be a moment. She might as well live in it.

Jenny Van Meer, *The Diva*

JENNY VAN MEER COULDN'T BE certain—certainty, she thought, inhibited an actor's gifts, and it was preferable to find comfort in ambiguity—but she believed she had something close to ESP.

She'd done some research on the subject (merely as a hobbyist!) over the years. Never for a role, just in keeping with her love of learning. What she had discovered fit her understanding of the way she saw the world, the way she sensed it. She often felt as though she could gather, from the air, what was expected of her to say in a social interaction, what was hanging right over the plate, the only-just-buried subtext that she might bring forward into text, and in so doing achieve precisely what she wanted.

The challenge, of course, was in the execution. Jenny was a woman of her generation, and a woman raised within her own family—she loved Mom and Pup, but, right up until the end, they let propriety reign. Encouraged her and rooted her on, but insisted that she keep her head on her shoulders, not become too good. And then there was what she'd learned as a woman within this industry, trying to remain appealing to financiers and directors who might be put off by a woman who said the wrong thing. Being forthright didn't come easily. There was a certain lack of humility in winning the conversation, in being so blunt, so . . . well. So Adria. And that's why Jenny had let opportunities go.

This was something she'd been trying to work out with Fiona, not that Fiona knew she was doing it. Jenny had chosen her therapist somewhat at random: there was certainly no shame in it, of course, but still, better not to give any ammunition to anyone who might think she was psychologically damaged by her particular lot in life, happy as it was in so many respects. All she'd needed, these past few months, and all that she might need for the next few, was a tune-up.

Fiona came with some particular advantages. She was willing to conduct her practice online, which suited Jenny just fine. No possibility of photos of her leaving a medical complex (not that photographers ever captured her unless they were staking out a Bitty Harbor type in her vicinity—and for that, Jenny was grateful, and sorrowful for the Bittys of the world). No need to worry about proximity at all. Jenny spent most Wednesday mornings—most weeks of the year—at her little place in the mountains up in Idaho. She'd been there full-time, except for her now-occasional jobs, for . . . who was counting? For years now.

This week, though, she'd been in Los Angeles, in a lovely hotel room that the studio had been good enough to rent, all so she could meet the stylist they'd hired for her. The thought of setting up an in-person meeting with her therapist, all the way out in Santa Monica, had barely crossed her mind.

It was 10:58. Jenny had packed for the flight, savored her coffee, then enjoyed some steps on the treadmill in the hotel gym. She'd detected eyes, sweetly eager ones, taking in her image as she ate the dish of sliced cantaloupe she'd ordered in the hotel restaurant after a healthy half-hour walk. She allowed herself the pleasure of very slowly, as if she hadn't known she had an audience, meeting those eyes, seeing their pleasure in realizing it was really her. Tourists. She gave them The Smile, The Nod. That, the coffee, the walk—it had all centered her, as much as she could be. And now, a minute to go.

A square burst into view on Jenny's neutral-toned computer backdrop. There she was, in some office, whose contents Jenny couldn't guess. All that was behind Fiona was wall; all that was in front of her was computer, was Jenny herself.

"Hi, Doctor."

"Hi, Jenny. Again, I don't have a doctorate."

Doctor or no, Jenny had to admit to herself that Fiona looked much more like a therapist than did the practitioner from *Who Is Lisa Farmer?*, covered as Adria's character was in attention-getting wooden beads and bold prints. Jenny acknowledged her thought that mistaking attention-seeking for character development was the Benedict way, and let it go.

"I think it's interesting that you want to give me credentials that I haven't earned," Fiona said. "And, if you like, we could talk about that."

A pause.

"Would you like to discuss that?" Jenny asked.

"It's your time," Fiona said, in a tone of voice as beige as everything else within the rectangle of her world that Jenny could see.

"Where do I begin?" Jenny asked.

Something just out of Jenny's reach hung in the air. She was grateful for the Post-it note that she'd, as she did every week, used to cover the little inset of her own face. Grateful not to see herself.

♦ ♦ ♦

JENNY WAS A STORYTELLER, AND EVENTUALLY SHE FOUND HER way there. She began by explaining to Fiona that it was really nice to have this space, this hotel room, these meetings of the past few days. It all seemed to add up to support, real support, from the studio.

"Win or lose," Jenny sighed.

"I'm interested to hear you mention the awards again," Fiona said.

"Well, it's a little hard to escape. It's why I'm here."

She tried to keep herself from growing flustered, tried to remind herself that one of the effective things about Fiona as a therapist, one of the things that distinguished her from the invasive, grasping woman Adria had just played, was that she knew nothing about the industry, or was, at least, willing to pretend ignorance in order to draw Jenny out.

"As nice as this support is," she went on, "sometimes I wonder if I wouldn't rather be home. A morning like this one, my goodness. I'd have fed the chickens, trimmed the bushes." She paused. "Looked at the sky."

"So," Fiona asked, "why not stay back? What draws you in?"

"Well, it's my work," Jenny said. "And a change of pace can be good."

She thought of the tourists' eyes—three sets: mother, father, daughter. All making their way through thirty-dollar hotel omelets, having been given a treat to remember when they were back home wherever. Jenny was the garnish on their meal. She wondered what they recognized her from, what they recognized her as.

"The hotel really is lovely." Jenny gestured around herself at the room she inhabited, then realized—no. Too theatrical. Fiona couldn't see any more of the room than the wall behind Jenny, of course. "More than I'd have paid for myself. And it feels—this isn't humble, I'm afraid." She smiled in what she hoped was a self-effacing way. "But it feels like a reward I've earned, to get their focus. To have a moment. My own."

"Then I'm delighted for you," Fiona said. "That sounds really nice. Not many women get celebrated in that way." She chuckled, with that therapist's trick of holding what she was thinking just beyond where even Jenny could find it.

"Yes." Jenny grasped for the next thing to say. "And I get to see old friends. Delle Deane. I don't know if we've discussed her."

Was that a spark of recognition in Fiona's eyes? No, no, just the sense of a new topic, new grist for whatever story she was working out for herself about Jenny.

"We worked together, oh, when she was just starting out, and she's a doll, truly. It inspires me to see and meet this new generation—and she is a true friend. I know she'll be there, at some of these events I'll be attending, and to get to reconnect with her will be just—" She felt the drama of herself casting her gaze to the heavens to accept the gift of Delle Deane, allowed it to happen. "It will just be wonderful."

♦ ♦ ♦

JENNY AND DELLE HAD WORKED TOGETHER ON *KISS THE RINK*, A kids' figure-skating movie that Jenny had made ten or so years ago. She wasn't always delighted to have to do things like that, movies so very far from the more artistic fare she'd made when she started—the animated franchise she stepped into a sound booth to voice every few years was worse—but a house in the mountains wouldn't pay for itself. Chickens needed feeding. So, back then, did her father.

So she had signed on and promised herself the next one would be something about which she felt more passionate—maybe she'd finally pull together the funding for *Judith of the Ewes*, based on her very favorite novel. But Delle, at seventeen, had been so vital and alive that it made this commercial experience feel almost like making art. Jenny hadn't had any prior knowledge of Delle before the cameras went up on the first day. Soon enough, she found herself relishing every single different take.

Playing a rebellious figure-skating phenomenon's coach could have been rote; the glare of disappointment when the skater shows up to practice with a bad attitude, the melting-away ease of a grin as the skater finally does what we've always known she was capable of, and hits the triple axel. But Delle played "bad attitude" five different ways in five different takes, and the face of triumph she made to be pasted on her skating double's body—that went five different ways too. Jenny had to adapt. Had to change. It was elemental. What they ended up using as coach congratulated skater was what Jenny now knew to be her signature Smile: lit from somewhere deep within, breaking across her face, lifting her cheekbones, reaching her eyes, with an unpretentious benevolence that suggested that anything was possible. The Smile was one that Jenny smiled for someone else's happiness, and it made her happy, deep-down happy. Delle had helped her find that.

Maybe that could have been her prize. If it hadn't been a kids' movie, for money. If they saw her differently.

But there were other rewards to work like that. Delle was just such fun.

"I always wanted—" she began. "We have talked about this. I always wanted a daughter. And Delle, well—we really had an intimacy. Still do."

Delle had texted her just a week ago to see if Jenny would be going up to the film festival too.

we need to tlk about ADRIA she'd written, with three little icons of a ghost, and then a yellow face vomiting up green slime.

The nourishment she'd taken from this, the weight of her anticipation that soon she'd know what Adria had done this time—she could hold this back from Fiona. The fact that it had gone on for a spirited thirty minutes of texting when she ought to have been doing upkeep on the house or reading a good book or just about anything else. She could hold that back. And she could hold back that she could tell, just tell, that Adria's movie had been the beneficiary of real money, real investment, while *The Diva* . . . well, Jenny had worked hard to make it an experience worthy of her time.

"We share confidences," Jenny said. "It's lovely."

"I think it's interesting that you connect Delle with family," Fiona said. "Like a daughter to you."

"Well," Jenny said, "there's—there's others, of course. Eleanor Quinn-Mitchell—I leave this afternoon for the festival, and I'll see her and Delle both there."

For all Fiona purported to be utterly blind to the world of the awards, Jenny knew, she *knew*, that Fiona hadn't been able to hide her recognition of the first (and still only!) Black woman to have won the top actress prize, those thirty years ago.

"And, well, we've never worked together, Eleanor and me. I've tried to find the opportunities for that, but—well . . ."

"But Adria takes them all," Fiona added. "So Eleanor is like family too?"

"Well, I don't know that I meant that," Jenny said. "Maybe you could call her a sister figure. If you were being generous. I reached out when she lost her husband, and we had a good conversation. We're going to get lunch later in the festival, if we can get away. Or apparently there's some big open-air meal thing up there tonight where we get to speak to the moviegoers."

Get to, never *have to*. To be grateful was its own reward.

"I wonder why you haven't mentioned yet that you'll be seeing Adria."

"Well, at the festival?" Jenny said. "I believe I heard it was up in the air as to whether or not she'd even attend." Last week Delle had texted her that Adria was being "typical" about going, which Jenny understood.

"I didn't mean the festival. I was just speaking generally." There was a hint of a sigh in Fiona's voice, Jenny thought. Her therapist knew Jenny was evading. "You've told me that she's going to be—that she has a movie out too—and that all of your memories, of, of—"

"Of being nominated," Jenny said. "And, yes, not winning."

"That all of those," Fiona said, "seem to feature her. I suppose I'd ask you how this time will be different."

"Well . . ." Jenny began, not knowing where she was headed. She supposed this was the part where no amount of intuition or ESP could get her around things, the part where therapy actually did work, or became work. The only way to the end of the session was through this.

"I do think this time will be different. I was younger then. I didn't have control over my emotions like I do now. It's been a lot of life."

Fiona leaned forward as Jenny continued.

"I've also settled my feelings a bit. No one wants to lose every time, but—maybe it's less raw now. Still, you always have that hope."

She would need to be warm, would need to present a face to so many people, would need to scale up what she'd done earlier over a plate of half-ripe melon—The Smile, The Nod—to all of her peers, all of the world. Why not start now? Suddenly, Jenny knew that she would make herself believe it, for these months ahead. That it didn't really matter. That this was all a fresh start.

"Adria has had so many chances," she mused. "And that's wonderful."

She felt herself meaning it, through the haze of rivalry and the prickle, always there when she heard or said that name, of feeling unseen, unheard, unwanted. Always second best, if even second. But she was forgetting that feeling now. It was working. She was feeling it. Contentment. Optimism.

"But, you know, one of these times?"

She laughed, a chortle that felt like it had the power to change the take, to shift her story into a different genre altogether. She gave Fiona The Smile, and gave it to herself too. Her image was blocked by a Post-it, but she could imagine the contours of her lips being beamed in, shifting the tone and lightening the pressure in the beige blur of Fiona's half-imaginary office. She felt it. She knew.

"I just have to hope," she said, knowing that it was something more than hope she felt inside. It was certitude. Doubt could come later. "I hope that this time, it'll be my turn."

Adria Benedict,
Who Is Lisa Farmer?

ADRIA WAS IN HELL!

Well, it wasn't hell. It was Colorado. Close enough.

Her phone was ringing, again. She didn't need to check—she knew. It was Howard, reminding her, as he had in multiple voicemails and text messages, that she had a contractual obligation to promote the film, and that now was hardly the time to make the studio—the streamer—regret investing in a story about an older woman, or a project centered on Adria Benedict.

But it wasn't centered on her, was it? If it were, she'd be getting dressed for the opening-night dinner right now, not sprawled across the bed in the nicest suite in the nicest hotel in the smallest town in the West, trying to block out the smell of the big bouquet of roses on the dresser, affixed as they were with a note from the studio congratulating her on her work. Under those circumstances, if she were planning to go out, she'd be mildly begrudging about it, only slightly, just because this was such a nice suite and she'd come so far, and it would be so lovely to sit. The roses would smell sweet, not cloying. There would still be the matter of her injured hand—although maybe, in her fantasy, it could simply be healed. In reality, it throbbed violently, still. No amount of hotel lotion, no matter how many more mini-bottles she called up from the front desk, could calm it. It looked grotesque, alien, like the surface of Mars. If she were the lead, she could be planning ahead to sitting front-row in a few months' time, telling herself a little joke about how everything comes with a price.

Of course it did. She already knew that. But that way, the fact of it would be funny.

What if it peels?

Either way, she'd be going to the awards. The dust would have settled from her having skipped all of the events here (she'd asked Howard, in her only call to him—terminated by her hanging up—to have his office book her a flight back to Los Angeles tonight); she'd be supporting, but of course she'd go.

And then what if it scars?

How red and raw her hand had become—not red and dry like a desert planet, that was wrong. Red like meat, like the ground beef her mother used to blend with pork and veal and roll into meatballs on Sundays. God, that turned Adria's stomach, the animal flesh beneath the skin.

There had been one time that Jenny was nominated and Adria wasn't; she'd taken six months off working at Dr. Golden's advice, and so there was no film to nominate. Of course, the same advice, to take time off, had never been given to Bill. She'd convinced him to watch the ceremony at home with her.

This was something to think about—something other than the throb, so alive in its ability to travel up and down her hand, and then the dull, dead ache beneath it.

It had been just after they'd spent Thanksgiving with the Thomases in Italy—Willy and Jamey both went to their wives' families that year, and Lindy was with some little friend of hers—and Linda Thomas had sent over a wonderful case of the Montepulciano they'd enjoyed together in Tuscany "just because," two days after Jenny received the nomination. Watching the ceremony, Adria had tried to explain to Bill that Jenny trying to hide her age by covering her hands in those horrible, tacky opera gloves was the very reason why she always lost. Hands were the first thing to age, as Adria well knew—hers gave her away too. But to hide them was worse. Jenny was too pathetic—she tried so hard to give the world what she thought they wanted that she never gave them a self.

It was the beginning of a real theory! It would have been good to talk to Bill about these things. Instead, he'd told her he thought she might be done with the red for the night, and eventually decided to head to the driving range; the one nice thing about watching awards shows at home on the West Coast was that they wrapped by eight or so. You forgot that in the room. All the eveningwear in the afternoon cast a funny kind of time-shifting spell. Adria kept watching long enough to see Jenny lose.

And that—that!—was why she couldn't wear gloves. It would look like she was trying to hide something. Three of these awards in quick succession, then a twenty-year dry spell. She wanted to break the record with a fourth; she had to be a her she'd never been before. Sex was never the point of an Adria Benedict performance, but neither was frumpiness; she didn't have to be cool, but she couldn't be Grandma. Not onscreen, at least. (Of course she loved Jamey's Rowan and Edie, *of course.*) Not yet.

One was Adria's limit these days, but she had earned it, and there was still half a bottle of tonic water left in the minibar. She used her left hand to prop herself up, gracefully as she was able, then shuffled her way to open a second little tubelet of gin.

♦ ♦ ♦

THE PLANE'S LANDING HAD BEEN AS BAD AS EVERYONE HAD SAID IT would be, and Adria had briefly thought they would hit the runway nose-first. It was a moment that thrilled her in its perversity; she knew that if they all died together, her name would come first in the headline. There was a comfort in that, and so, for all her carrying-on during the turbulence, she didn't have the same reaction upon impact that the others did. She sniffled a bit, sure, but mainly about the pain in her hand, the hand that would sadly soon be holding a trophy for supporting Delle. Not about the landing. *Who cares about that?* Everyone cried upon descent, they said: well, people were all the same, except when they weren't.

She'd rushed off the plane—thank God Howard's office had arranged her own airport transfer (and charged it to the streamer). Adria had burbled over her shoulder about how she needed to get to the hotel to get her hand looked at. Looked at by whom? Stupid thing to say; the streamer man had called after her that they could look into getting a local doctor to come by her room and tape her up before tonight's dinner.

Tonight! There wasn't going to be a tonight. Tonight she'd be on the next flight out, the one Howard was going to buy her. Holding a cold glass of a first-class gin and tonic up against her hand between small sips. Feeling the hand heal as the lime effervesced into the bubbles into the liquor into her bloodstream. And then she would be home. She should probably call Bill. But she couldn't bear the idea of hearing him disappointed she'd be home early.

The phone rang again. Adria debated answering. If it was Howard, it was probably about time for her to obtain the flight details he'd be passing on—right? She flipped it over and saw the name of the man from the streamer. A whole new debate, conducted in the few seconds before Adria figured it would go to voicemail; stirring up a fresh wave of needles across the back of her hand, she picked up the call, set it to speaker so as not to have to hold it.

"Adria." The voice, with the untrained boom of a tuba, echoed off the walls. "How are you?"

She sensed real concern, but couldn't place its object. For the movie, no doubt. Not for her. Not for the well-being of a supporting actress.

"I'm not sure," Adria said. "If I'm being realistic, I don't think it'll scar. Nothing like that."

"It certainly looked painful," the streamer man shouted. "We can still call and get a doctor to you—to your room. I take it you're there?"

"I don't think that'll be necessary," Adria sniffed. "I'll wait to be seen in Los Angeles."

The air, somehow, seemed to get thinner. How high up were they, anyway? "I don't know that I'd wait three days, if I were you," the voice said, sounding like an actor at a table read, only now familiarizing himself with the beats of the script.

"No, tonight. I'm—I'm going to leave."

"Then I think we have nothing left to discuss without involving your representation," the voice said. There was such a coldness to people like him; that was what it took, Adria knew, but it could still stun her. "Including your attorney."

"I don't know that we—" Adria began. The line went dead.

This was bad. Maybe she ought to have been picking up Howard's calls.

Her phone rang again: Delle. Adria controlled the sudden urge to throw it across the room. All that would give her would be a ruined hand *and* a ruined phone. And a ruined campaign.

She already knew what Howard would say: That she'd really done it this time, that even Adria Benedict couldn't count on things breaking her way 100 percent of the time. That a win for supporting was still a win, and a loss of face—she could only imagine what they'd write if it got out that she'd skipped the whole festival over a bruised ego as well as a burnt appendage—was something else altogether. She never lost. She'd just have to find another way to win.

This last part wasn't Howard. It was her. She took a swig of the gin and tonic, finished it off. She would have to go tonight, wouldn't she, as badly as she didn't want to.

Who else to call? Not Howard, not yet. Let the hammer fall just a bit later, once she was out of options. Not Bill. For a wild second or two, it felt as though it ought to be Lindy, but that wasn't right. Not right at all. Let her enjoy being a student—still, at Lindy's age, a student!—without having to worry about her mother.

Maybe it was time to leave the room. To see what it would be like. When she did what she had to do tonight. When she made herself act as if she wanted any of this. And to get away from that awful bouquet. Something in this room was really starting to smell of rot.

♦ ♦ ♦

ONE MORE FULL MINI-BOTTLE OF HAND LOTION, RUBBED IN AS firmly as Adria could bear, until no greasy sheen remained. She pulled the sleeves of her sweater down low over her hands, held them in fists like a child. She knew this would stretch out the sleeves—as she was always telling Lindy. And it would stain the right sleeve with lotion besides. But what was a $350 sweater right now? She just needed to test it. Test herself.

Maybe it would be easy! Howard had told her that stars just kind of milled around in street clothes—that was the point, to show that the Adria Benedicts of the world were just movie lovers too, normal enough for a fan to admire without developing an inferiority complex. No one would bother her until dinner, when she was on display. And that was part of the job. She thought of the dress she'd brought, a simple early-fall cotton thing with cap sleeves, to be worn with a nice little wrap. *Where can I find opera gloves,* she thought, *in the middle of fucking nowhere.*

She was unaccustomed to the feeling of thinking ahead twelve hours and having no idea what might end up transpiring. She'd be here, or home; she'd have gone to the dinner, or not; she'd be lead, or supporting. As she walked to the door, she was possessed by a new resolve. She *would* go to the dinner, wouldn't she? If she could make it out of this room. It would be a great surprise, another remarkable Adria Benedict moment—the way the whole team's faces would light up, if only with shock, as they saw her. Things would work out for her, just as they always did. The hot coils running across the surface of her hand were just a reminder of something she could overcome.

No sunglasses for the hotel bar. Too easy to come across as above-it-all; she had to simply trust that no one would meet her gaze. She walked down the hall toward the elevator, holding her sleeves tight. The rub of cashmere on burnt skin was growing almost pleasurable, its predictable jabs of pain a way to mark time passing, time until this godforsaken exercise was all over.

Adria was starting to relax into the buzz of two drinks. She could do this. There, at the elevator, was someone, but not Delle, thank goodness. Clad nicer than Adria, in a tailored pantsuit that suggested actual effort, not just the effort it took to look effortless. The woman's head turned.

"Adria," she said, as if she'd been waiting for her. "Hello."

"Eleanor." Adria exhaled, made herself display a kind of mirth. "Oh, Eleanor. I am so glad to see—what are you doing here?"

Adria knew Eleanor Quinn-Mitchell hadn't worked, by some combination of circumstance and choice, in, what, seven years? The poor thing, losing herself in taking care of her husband as he died. They'd had such a partnership in the later years of Eleanor's working life, Adria knew—and even if they hadn't, it still seemed such a blow. To lose Bill . . . well, Adria couldn't fathom it.

But she would have kept working, she knew. Even in grief. That would be her solace, her heroic self-preservation, her finding a way forward. *That,* Adria had thought as she heard stories of Eleanor's retreat from the world, *will never happen to me.*

"I'm in a movie this year, Adria." Eleanor's tone was even. "*The Glass Menagerie.*"

"Oh!" Adria said. "I had no . . . Forgive me. I hadn't known."

Good for Eleanor. Coming back. To a place she shouldn't have left so long.

"It isn't much." A certain tone of resignation had entered her voice. "They're giving me one of those special tributes here, but it isn't much."

How had Adria not known? Eleanor waved her hand in the air dismissively, as if to bat Adria's thought away.

"I don't mind telling you," she said, "it could have been better. The girl playing my daughter . . ." Eleanor raised her eyes to the ceiling and exhaled, hard.

Eleanor had always been so easy to talk to! Why hadn't Adria made more of an effort to cultivate her all these years? Well, perhaps now was her chance.

"I had a similar thing happen to me," Adria said. The elevator door opened, and they got in, Eleanor first. It was the two of them alone, for a few moments. "And now I'm stuck here with this . . . twenty-something . . . from my movie."

Eleanor nodded slowly, stoically.

"We worked it out so that I'd be representing the movie here, and Miss Contessa would be elsewhere. She's shooting a magazine cover, I think." Eleanor exhaled. "Seems like something she'd be best at."

The elevator doors opened—were they at the ground floor so quickly?

"Say." Adria attempted to sound cordial, chipper. "Want to join me for a quick drink? Lobby bar?"

"I'm sorry," Eleanor said as the two walked into the lobby. "I really am." She looked at Adria for a long moment. "Because I've always admired you. I just need a little time to myself. Being here—it's a lot to take in."

Eleanor moved toward the door, and Adria felt an urge to chase her, to be like that poor girl Bitty and confess how much she just wanted to spend time with her. But Adria didn't move.

"I was just coming down to get some air," Eleanor said with a goodbye nod.

Adria watched as Eleanor made her way into a circular driveway lined with pines, then walked out of her line of sight.

Adria hadn't realized Eleanor was working at all, so they might not have had much to talk about. She probably could have made more of an effort with Eleanor over the years, but Eleanor was so withdrawn, and the whole litany of expectations she faced, first Black winner—Adria couldn't easily relate to much of Eleanor's story, and it didn't come naturally for her to be seen trying.

She hadn't thought about her hand the whole time she was with Eleanor.

So, the lobby bar. No one would be there. Well, fans of movies, even her movies, maybe. But they'd give Adria her distance, her privacy, allow her to gather herself before she had to face the whole world. They would allow her the space to figure out how this story about herself could be made coherent.

Where did Eleanor go? Adria wondered. She herself had been so wild-eyed on the ride from the airport that she'd barely noticed there wasn't really much around. Just a vale of trees. Maybe Eleanor was off hugging one. She'd always been a bit of an odd bird. There was more than one reason she'd been set apart from the rest of them, maybe.

Oh, be nice. But where *was* the lobby bar? Adria had heard there was one, somewhere. She had a theater-class inclination to spin blindly, to stick her finger out as she twirled, and to follow it once she'd stopped. But that was silly. Someone might see. She sneaked a glance at the balled-up cashmere in her hands, seeing an oily bleed of lanolin through the oatmeal-colored sleeve. This sweater wouldn't come home with her. She'd figure it out.

She cast her gaze around the lobby: front desk, sitting area and fireplace, elevator, the end. She'd never find Eleanor, didn't know that she wanted to, but why not venture outside? She walked out the front door.

She'd barely registered the outside world on her plummet from airport to hotel, but now—ah! The air, did it feel good against the burnt skin of her hand? Maybe it did! She loosened her grasp on her sleeve, let it go entirely.

She looked to her left—just the side of the hotel, buttressed by more tall trees, ancient and dignified. And then to her right. Wait. *That* was it! A set of chairs casually strewn around a fire pit, not yet lit; a small bar set up against the exterior wall of the hotel, with a white-jacketed bartender behind the counter, making use of good weather while he still had it.

What harm would it do to have one more gin and tonic in the sunshine? She started walking toward the bar. And then she noticed. Not just the chairs but the people in them. Delle's back was toward Adria, but it was Delle—same grubby outfit, same choppy and two-toned haircut, same haughty attitude in the shoulders. And there was Jenny, facing Delle, facing Adria, looking somehow different. Just older than the last time Adria had seen her. But beyond the slightly more stooped posture and behind the wrinkles, less controlled than last time, there it was. A face Adria recognized so intimately, it was as if it belonged to an old friend.

Delle and Jenny were happily chatting, it seemed, with Delle's back hopping up and down in raw and unaffected laughter. At least it sounded unaffected. Jenny, in some god-awful denim shirt—*so she's a cowgirl now?*—cackled. Adria could hear it now.

She tried to look away, but not before Jenny caught her eye; then Delle turned too. The younger woman stared blankly, as if truly confused for the first time that day, while Jenny seemed to gesture Adria over with her eyes, made some tractor-beam maneuver to signal that Adria ought to come say hi. Adria never quite knew how Jenny did it, managed to get inside her head, managed to weaponize Jenny's own need. She mouthed *Sorry!* and turned around, walked back into the lobby, and felt herself stop just short of breaking into a run as she came toward the elevator.

Back in her room, she dialed the number, one she knew by heart.

Her hand burned anew as she held the phone, but it didn't matter. It had come, she knew, to feel righteous, a symbol of her martyrdom. Or at least the hand thing wouldn't matter, once she'd gotten the world to see it her way.

"Howard," she gasped into her phone as soon as the line connected. "Howard, we need to figure something out. Don't let them bring in lawyers." Her breath, she realized, was ragged. She forced herself to slow it down. "I think we've all made our points. I'll do anything they want me to if you figure this out. If we set this right."

She listened to his assurances. She was doing the right thing.

"And, Howard?" she said. "I'm not speaking to him, but when you talk to the man from the streamer, can you tell him I'm being agreeable? And can you have him send a doctor up? I need my hand looked at. Before the dinner tonight."

From "Bitty Harbor Hits Different," cover story
in a men's magazine's November issue

I'm on the verge of telling Bitty Harbor my grand unifying theory of what it means that an icon-in-the-making—the nuclear-grade bombshell who played the lead of some of the last decade's funniest comedies, all grown up at twenty-eight and ready to leave childish things behind—is now playing one of the key figures in the Late American historical parade. Then I catch myself looking into her eyes.

An elliptical shape in which one could lose oneself, coolly hooded as if concealing some deeper inner self no red-blooded American man could resist trying to find. Hazel at the center and ever-so-slightly bloodshot in a manner that hints at tears you wish you could have been there to dry, they're what a college friend called "girlfriend eyes." The kind you want to look into to see your future. Or hers. Maybe, if you're a profoundly fortunate man, those two can be congruent.

But today, my future entails nothing more than a few rounds with a girl who can more than hold her own at the bar. "My publicist wanted us to go mini-golfing," she says, rolling those eyes (those eyes!). "But that seemed so corny." She picks up her second vodka and cranberry, the drink some call a Cape Codder. It's a nod, perhaps, to her own roots in New England, emerging from rural Maine as something close to a fully formed star. Or it just fits the moment: crimson as passion, and strong as she's needed to be to climb the Hollywood heap. She twirls the straw, smiles a heart-melting smile. "And I've had tough experiences with magazines." She takes a sip, bats the thought away. "But I feel really safe with you."

That voice—so familiar from finding the way toward the punchline in comedies like *Beach Girls* and the *One Crazy Weekend* franchise. (A certain stripe of Elder Millennial man may, after a couple drinks—Cape Codders or otherwise—admit that he has her "you're a pain in the vagina" monologue from *Another Crazy Weekend* committed to memory.) The voice is musical, with a touch of rasp, all in service of something a little daring. (Perhaps only Hollywood power publicist Leanna Finch's favorite client has the nerve to tell her when her ideas aren't working.) This is the kind of voice that could make you envy Lyndon Johnson. Even though he's dead.

She takes the lime from her Cape Codder, puts it in her mouth, bites down. "Oh my God!" she laughs. "I thought that would be funny, but I always forget how tart it is!" Her hair, styled in the sort of loose curls whose effortless appearance means you know they took all day, has fallen over one of her eyes. It would be churlish to complain.

What does it mean that a generation of American males' favorite fantasy is strapping on a skirt suit and pearls? She'd tell you it means that she's ambitious. "This was a really great part—the history is so interesting," she tells me. Her voice falls into an alluring whisper as she goes on, turning the narrative of getting cast into a battle, or a seduction. "I had to fight for the role. But Lady Bird's a fighter too." But maybe, if only subconsciously, it's a signal that she's a star from a different era, crash-landed into our own fallen, post-movie-idol world. Playing opposite Webster's-dictionary-defines-Alpha-Hunk-as type Josh Jorgen, Bitty's Lady Bird seems always to need his protection—even when she's standing up for her man and her family, a new quaver has entered that voice, a new huskiness. And that makes us want to protect her too.

"Whose round is it?" she asks, those eyes (yes!) twinkling once more. Suddenly, she's not the fragile movie star. She's the good-time girl from inland Maine, the one who put state school on hold to pursue fame. (And she swears she's going to finish her degree someday! Say a prayer to the ghost of Lady Bird Johnson that she doesn't: just like girlfriends since time immemorial, she majored in art history, but this is a woman who belongs on the big screen, not cloistered in a dusty museum wing.) It's her turn to head to the bar, if I'm being honest. But I tell a lie. Because Bitty Harbor is the kind of girl for whom you get the drinks.

Bitty Harbor, *Lyndon and Claudia*

"BITTY *ISN'T* MY REAL NAME," Bitty said.

She leaned forward slightly, as if inviting the viewer into a secret, making fleeting eye contact with the bland, unbothered camera operator before returning her attention to the camera's glass iris. As this format cut out her interviewer's whining, sharp voice—he "*had* to ask" if Bitty was her real name, with the verb pitched half an octave up—she'd been told to frame everything as a complete sentence, as if it all were a series of original thoughts she just wanted to share.

She did her best to adjust herself, to shift her weight imperceptibly in order to feel comfortable in the bathrobe the magazine was making her wear for this video. She went on.

"But it's also not exactly a stage name. I was the youngest of three growing up in Maine, and the only girl, and my middle brother—his name is Robby—couldn't really pronounce 'Katie.' And I really was itty-bitty! It just seemed fun, and it made me . . . stand out."

She trailed off, letting these last two words evaporate, hopeful they might become inaudible as she spoke them. She'd lost the thread of a perfectly serviceable answer just before she finished giving it.

"And you're certainly not so bitty anymore!" the interviewer remarked.

Bitty gazed at him with what she hoped was a calmly appraising look. She'd never been good at the sort of hauteur she supposed a performer was meant to suddenly develop with a certain level of success. And it was hard to present as being above anything when she was attempting to look relaxed in a fluffy white bathrobe that kept slipping open, along with concealed shapewear and a full face of makeup.

Leanna made a gesture toward clearing her throat. Bitty had to complete this video to give the magazine something to put online with the Movies Issue cover, but she just hoped it'd be over soon. She assumed the journalist felt the same.

"I just mean," he said, "that your career is so *big*. Nothing bitty about it."

Bitty turned to pick up the bottle of water that had been placed out of frame. At her request, it had been placed to her left side, so that when she picked it up, she could sneak a glance at Leanna. Her publicist had the bearing, right now, of a sagacious elder, wise to all the chaos of the world but enlightened enough to be able to see the bigger picture. Or at least the less bitty one.

"I'm sure this is, uh, out there, that people know it," the journalist continued, in an unconvincing pantomime of as-yet-unfulfilled curiosity, "but just for fun, what's your, uh, real name? Your legal name."

This last part was less a question than a challenge—the word "legal," delivered in the tone of a process server handing over a summons, gave the game away—and Bitty felt grateful that she didn't have to respond spontaneously. She wished that Leanna hadn't convinced her, back then, that this stupid childhood nickname was so stickily memorable.

Even as she rolled her eyes to some degree more than "slightly," to ensure the journalist would notice, she kept herself from looking at Leanna. It felt like playing the game on easy mode to have her publicist bail her out now. Bitty felt a strange surge of pride that was almost as destabilizing as the waves of nausea that came every few minutes: Look at her! Doing this when most would be sick in bed!

"My name is actually Katie," Bitty said. "That's the name I was born with."

"Wow!" the journalist exclaimed. "Katherine Harbor?"

Maybe she should have agreed to do what some of the other women would be doing today, once Bitty left the set and her peers, the women with less powerful publicists, were allowed to enter. Leanna had told her that some of the women would be interviewing each other, but that it seemed like a bad idea to share the spotlight. Bitty could understand that.

But think of how much better it would have been to get asked questions by Contessa or someone, rather than this clown! He reminded her so much of—well, every interviewer. Including the guy whom she'd had to talk to for a men's magazine a couple of months ago. She'd suggested they go to a bar just to make the hours-long interview more bearable. But he didn't seem interested in her movie at all. Or much of anything beyond his idea of her. It was easy enough to play into that idea, to be flirty, goofy. To be the kind of girl who laughs when nothing is particularly funny. But it was a little depressing too.

"No, my legal name is Katie." Bitty was smiling too hard.

"Can you actually," the journalist said, "just because it's so interesting that Lady Bird was also a nickname—can you say that as a sentence that's kind of like, 'My legal name is Katie,' and then maybe explain why—the whole, it's a nickname, but it's a legal name, but you also have a nickname, of it all?"

She wanted to tell him that it wasn't that serious, that everyone knew Adria Benedict was a made-up name too, that at least "Bitty" came from a family nickname, that there was a meaning to it. It was something that Bitty had kept from her real life, before all this. But she couldn't. She envisioned something cracking, pieces of her face falling to the floor like porcelain as fault lines emerged from her brittle smile. At that moment, a near-unbearable tension headache seemed to quake across her skull, with its epicenter in her pressed-together lips, perfectly colored and lined. She had to say *something*.

"Of what all?" she asked, her voice flat and dry.

"Maybe," Leanna said drily, "we could move off of the name concept."

"Good, uh, good by me!" the journalist said too loudly, as if Leanna were in another wing of the building, rather than simply out of the camera's line of sight. And then, to Bitty: "You know how it is . . . everyone has things they want you to ask, and sometimes they're silly, but . . ."

Bitty decided that, having deployed her bad cop effectively, she could be merciful. She gazed at him with as soft and limpid eyes as she could conjure. Yes, she did know how it was to be asked to do things that were stupid for work. She was here, wasn't she?

♦ ♦ ♦

LEANNA HAD INFORMED BITTY WEEKS AGO THAT, ALTHOUGH she'd talked Ceridwen Darby's team down from forty-five minutes to thirty for the video interview, Ms. Darby herself would not budge on the concept. The idea was, as expressed in an email Leanna read to

Bitty over the phone, "taking readers behind the glamour"—and so, after Bitty had posed for the cover shoot, she then had to change into a bathrobe and act as if she'd been caught getting ready.

Maybe, she'd thought, as she walked triumphantly out of the photo studio back into the dressing room to change, this was really acting!

Leanna had accompanied her back to the second studio where they were now shooting on video; it was hard not to notice how strangely quiet it felt, how eerie not to have all of the other girls who'd eventually be on the cover with her. It was good of Leanna to ensure that Bitty would get to shoot alone, she supposed. But there was alone, and then there was . . .

Now, sitting here with the journalist doing the video interview, she felt a gnawing hunger. She knew she'd been wrong to pass up the food—it was always the same thing at shoots like these, the tureens of quinoa with the chopped-up red bell peppers or the arugula salad—but taking a plate would have felt like an admission, in front of Leanna, that she needed something to get her through.

And she was stronger than that!

"A-anyway," the journalist continued. "Can we talk about *Lyndon and Claudia*? More people will have seen it by the time this issue is out early next year, and you're amazing in it."

Bitty smiled at the praise. That was easy enough to do.

"So, I guess my question would be, when was the first time you ever heard of Lady Bird Johnson, and what did you think of her?"

These questions were murder, and the culprit was being allowed to escape. How awful that he'd be edited out of the final video, forcing Bitty to act as if she were speaking to herself, along these inane lines he'd set forth for her.

". . . How strong she was, just, really, a pillar of support for her husband—and for the whole country, you know," Bitty said, rummaging through her thoughts.

Just two nights ago, she'd been flipping through a magazine that had come to her house, with Delle and Adria on the cover. She knew better than to read it, but she had indulged, and she couldn't control how envious she had felt when she'd seen Adria refer to Delle as—what was it? Another daughter? She'd said all this to Josh last night, and he just laughed, told her that Delle Deane would be lucky to have half of Bitty's talent, and gently slugged her in the arm. That felt good. But she hadn't gotten it out of her head. It made her wonder about Adria's real daughter, Lindy—Google said she'd gone to Princeton, was a grad student somewhere now. Not many photos of her at awards ceremonies with her mom. Bitty would have been at every one.

What must it be like to be so proximate to greatness—like Lady Bird, married into it as a wife, or like Lindy or Delle, born or adopted into it as a daughter? It made Bitty so sad. She had wanted, the night she'd looked Adria's daughter up, to plunge into another reality and become Lindy Greenaway. (Lindy couldn't possibly be Lindy's real name either, right?)

For now, she was simply Bitty. And thank goodness she had memorized the part she was currently saying, about how highway beautification was a symbol of Lady Bird's faith in American potential. She hoped that she hadn't let her voice drop into its lower, hoarser register as she'd been thinking, that there wouldn't be recorded proof that, when she'd woken up this morning, she'd noticed all but one of her pack had been smoked before bed.

Why be negative? Bitty felt a surge of pride burst through the pulsating agony residing somewhere behind her forehead. This shoot, this day, was definitely different from before. The last time she was on the

Movies Issue cover, she and Delle had been interviewed together, but just for the print issue. No video cameras were there to capture Bitty squirming, but they only used two quotes from her, both of them trite and silly. She'd told herself then that press was just for fun. But this was her chance to do something a little more serious!

"Were you worried at all that the character might seem a little retrograde today?"

Bitty was fighting through haze and itch—why were her upper arms suddenly so prickly and irritated? Was it this robe, whose purported comfort ended up making her feel nervous and ill-at-ease, without the girding structure of the normal press-day costume? Did hangovers change after twenty-seven? Or did everything? But beneath or just beyond it, she felt, in a funny way, proud. This guy thought she was smart enough to answer a question about politics.

"Well," Bitty began, tilting her head and squinting, as if gazing through a pair of glasses.

This was her literary moment. Maybe actresses could be historians too! Maybe that'd make this job something to be proud of, something a little less vain.

"—I'm sorry, I have to butt in," chimed Leanna, who, from Bitty's perspective, wasn't and didn't. "We were really just—I have to admit—thinking that this was going to be a little more about celebrating the movies of this year."

"Totally, totally, it is!" The journalist flushed, his voice strained and reedy.

Witnessing his abasement was even harder when Bitty considered that it was being done on her behalf. She glanced at the cameraman, and he gave her nothing. He'd been here this whole time, Bitty marveled, forgettable even as she was endlessly angling herself toward the machine he operated. He was silent and unobtrusive, just another figure in the glutted economy held up by people like her begging for awards. And he was, perhaps, the second-most-competent person in this room.

"It's just . . ." The journalist seemed to choose his words, over and over, with such exceeding care that they ended up sounding offensively careless. Or maybe, it hit Bitty, she was still just a little fucked up. "I think we all agree," he began in tortured tones, "that the role of the First Lady has changed a lot . . . and the role of women more generally . . . since—"

"Got it." Leanna was, for once, looking up from her phone. "Maybe we can have Bitty explain why she thinks Lady Bird Johnson was *ahead* of her time, actually."

"That is definitely another way to put it!" the journalist blurted.

"Great," Leanna said serenely. "Bitty, are you ready?"

This last part sounded vaguely threatening for the first time today, and Bitty couldn't be sure why—she and Leanna were on the same team. Was she ever not ready, when it came down to it, despite the occasional obstacles that Bitty was more than entitled to set up?

"Yep!" she said, and began to describe what a unique partnership Lady Bird and Lyndon had shared, and how it was actually not unlike the partnership she'd had with Josh, and she was lucky he'd been able to take a break from the comic-book universe to shoot this movie with her, ha, and the real Lyndon was six foot four, so she was lucky she had the real-life Scubaman towering by her side, double ha. (If only Josh were here! He always handled these types of things well—she'd watched his talk show interviews online. He had such good answers when they asked him about all the historical research he'd done into LBJ. She felt an odd kind of safety imagining his steadiness, the way he knew just how to express himself in all the ways she never could. He got asked different questions, and that helped too, of course.)

At least she had the security of having memorized her spiel about Lady Bird months ago. And it didn't feel untrue: she'd been lucky, in taking the first offer she'd gotten after losing out on *Who Is Lisa Farmer?*, that this part actually gave her something to dig into. Schizophrenia opposite Adria would have been a dream (imagine getting to learn from her as a scene partner!), but there was something, at least, in independent-minded beautification with an accent opposite Josh. He'd been, for once, not as bad as his reputation suggested. Much better, actually. They'd met on the chemistry read—he was guaranteed the part, she figured, but there were a few potential Lady Birds waiting to take flight—and he approached her, right before they began reading, with a smirking swagger that suggested he was already deep in character. He wasn't—that was just how Josh was.

"Bitty Harbor!" he'd said. "I'm such a fan." He'd kissed her hand—such a silly, stagy gesture, but there was something in his bearing that undercut the goofiness of all six and a half feet of him bending to find her hand, something that added a touch of self-aware comedy to it. Then, straightening to full height, he'd mentioned a tiny independent horror film she'd made, one where she'd found so many new ways of expressing herself while playing the mom of a five-year-old whom she needed to protect from the dangers in the woods around their home. (Turned out the dangers were all in her head; the danger, in fact, was her.) It didn't have any sort of budget and she'd shot it in twelve days and she was proud of that, proud she'd gotten through, but it also meant that it was barely released. No one recognized her from *Mother in the Forest*; everyone knew her from the string of raunchy sex comedies she'd made when she was first starting out. But he'd known, somehow, that she was proud of it. It had been easy, dangerously easy, to act as if she had loved him for a long time.

Once she got the part, the director seemed more interested in just moving through the setups than saying much of anything about her performance. The early days were lonely. But gaming out their performances together over drinks after the shooting day was done had let Bitty feel like she was in a funny sort of control of things. That was what Leanna would never understand, the way that loosening up her mind after hours helped her feel more open to possibilities, freed from the self-consciousness of being Bitty Harbor.

The day that she didn't feel like she could keep on going, Josh had helped her out, getting the girls who played their daughters off the set and convincing the director, so eager to push ahead, that the production could halt for just a few hours.

"We help each other, Bit," Josh had consoled her, when she knocked on his hotel room door that night to say thanks. "You know that." He'd offered to come back and make sure she got into bed all right, but she had known that there would, eventually, be a time he came to her room, and she wanted it to be perfect. In the meantime, this was how they helped each other. It helped her performance as Lady Bird to know that her Lyndon was endlessly behind her. Bitty had Josh's back too. She had worked so hard to give Lady Bird, to give Claudia, a strong backbone, like in the scene where she stands up to her philandering husband, tells him that he needs once and for all to commit to her. She'd lent Claudia a self-sacrificing nature without being melodramatic, a stoic elegance that felt far from Bitty's own self—Josh had talked her into underplaying the scene where she uses her family inheritance to buy a radio station with Lyndon, to make it feel like a quiet, contemplative decision she half-regrets as she finally commits to shifting from Claudia Taylor to, well, you know.

She had tried to imbue in Claudia's softness and her delicateness an exquisite sensitivity, a taste for the simple glories of nature that reminded her of her mother's love for the yellow flowers she brought home once every couple of months and refused to toss until they were sagging. Claudia loved beautiful things, and she loved her children: she wanted better for them. The First Lady's big project had intrigued Bitty when she'd first read about it in the weeks before flying to Albuquerque (which, for tax reasons, was standing in for Texas): Lady Bird hadn't wanted to abolish highways or to find better, cleaner ways of moving people around the country. But, stuck with the reality she had, she wanted to make it nicer. Bitty could understand that.

Maybe she could save this for one of her acceptance speeches over the course of the season; better not to risk it at the ceremony where they gave you champagne first. Or she could just keep it for herself. Either way, she was speaking along more banal lines, for now.

". . . There's a special kind of power, I think, in that behind-the-scenes support she had to offer," Bitty said. "It gives you a lot to work with, imagining the stuff that isn't public."

"Did she remind you of any strong women in your own life?" the journalist asked.

Was she supposed to say her mother? And, if not, why was that always the first thought? Bitty was stalling, flailing. And suddenly something bloomed on the side of the sunbaked highway of her hungover mind.

"A strong woman doing whatever it takes behind the scenes to make sure the boss looks good?" she asked. "She reminds me of my publicist."

The journalist snorted, and Bitty put on a sort of high-spirited giggle, the one she hated watching herself perform on talk shows. But it was a move that she understood, in a painful agreement with herself, "worked." And she could work it. Tossing her hair back in laughter also allowed her to sneak a look at Leanna, who was now looking back at her somewhat quizzically. Strange, given that Bitty was now fucking acing this.

"O-kay . . ." Leanna said, isolating both syllables. A different nausea announced itself—not the one that had been coming and going, but a deeper, pit-of-stomach feeling she associated with childhood, knowing she'd failed another test and waiting for the teacher to reach her desk, to drop off the paper with "SEE ME" written on the top. Finally, Leanna's laugh emerged as a dry crumple from the back of her throat, and Bitty knew, as her publicist spoke, that it was Bitty, and not the journalist, who was really in trouble.

"You are *not* using that."

♦ ♦ ♦

"I THINK THAT WENT PRETTY WELL!" BITTY SAID, FALSELY bright, as they walked back to the dressing room.

"Mm." Leanna was busily typing into her phone. "Sorry. A minute."

They reached the dressing room, Bitty walking in first, feeling both as though she wanted to grab on to the doorframe for support as she crossed the threshold, and as though her grip might slip and Leanna might see. She got in fine. It was fine. She was back in jeans before Leanna looked up from her phone.

"Sorry. It never ends." Leanna sighed. "It went okay." That word again.

Bitty didn't respond, couldn't. She was so close to having her last social interaction of the day, she thought. So close to the car ride home.

"I just . . ." Leanna stopped herself, started again. "Well, for one thing, Ceridwen wants to meet you, but I'm putting her off for now.

She's not here yet, and I'm telling her team that you have a hard out. There'll be another opportunity. I think the cover shots got strong enough by the end that you'll have a shot at the front fold regardless."

"That's cool."

"I've also asked them to take out some things." Leanna chortled a bit. "The name stuff is good, even if it ran on too long. People are curious about Bitty, Bitty!" She laughed in a choked way. "Then at the end, when you talk about your favorite ice cream flavor and, sorry, even when they asked you to play Fuck, Marry, Kill with the presidents from the sixties, that's fine. You did the right thing killing Nixon—and of course you had to marry Johnson. You stayed on-message."

She suddenly looked graver than she had yet today. Bitty constrained herself from the urge to look away. "But, and I am *really* sorry," Leanna went on, "there'll be other times you get to talk about Lady Bird and what she meant. And this isn't that time. We'll practice some more. And you look ridiculous talking about it in that bathrobe, first of all."

Bitty's cheeks flushed. "This is what they're making us all wear."

"If the other reps are smart, they'll make sure their clients just talk about ice cream and party games too."

Somehow, this was the first time today that Bitty felt tears rushing to her eyes; it was a relief of sorts. It was a place to put all of today's aches.

"What other opportunity is there going to be?"

"I don't know, we'll get you on late night. You'll be a little more prepared. I mean, you're always prepared. But, you know." Leanna sounded grim. "I'll just call the car around. We can discuss on the way to drop you off."

"You know they never let you talk about anything real on late night. You know that!" Bitty couldn't let a tear fall. "Just like that dumb interview you made me do with the men's magazine. And I really did all the research. I really know Lady Bird."

"Let's not talk about that piece." Leanna made an emphatic direct hit onto her phone screen with her index finger. "You just seemed . . . nervous today. Okay? You just seemed nervous. And I don't think you always realize how uncomfortable you can look when you get nervous. We got the photo. It'll look great. This video—it doesn't matter. Let's not let a bit of, you know, nervous energy throw us off. Big day."

Wasn't there another word Leanna could have used, over and over, than "nervous"? It made Bitty sound so weak! Bitty glanced at her publicist, once again tucking her chin to gaze into her phone.

"Thanks for not telling me in advance that all I had to know for this interview was how to talk about ice cream and my stupid name." Bitty felt hot suddenly. "Maybe if you'd done your job, I wouldn't have looked like a *fucking* idiot."

Leanna inhaled audibly. Bitty counted to five before she spoke, but maybe she was just counting too quickly. When Leanna spoke, it was a demonstration of her gift for whispers the likes of which Bitty hadn't witnessed since, well, the last Movies Issue cover.

"Bitty, I've known you a long, long time," Leanna said. "I know your brand of cigarettes. I know that you never eat on a shoot, even when you are only punishing yourself. I know that for whatever godforsaken reason, daffodils are your favorite flower. And all I'll say right now is that this is going to be a long awards season." She placed her phone into the purse slung over her shoulder.

"What I mean by that," Leanna continued, "is that I am going to try to hold your hand—literally, when I have to—but I need you to do your part. You did an exceptional job in the movie. You did an okay job today. Not as intense as you can get, which I'll take as a credit to my teachings."

Bitty tried to summon something from Lady Bird—her optimism?—that would allow her to take this as a compliment. She was coming up empty. Lady Bird had backbone.

She was so tired.

"But knowing you as long as I have means that I do know how you get. You need to be careful with yourself. And you really need to—I'm sorry, okay?—you do need to watch the drinking."

"I know," Bitty said, so quickly that she startled herself. "It's just, it's . . . it's been hard." She tried to find the thing to say that would earn a retroactive forgiveness, and a future indulgence. "I don't know how to explain."

"Think of it this way," Leanna said. "I loved what I saw on the photoshoot today, and I'll love it more when they're done fixing it up. But I think we both know that alcohol, leaving aside all its other aftereffects that you've experienced today, has a lot of calories. And you can't wear that big cover-up from the shoot to the awards." Leanna grinned. Of all the fucking things to do with her face. "Now, can we hug it out?"

Bitty stood silently, accepting Leanna's embrace. She moved her arms in the proper ways, felt the head of Leanna's compact body and of her own embarrassment rinse away the memories of the scratch of the cotton robe. She felt whooshes inside her skull as the long-hoped-for quiet in her brain began to delete some of the hardest parts of today, and to put others in storage for safekeeping, to deploy at some future low moment, to beat herself with further.

The blessed silence broke, with a series of dings from Leanna's purse.

"I'm sure that's our car," Leanna said. "Come on. We're just beating Contessa coming in. I know you love her, but. Maybe another time."

"I'll call my own car in five minutes." Bitty's voice was just the right side of a mumble. "I'm taking a minute. I just don't really have anywhere to be."

Leanna stared at Bitty, seeming to want something more.

"I'm sorry I yelled at you," Bitty finally said. She spoke so quietly she could barely hear herself. But she'd known Leanna understood her apology, and accepted it. She always did, in the end.

"Okay." Leanna looked directly at Bitty with her face held in a flat, emoji-esque neutrality. "Just take care of yourself, Katie. It was a long day." She widened her eyes, pulled the corners of her mouth sideways into a horizon of emotionlessness. "The first long day of many, right?"

Contessa Lyle,
The Glass Menagerie

Contessa had always hated the smell of smoke, even before she first met Bitty.

She could pick up the scent on directors' shirts on *Nina in Charge* when they huddled with her to give her notes on how surprised she was supposed to act when Nina faced her latest setback. She'd sensed it on her director from *The Glass Menagerie*, when he came in close and used his hands to position her body just the way he saw Laura—never mind how he saw Contessa, she supposed. She could even summon it from her first shoot, the car commercial where she'd delivered the slogan at the end. The actor playing her dad, she'd thought each time he had to do a take hugging her, smelled sort of moldy. Like old, stuffy air, unable to move freely, dying, molecule by molecule, on his clothes.

She didn't really judge—couldn't imagine smoking, but didn't judge—she just loathed that stink. So she tried to give Bitty as wide a berth as she could as she came into the studio. Bitty, it seemed, was always smoking, or just coming from smoking, but however much she did it, it didn't seem to quiet her anxieties. Whenever Contessa saw her,

Bitty was jerky in her motions, like she was trying to rehearse how to have a conversation while actually doing it. She'd thought about joking with Josh about it, but she knew he was pretty loyal to his costars; he acknowledged Bitty was intense, sure, but the most negative thing he'd really said about Bitty was that it was "intimidating" that she could match him glass for glass.

Which even a girl who'd only been drunk three times in her life knew wasn't actually negative at all.

"There she is," said Melanie as they got out of the car.

Bitty was standing on the curb, cigarette held down by her hip, seeming to watch the smoke break into particles and drift into space. She was wearing loose jeans, just the wrong shade of blue, Contessa thought, and the wrong fit—neither cool for being bleached-out and faded in a chic way, nor cool for being that deep, freshly purchased indigo. These just looked like they'd been washed and dried too many times, and hung awkwardly off Bitty's small frame.

There was no avoiding her; Bitty was close enough to the front door that to not acknowledge her would be a purposeful act of unfriendliness. And they were friends, sort of—right?

"I know," Contessa whispered to her mom out of the corner of her mouth as she slammed the door, hard enough to worry it'd get Bitty's attention. She wanted to give herself a minute, two, before she had to deal with her.

Then they were to the curb, and there was Bitty, seeming to lunge for Contessa. At least that's how it felt; Bitty took two rapid steps toward her, still holding her cigarette in her right hand but extending the left one for a hug.

"Oop!" Contessa exclaimed with a smile as she dodged the ash. "Don't want a burn!"

"Oh, uh," Bitty stammered as she adjusted her position, then glanced down at her right hand as if she'd forgotten what she was holding. "Right." She took a drag, gently, as if sipping a hot coffee. "Sorry, Contessa."

"It's no big deal! At all," Contessa said, laughing nervously. "Anyway. I'm paired up with Davina Schwartz for the interview. You did yours solo, right?"

"Right." Bitty dropped her butt, ground it into the pavement with her heel. "It just—it seemed like a good idea."

"We really can't stop," Melanie said. "We're late. Contessa wanted to squeeze in spin class *and* a stylist session before this. Most girls don't work their managers this hard."

Bitty was staring so blankly at her that Contessa felt a little shocked when she eventually spoke.

"Gosh," she muttered. "I just, uh, woke up and came straight here."

She looked at Melanie with what seemed to Contessa a strange searching expression. She was so unlike Lady Bird in the movie Contessa had now seen twice. (Josh was in it, so.) Lady Bird always knew the right thing to say, and said it forthrightly. A tremble in her voice, appropriate for the role, but forthrightly. Bitty made her that way, somehow.

Eventually this lost, curbside version of Bitty came out with, "Well, I've been meaning to call a car, so," and pulled out her phone, did nothing with it.

It was funny seeing Bitty in her street clothes but with a full face of photoshoot makeup, Contessa thought. Funny that she hadn't bothered to wash it off. Even though they'd all, she knew, received briefs telling them that the makeup concept was supposed to look, on-camera, like they were wearing no makeup at all, Bitty looked spackled, smoothed out. Surreal, like a painting of Bitty Harbor done by an unskilled but enthusiastic fan.

"Cool!" she heard herself say. "Well, have a good day, Bitty."

"Do you want to—" Bitty began, caught herself, kept going. "Would you ever want to hang out? Maybe we can ask Josh too. He really likes you!"

"Josh is the best," Contessa said. "But this is such a busy time. I'll see you at these things, though! I think we're both supposed to be at the panel in a couple of weeks, right?"

"I'm so relieved I'll know someone at these things." Bitty sounded morose. "Assuming . . ."

"You'll get nominated!" Contessa said. She hated that she really believed it. Josh was incredible in the movie, but Bitty, too, had done everything she was supposed to. She gave Bitty a little wave, told her to have a great day, set off.

But Bitty seemed to want to keep talking, addressing Contessa's back as she walked away. "Just so you know, the questions—they're kind of stupid."

"Ugh, I know, they always are!" Contessa shouted as she picked up speed, turning her head just enough to avoid the impression of being impolite.

♦ ♦ ♦

"LET'S TALK ABOUT WHAT DAVINA'S GOING TO ASK AGAIN," MELAnie said as they approached the dressing room. The outfit Contessa would wear on the cover had been agreed upon weeks ago, and would be hanging on a rack with two just-in-case alternates. They were going with something super-princessy, big poofy skirt and fitted bodice; there would be time to take risks later. (That's what this morning's planning session had been all about.) But Contessa paid just enough attention to @ContessaHive and @BestOfContessa, and all the other social media accounts run by her fans, to know that wearing a showstoppingly big dress was giving a public that still mainly knew her as Nina exactly what they wanted.

And that might mean she'd get the front cover! They walked into the dressing room, still empty. Apparently Davina was already ready for the conversation they were going to have. Hopefully they'd make it seem natural for the cameras, even though they were actually meeting for the first time. But maybe that would be better. No preconceptions.

Her phone . . . right. Her phone was in her purse. Had to make sure her mom wouldn't look through her purse, which of course she wouldn't, why would she. But Contessa had to make sure. She really wanted to text Josh, but the safest move would be to surreptitiously leave the bag on top of a high shelf so her mom wouldn't even notice it. But then, if she *did* notice it, she might wonder why Contessa was hiding it.

Why was it such a big deal? It wasn't like he was going to text anyway.

What a sad thought! Contessa indulged herself in a moment of self-conscious drama, of self-pity. It beat thinking about whether or not she was going to get nominated.

That had been one of the first things Josh had said to her that made her swoon, hadn't it? "Hello, our future best actress." He'd been brought on last-minute to *The Glass Menagerie*; apparently he had a week free in his schedule, and the Gentleman Caller character only required a few days on set. His agreeing to be in the movie kept the funding from falling apart, as it continually threatened to. Eleanor had grumbled that it was strange to have an all-Black production of this play that ended with everyone focused on a white man coming for the last few scenes, but Contessa was just glad the movie was getting made. She'd never even seen the *Scubaman* movies, back then.

She'd watched them all now. It was really exciting to see Josh fighting off sea monsters—he looked so good, especially in that one instance, every movie, where they found a way to rip his wetsuit off. It was especially crazy to think that this was a guy with whom she shared . . . something. They hadn't had sex. Obviously. Hadn't done more than exchange a kiss on the hand when they first met—when he bent down and kissed her hand, as they met one-on-one to work out some ideas for the blocking of their scene, she'd impulsively done the same thing, smirking as she looked up and met his eye. There hadn't been any improvising allowed on the *Nina in Charge* set; it felt thrilling to be able to live in the moment. Like an actress, or a woman.

He'd met with her alongside the director, with Eleanor and Jimmy, the other actors, and her mom all present. They'd all exchanged numbers, but the first text had come as a surprise.

wanna meet in your trailer?

jsut to work some things out

After their courtly, charged gesture of trading kisses, that's what they did. They'd worked through how Laura might act on a date. She was impeded in her movements, and, as Contessa played it, first tried to hide it, being as still as possible. Then she might grow a bit more comfortable in displaying her frailty as she—tragically!—got comfortable with the suitor who never cared about her anyway. She might show him a little of how she moved through the world, seeking a kind of acceptance she'd never believed she might find.

"Hello, our future best actress."

That's what he'd said at the end of their third meeting, the end of Josh's third and final day of prep. He was going to shoot for a couple of days, and then he'd be gone. She was getting really comfortable with how Laura moved. How the Gentleman Caller moved to accommodate her. Laura had been crazy to think it might be love. But, as Josh looked at her admiringly—realizing she was nailing it—and did that thing guys do where he pulled his hand down over the corners of his mouth, like he was stroking an invisible beard, Contessa began to think she might not be.

They started texting more after he wrapped. At first jokingly: She sent him a paparazzi picture of himself in which he looked a little gawky, caught between sips of his matcha latte on the street, his lips green like—wow, she never spoke like this—like he'd just eaten out the Wicked Witch of the West. (Where had that come from?) Then he sent her one in which her hair looked a little matted leaving spin class (how'd they find her?) with the comment

rode hard, i see.

Then he said it'd be fun to do a spin class together, but getting on the bike seat was always a little uncomfortable. Then she had joked, knowing something was coming, that it was probably hard when you were six foot whatever, huh?

It *was* hard! But his height wasn't the only reason! And he showed her because he knew she'd be cool with it. She'd been the one to kiss his hand back.

"Hello?" Melanie asked.

"Right! Sorry, where were we?" She opened a random drawer at one of the many vanity mirrors in this dressing room, tucked her purse into it. Good enough. She turned toward her mother, away from the mirror.

"So Davina Schwartz is asking the questions, but the magazine writes them. Well, they suggest them." Melanie made air quotes around "suggest"—she had to be the last person in the world still making that gesture, Contessa thought. "And we had the team tell them not to ask about Eleanor, and they said they'd limit it to one question. Remember, just tell Davina that you think there's room in the category for both of you."

"Ugh. Why couldn't Eleanor just—"

"Why couldn't *you* just," Melanie spat. "You could have won supporting, easy. But it's your choice, and I have to respect it."

"Yeah. We also told them not to ask about—"

"They're not asking about the director, and they're not asking about Jimmy," Melanie said. "They get two questions about *Nina*—a question and a follow-up." She flicked through her phone. "Oh, here it is. Davina is going to ask you to play Fuck, Marry, Kill—what the fuck?—with Tennessee Williams plays? No," Melanie groaned. "We're not doing that. And then something about your favorite ice cream flavor."

"I can handle that," Contessa said. That was, she supposed, all that was left for her to talk about. Eleanor froze her out on set, the director just gave her orders, Jimmy pushed her around—so much for the collaborative environment she had hoped they would have. And they could ask about Josh, but they'd prepared for days for him to only be in the movie for a few minutes. She knew plenty about Tennessee Williams, but apparently all that research was only good for some weird party game she was going to play with Davina. (She supposed she ought to kill *The Rose Tattoo,* if they asked. That one sucked.) It would be nice if someday, Contessa thought, she made some work worth talking about.

But for now, she would be discussing ice cream.

"Just do a good job out there." Melanie looked over the dress hanging on the rack, waiting for Contessa to give it weight. "I know you will."

♦ ♦ ♦

"SO," DAVINA SAID.

The two were sitting in armchairs placed at a forty-five-degree angle, so that they could, moment-to-moment, look at each other or cheat out and catch the camera's eye. Davina was wearing just the same thing Contessa was—a white robe, a full face. Well, Contessa presumed, she probably had the same thing on under too: a whole system of shapewear just to make sure she looked trim and to make sure that, if the robe slipped, nothing too bad would be revealed. But there was something odd about Davina, something in her "So," the pull on the vowel, the upturn of the corner of her lip, that made Contessa wonder if she had anything on under there at all.

Better not to worry about that! Davina could take care of herself. She didn't need her mom with her, did she? Contessa was in no position to judge.

"As we wait," Davina said, "did you hear anything about how the morning went?"

"Well, I saw Bitty in the parking lot." Contessa wasn't sure how much to disclose, what there even was to disclose. She felt a loyalty there somehow—Bitty wasn't a bad person or anything like that. "She seemed really worn out."

"I had a little meeting with Ceridwen Darby before coming in." Davina stopped herself, seemed abashed. "Surely you did too?"

"Mm." Contessa was content to play coy on this one. Maybe only the serious actresses got to meet the editor.

"And she said—well, let's not play the game of pitting women against other women." Davina pretended to bonk herself in the skull with her fist—*bonk, bonk, bonk*. Her terrycloth sleeve rolled up, revealing a gold bracelet with fine and delicate links. *So pretty,* Contessa thought. So funny that Davina didn't otherwise do too much with herself; they weren't supposed to look made-up, Contessa knew, but still, her full face of makeup was beige-on-beige-on-beige. Not even a little highlight. And her hair was just kind of . . . there, slicked back as if she was trying to forget about it.

"But apparently," Davina went on, "it was a bit of a challenge getting Bitty through." She chortled slightly, giving Contessa an invitation to join in.

Contessa had just met Davina for the first time moments ago. Had felt strangely appraised by her, as if Davina had been sizing up a racehorse, or a piece of art to buy. Or a woman she'd beat, easily. For an actress (and a good one! Contessa really liked *Andronicus*!), Davina wasn't very good at concealing the ranginess of her eyes. *The competition has begun,* Contessa thought. But it ought to feel more fun than this.

"Well," Contessa began. She laughed too, a little. It was mean to Bitty, but it would be meaner to Davina not to indulge her. Davina was right there. And all of a sudden, she smelled it again. The smoke. Had it gotten into her skin? Could Davina tell?

"She's so talented, is the thing," Contessa said, feeling futile, silly.

"Yes, yes," Davina said. "I'm going to watch the Lyndon movie soonest. I'm sure it's wonderful."

"All right," came a voice. "We've got the camera set, and you're both mic'd up, so—whenever you're ready. Just what we prepared."

Contessa shared a significant look with Davina. It felt significant to her, at least. They were in this together, for the next twenty or so minutes. Scene partners. And as odd as Davina had already proven herself to be, Contessa thought, hoped, that they'd get equal billing. That they'd give each other that. Maybe there was something to be learned from her. About how to build a career. Even in the moments when people weren't looking.

"I'm Contessa—" Contessa said.

"And I'm—" Davina cut in. "No, no, sorry. Sorry. Take two. Please, forgive me. I'm usually better at the timing."

Contessa smiled like one of the saints she remembered from church growing up. Like the Virgin Mary, whose big blue dress always reminded Contessa of a princess. It was this easy to be penitent. To get the advantage.

She made the *three, two, one* countdown signal with her left hand. Trusted Davina was watching, because—well, they were opposite one another, and she'd also gotten an odd sense that Davina was always watching. A sense she hadn't felt since working with Josh, which was obviously its own thing. But still. She trusted herself.

After her pinky came down, signaling the expiration of *one*, she took a breath, tried again. "I'm Contessa Lyle."

"And I'm Davina Schwartz." Davina had picked up on it. This could be simple. Like tennis. Or not even that complicated. Like playing catch.

"We're here for the Movies Issue cover," Contessa sang out, content in her knowledge of how easy this would be. Her phone could be exploding, could be bursting with the fullness of Josh—or it could be sitting silent. She'd find out, wouldn't she. But either would be fine. For a satisfying, overdue moment, she felt herself not caring. It just felt so good to be performing for the camera. To be doing a version of what she loved.

"Well," Davina said. She was halting, but Contessa willed her to keep going. Gave her a look with a little iron and lead in it. Contessa knew that the final edit would come in close on Davina here. And she knew that her own furrowed-brow intensity, in the very unlikely event the editor chose a wide shot of both women, would read to her fans as her being Nina. Trying to figure things out. There was a little cuteness to her glare still. Maybe that would go away as she got older.

"Right!" Davina met Contessa's eyes for just a moment, then squared her shoulders, seemed to remember where she was. "We're here to celebrate the year we've had. And we always start videos like this with a fun one."

"I know," Contessa began. She realized as the words came out of her mouth that she was going to need to take this one again. "I know!" More brightly this time. "And I love that!"

"So," Davina said. She suddenly looked game. Even playful. Maybe this was what it was like for the people who acted opposite Davina Schwartz onstage back in London; Contessa had looked up old reviews. No one had ever written such nice things about Contessa. Maybe no one ever would. It felt good to be on the receiving end of Davina's full attention, and intimidating, and kind of sad. Because, Contessa realized as Davina clicked in, the woman sitting across from her, goofy as she was, had a genuine talent.

"Contessa." Davina brought a certain grave commitment to her lines that only emphasized how silly they were. "What is your favorite ice cream flavor?"

But Contessa had her own way to play things. She knew that. And she might not have had classical training, but she'd done the work. She could see Davina break into a smile, a real one, all her teeth, as she said what she'd rehearsed, six words with a perfect little pause at the halfway point. Clever like Nina, vulnerable like Laura. All Contessa. So what if she didn't really like ice cream at all? That didn't matter for the performance. To think of what Bitty had passed up, not doing a conversation like this. Not proving that she could hold her own. This was, Contessa suddenly realized, the fun part.

"Vanilla soft serve," she said proudly, just cutely enough, seducing Davina, and the camera, and everyone who'd be watching someday soon. But being innocent too. Innocent, but not naïve. Perfect. "With rainbow sprinkles."

She swallowed the saliva that had built up in her mouth, looked back from the camera to the strange but not-quite-impossible woman sitting across from her. Then a grin, and an inquisitive, inviting tilt of the head.

"What's yours?"

Davina Schwartz, *Andronicus*

"JUST DON'T LET CONTESSA ASK you too many silly questions."

That's what Ceridwen had said in Davina's dressing room as Davina finished getting made up. It felt strange and unconventional for an editor to sit in while Davina was being polished into a slightly more refined version of herself, but that odd woman, the vowels in her name somehow unfindable no matter how many times she reintroduced herself, had insisted.

Ceridwen hadn't quite reminded her of British journalists, with their rapacious eyes and the quick ticking of their questions. They were always waiting to catch you in a misstatement, waiting to find the slip that would allow them to write that you were, well, gay. Instead, Ceridwen had reminded Davina, honestly, of a fellow theater actor.

And that, she supposed, she could work with.

"How do you mean, Ms. Darby?"

"Ceridwen, please. Ugh, I do apologize—Mum and Pater go to Wales for their honeymoon, and I'm simply fucked for life, aren't I?" Utter theater actor. "Well, I am not such a micromanager that I tell them what to ask. But, you must know this, you've earned your place in the firmament. You're not a Bitty Harbor, not a Contessa Lyle."

Davina hadn't been sure how to take this, other than as a roundabout observation that she was not young. Certainly she knew Contessa was . . . she was special. Davina had tried to adjust her bathrobe so not too much of her décolletage would be showing for the video shoot.

"You can do this," Ceridwen had said. "It's silly, but you can. Just another hoop to jump through before the final prize. Just imagine you're Adria Benedict. Even she has to do things like this nowadays."

Davina had reddened. To be compared. To Her. Could Ceridwen really believe they had much of anything in common, she and Adria? The moment had hung there, beautiful and shimmering. It was iridescent, too good to last.

For Ceridwen had suddenly let out an ungainly guffaw.

"You poor thing," she had said. "These stupid bathrobes. What was I thinking?"

♦ ♦ ♦

"CHOCOLATE, I THINK. WITH A HEAPING AMOUNT OF HOT FUDGE and nuts." Davina's favorite flavor of ice cream was none. The second best was a little mango sorbet, if she was indulging. But this was no time to be a snob. Be snobbish about your work, if you must, but not your food intake—this was, after all, America.

"That's my favorite flavor," she went on. " 'Favourite' and 'flavour' both spelled with a 'u,' of course."

Good, she'd remembered to do that. She was British; she was prestige.

"Okay, that's settled." Contessa smiled. What seemed like a tense exchange or two had passed between them in the early going, but things were getting easier. It was hard not to resent this young woman for how easily her beauty came to her, how transfixing was her fleeting anger—but then a smile came, and it was just simpler to forgive everything. To lose oneself in her.

"So," Contessa said. "We're the two theater girlies this year. You're in *Andronicus*, and I'm—"

"Laura Wingfield!" Davina shouted out. She realized as she said it that she'd cut Contessa off. Couldn't stand the idea of seeing even a moment of frustration on that brow, seeing those perfect eyebrows raise as Contessa took the line again.

Thank God. Contessa kept her smile affixed; she was willing to play along. Maybe, somewhere in there, she had the makings of a theater actor too.

"Exactly!" Contessa said. "So, I have a little game for us to play." They'd been prepped well—Davina knew that the director of this video, standing out there somewhere and silently watching them perform, had offered them the chance to hold index cards with their lines on them. Both had turned the cards down.

"Fuck, Marry, Kill," Contessa said. She laughed, and Davina wondered if the camera would pick up the extent to which she'd seemed to push herself toward laughter. "Okay," Contessa continued, pushing an invisible lock of hair behind her left ear, "so your options are: Romeo, Hamlet, and King Lear!"

"Let's start with Lear," Davina said. "He has money and is expiring soon. Seems like the marrying type." Davina let out a guffaw that she was certain she reined in before it became a cackle. Contessa started giggling, more naturally mirthful than she'd seemed when introducing the game. *Can she know these plays?* Davina wondered. *She can't have gone to school for very long.*

Funny that they'd chosen men to ask her about. Well, she and Beth had always wanted to keep their lives out of the news. Now she was being asked to play a supporting role in this campaign-season play, Lady Capulet to Contessa's Juliet. (As for the concept of "Fuck, Marry, Kill," she supposed Juliet had rather done all three to poor Romeo.)

"This isn't in the script," Contessa said. "But, honestly, I'm really curious. Was there a time you really fell in love with stage acting? I've never tried it, and I . . ."

She trailed off, fell silent even as Davina silently tried to cue her—*and you what, Contessa? And you'd like to? And you're scared?* She waited one more moment before jumping in to finish Contessa's thought—she couldn't quite trust herself with timing nowadays. They'd been told they were allowed to riff, so Davina didn't bother looking around to see if this was all right. The magazine would cut it out in the edit anyway, if it wasn't.

♦ ♦ ♦

THE ANSWER WAS *WHO'S AFRAID OF VIRGINIA WOOLF?* IT WAS twelve years ago. It had been Beth who'd encouraged Davina to do it. Davina had just won a British television award for a crime series where she played a tough (but sensitive!) police detective. It was a coup, but she'd never felt farther away from herself as an actor. Never felt less artistic; clock in, clock out, make herself produce tears over a cadaver.

"Isn't it what you want?" Beth had asked in bed one night. "A challenge?"

This in response to Davina listing all the reasons why returning to the stage, this time, in this production, was a mistake. Director untested. Costar a notorious drunk. Too young for Martha. Too soon since the last revival. No new idea as to why this, why now.

"You're the new idea," Beth had said. "Think of what we did in uni. What you did just five years ago in *Anything Goes*. You'll make it your own. You always do."

What went unsaid was that, this way, unlike her cop show, she wouldn't have to be on location far away in Scotland. She could practically walk to the theater. Beth and Davina had agreed to start talking about a child, how that could happen, if it even should, in a year's time, when they both turned thirty-five. This was, perhaps, the final moment something like this could happen. And Beth was encouraging her. Ran lines with her, talked her through the early rehearsals, when the whole world seemed against her. Held Davina as she sobbed when the reviews came out—there really was nothing worse than a British journalist. Just sat there and took it when Davina told her this was her fault. That Beth's blind faith had humiliated her, that she was only living vicariously through Davina's success because she couldn't find work herself. Beth had been sitting, not front-row, never that, but in a prime aisle seat six rows back on opening night. Was careful not to comment when Davina's hand slipped, only slipped, from around the waist of the actress playing Honey down to her posterior during bows. They always understood each other.

It had been an artistic failure, that production. And a flop. But it had brought Davina back to herself. Now, with these years on TV, this film, it was her time to make money for their family of three. But back then, storming across the stage each night—before the reviews came in, before it became painfully clear the experience would end in failure? That had been her freedom. It was easy to forget how unfettered she'd felt onstage, when Davina thought about the tough parts of that production of *Woolf*, the old leathered spittoon who'd played George, the crowds dwindling night after night until the mercifully early close. It was easy to forget, too, that Beth had believed in it hard enough for them both.

"I fell in love with theater acting doing *Anything Goes*!" Davina said. "It was my first production on the West End"—she stopped herself, let out a cough so light she was sure they wouldn't need to edit it out at all—"that's the Broadway of the UK, and I had to learn to tap-dance." She grinned, gleamed. "What fun!"

♦ ♦ ♦

IT FELT GOOD TO IMPRESS CONTESSA, NOT LEAST BECAUSE IT served the purpose of the video. If someone as young and intellectually undeveloped (or so it seemed) as Contessa was carried along by Davina? Well, then that meant she wasn't as abstruse, as strange, as out of place as she sometimes felt.

And there was another thing. Contessa might not be much of a conversationalist, but—Davina could admit this, Contessa was just old enough that it fell short of bad taste—she'd had a bit of a crush on her in recent years. From afar, never having met. But cameras didn't capture it all, clearly—Davina hadn't been able to sense the potency of her aura, the rangy physical power of her youth. Her strong legs, powerfully built for such an otherwise slight girl. Davina had always been drawn less to the explicit or blatant than to the allure of what was held in reserve underneath, and—why not admit it?—Contessa's bathrobe, pulled higher and tighter than Davina might have expected, revealed just enough of what seemed to be perfectly shaped breasts.

"So, I'd like you to teach me some British slang." Contessa rolled her eyes ever-so-slightly at the silliness of the prompt she'd been given. Things had seemed so promising when she asked her own question, but evidently that was just to be a moment. Ah, well—some actors really needed their scripts. "Is the trunk of a car really called a boot over there?"

Davina could have redirected her, pushed back to the question about theater, asked where Contessa's ambition really lay. But who had the energy? British slang it was. While automatically running through boots and lorries (surely Contessa wouldn't ask about what Davina's countrymen called cigarettes), Davina let her mind wander. She thought about Rory, whom she hoped to see later tonight. They could talk about how Ceridwen had compared her to Adria Benedict. But not too long, better not to brag. Or to let Rory see how much a thing like that meant to her. The vain actress, still chasing her idol. Or they could talk about the new film Rory was prepping. Maybe Rory would find a part for Davina in her next project—it was so appealing, Davina thought, how industrious she was, how she was already on to the next thing.

Or maybe Rory would just see how well Davina was playing this odd role into which she'd been thrust, the actress on the campaign trail. How well she handled having to wear a bathrobe to take viewers behind the glamour, even though she'd never had much glamour in the first place. How elegantly she showed the world just enough to amuse them.

And Beth would need some tending to today, wouldn't she.

"And when you're very happy, you say you're feeling chuffed," she heard herself say. "And I'm very chuffed to be here with you."

They had a few questions to run through about *The Screaming at Salem*. Maybe if she had a better team, the kind Adria surely had, she'd be freed from answering entirely, rather than just using her best judgment. (But then, hadn't she been told that even Adria didn't get what she wanted all the time, that she was causing some sort of chaos in Colorado? No matter. Just gossip.) She had to trust that the editors of this video would find the moments where she was being ebullient and witty, and ditch the ones where she was refusing to answer whether or not Hazel Prewitt had really died when Prudence pushed her off the cliff in the finale of season three.

Playing the witch was too easy: all she had to do was sneer. But it might be fun, Davina thought, to play Martha now. She'd do it properly. If she won, maybe they could put together the money to stage it in New York. Still far from Rory in Los Angeles, but an ocean away from . . .

She'd win. And it'd happen. And then perhaps Mary Tyrone in *Long Day's Journey into Night*, maybe even Blanche DuBois—a very slightly older Blanche, but plausible, still plausible. Now was the time.

"I have such fun playing Prudence Snell, I must tell you," Davina said. "But I'm every bit as excited about Tamora, in *Andronicus*."

"Yeah, she's such an amazing character!" Contessa grinned, then feigned a shudder. "Tamora really scared me."

"Actually," the director's voice came in, from somewhere beyond the lights that illuminated both women's bathrobes into dazzling bursts of white, "that's time. We have everything we need."

♦ ♦ ♦

DAVINA LEVERED HERSELF OUT OF THE CHAIR, READY TO HEAD to the car, no one to meet, no one to hold her up. Perhaps, she thought, Contessa would see her lack of a team around her as a sign that she was low-maintenance, earthy, an actor rather than a mere celebrity. But, really, it would be good to have a publicist based here; her life was here, was it not? Why was her team still in London? Extant loyalty to Beth, Davina supposed, not that Beth would believe that. She nodded to Contessa and was surprised when the younger woman approached her, arms outstretched.

Contessa's skin exuded enough heat to make Davina realize, all of a sudden, how cold they had been keeping the studio. It felt like a comfort, so much so that Davina reminded herself that after a socially appropriate length of time, she'd have to let go. How assuring it felt, Davina thought, to hold her. Even for a moment. So Contessa had gotten tongue-tied. So even when she'd recovered, she was content to follow the script. She was young. Not everyone needed to wear their ambition all the time.

They parted, and Contessa smiled as she might at a favored aunt. Crossed her arms, which had the effect of pushing up her breasts slightly.

She has no idea, Davina thought.

"I wish they'd let us talk about our movies more." Contessa spoke quietly enough to make sure the director and cameramen wouldn't hear. Then stuck her arm up, practically shouted: "Thanks, you guys! This was great!"

"The talent is moving!" a voice shouted from off in the distance; Davina knew they ought to clear the set, but she couldn't move until she'd finished with Contessa, gotten out of their conversation whatever it was this beautiful girl would share.

And Contessa wasn't on the move either. She turned back to Davina, went on: "You know, I actually had stuff I wanted to say about playing Laura."

Davina didn't want to confess, couldn't, that she hadn't yet seen Contessa's *Glass Menagerie*. She had the screener, it was just—when was she supposed to find the time to watch a movie? But she had to say something.

"Yes, right, well, I do love Tennessee Williams. And who doesn't. How incredible—er, how interesting, to recast that play with a Black family."

Stupid! Contessa was gazing at her with a look of bland forgiveness, like Davina was a schoolchild who was pestering Teacher.

"Yeah." Contessa smiled. "It was a lot to think about, for sure!"

"You're going to need a better answer than that, Tess, for the rest of this season." A white woman who bore a resemblance had trundled up. Must be her mother. "Not every interview is about ice cream and party games."

"Yeah, but we're just talking," Contessa said with a pout. "I actually do watch the movies. And yours was incredible."

"I've been meaning to watch yours." Might as well just tell her she hadn't bothered yet. They were just talking, after all. "I'm hoping to catch up on all of the films the next time I'm on a plane back—back to London."

"Oh, when's that?" Contessa said, seeming to take a step toward Davina, to want to share a confidence.

No, she hadn't. She was moving to get out of the studio, to allow Davina to head back to the dressing room and get back into her clothes and return to the rest of the day she'd planned, to whatever version of her life was playing out now. She looked at Davina guilelessly, flicked her eyes down as if to make sure she was still holding her purse.

Davina was boring her.

It was refreshing, in some perverse sense, to know that there were still some things that Davina wanted, in this charmed era of her life, that lay beyond her grasp. If Adria, somewhere in Colorado, couldn't get all that she desired, maybe Davina was in good company.

"I'm not sure," Davina said, to this beautiful girl who was, she knew, just talking. Just being polite. "I think I won't be going back to London for a good long time."

Jenny Van Meer, *The Diva*

IT HAD BEEN SO NOURISHING, Jenny thought, as she buckled herself into her first-class seat, to be among her people.

Not just dear colleagues like Delle, or even the team behind Jenny's movie: the director who'd supported her, the producers who'd chosen her. They were all there, all wonderful. But the people! The ones who were there just because they loved the art of film. They got it—got her. And the ovation she had received after *The Diva* screened: well, it just felt *good*. To be watched so closely, and to know that they believed her, believed in her. She felt a bit like Maria Callas as she walked in front of the screen, absorbing the praise, letting herself feel it. (Only a bit, of course. Better to leave poor Maria on the set, where she belonged.)

The questions from the audience had been so real, so penetrating. They'd truly understood Maria's story. She had come alive for them, and they had cried for her sorrow, cheered when her voice soared. They hadn't expressed any of Jenny's own occasional, fleeting doubts—that she was too old for the role (she was, wasn't she, a decade and change older than Maria had been when she'd passed), that she hadn't sung the part herself, that the whole thing looked (if you stared closely!) a bit off, a bit cheap. She was too close to it to know how it all seemed to an audience member coming in cold. But the applause told her that her performance had carried the day. She'd transformed into Maria, and in so doing had transformed the movie into art. Jenny had done good. Done a good thing. She'd have some happy news to tell Fiona this week, wouldn't she.

Jenny nodded politely at her seatmate as he plopped himself down—he looked like a man traveling for business, button-down and slacks, holding the same newspaper she was, unremarkable in every way. She gave a 10 percent–muted version of The Smile, then looked back at her own paper.

There is so much going on in the world, she thought, *for people to be so concerned with me. For me to be so concerned with myself.*

But it was just for a few more months. And getting to feel that love made it worth it.

The Diva hadn't been easy. Nothing ever was, but this one: my stars. How amazing, how truly incredible, in the literal sense, that it had been made. With her in it. Yes, there'd been no money, and yes, her being cast had been a bit strange. (Who must have turned it down? she wondered. Besides, well, Her.) She'd been bolstered by a kind director, a talented cast. But, if Jenny was being honest, she felt wonderstruck that it was her at the center of the frame. No matter how unsuited she might have felt, someone, some entity in this town or beyond thought she had what it took. She had thought those moments were behind her. How nice to know that there were still mountains to climb.

"Anything to drink before we take off?" the flight attendant asked. A man—a gay man, Jenny thought. She felt bad for a moment, profiling him off the slight sibilance, the zazz on the *th* sound in "anything," but of course there was nothing wrong with it, nothing at all. Some of the most talented people in the industry . . . !

"Coffee, please," the businessman next to her barked. "I take it black."

"Oh, I don't know," Jenny said. "Maybe an orange juice?"

"You mean a mimosa?" The flight attendant winked; catching it felt like a small prize.

"I couldn't." She gave it a topspin, an actressiness, a bit of gush, because they both knew that she'd say yes. Why not make it feel like a give-and-take? The attendant, of all the people on this plane, would recognize her, wouldn't he? She'd found that gay men seemed to especially love her, had once found an article about a drag club that hosted a Night of a Thousand Jennys. She couldn't take offense—some of those costumes had really made her laugh. Who knew why gay men loved her? Who knows why these things are the way they are?

"You sure? You don't need a little something just to get through takeoff?" The attendant grinned. "The ascent is a little steep."

Jenny had been much more restrained upon landing in the mountains this time than she'd been in the past, although she still resented the rolled eyes from colleagues when she wept a few years back. Not really fair, was it, to judge an artist for being dramatic.

"Oh, I know," Jenny said. "I came in the same way. So I'll take a little." She stretched this word out—"leeeeeettle"—to convey that a lot would be okay too.

Another wink. What a gift it was, to be able to know the way these things worked out, to be able to make people happy by playing the role. She raised the glass slightly as the attendant handed it to her, gave a serene nod.

"My name is Mark," he said, "and I'll be taking care of you today. You both. Anything you need."

"I won't abuse the privilege, Mark." Jenny beamed at him. "Thank you."

The businessman sighed slightly. It was time for the interaction to end, and Mark sensed it too. He moved on to the next row.

They'd be taking off soon, Jenny knew, and then it would all happen quickly again. Car booked by the studio waiting at the airport, hotel check-in expedited. A nice soft bed, maybe flowers congratulating her on the premiere. On how well she'd done.

The director had been right, she thought, to insist that she lip-sync to Callas's classic recordings. Of course, Jenny prided herself on doing the work, but it wasn't realistic to think that she'd become an opera singer in her midsixties, was it? Not with the limited time they had to shoot, at least. The decision freed her up to concentrate on thinking, deeply, about what Maria had felt like, being left by Onassis so cruelly. Embodying the woman, that wonderfully expressive woman. All that talent in one person, and so alone.

Delle had been reassuring about it too, when they'd gotten a drink. She'd been kind about the special effects that had been used to make Jenny look younger in some scenes, which had, at first, made Jenny feel kind of funny.

"It was really moving to see," Delle had said. "Made me think about time passing, for you and for Maria. And about how lucky I'd be to have a long career like yours."

It took some doing, when they sat down for drinks, to move Delle past talking about Adria. Dignity dictated that Jenny not take too much pleasure in hearing about Adria's suffering. The burn certainly sounded painful, although Jenny now knew that Adria was fine; she'd shown up at the dinner with it taped up, and was absolutely ebullient with her director and with Delle, posing for pictures with her arm around the younger woman.

Delle had texted Jenny that night, after the dinner, that what she'd known would happen had happened; Adria's blockade, and her performance of a sudden change of heart, had worked, and it'd be Delle in the supporting actress race. Jenny had declined her video call, sending back a text message that it was too late and she was in bed, because she just knew what it would be. And she couldn't watch Delle cry.

So they'd be competing again, Jenny and Adria. Of course. Of course Adria hadn't spoken to Jenny at the dinner, and of course Jenny knew not to call attention to it. She'd tried, just as she had when she spotted Adria looking so lost at the hotel bar, to look inviting, to make clear she was open, ready to say hello. But that was Adria's way. It worked for her. Clearly.

Something more, perhaps, to bring to Fiona. Although wasn't that just the worst thing, in some ways. To have nothing to keep for oneself, nothing to hold on to. Maybe she could keep one more secret. Just for now. There would be more of Adria to discuss with Fiona soon, more of this process that Jenny knew would grow harder as it wore on.

It hadn't always been such a marathon, had it? It was more forgiving back then. Or maybe Jenny was just younger. Anyway, talking about Adria might just look like gloating. So much was going so well for Jenny. Right now.

Delle really had been wonderful about the way Jenny looked in the movie. She was so guileless; coming from someone else, the words might have sounded like idle flattery. But Delle couldn't be anything but honest. The things she had said about that other young woman, Bitty Harbor—Delle was simply constitutionally compelled to say whatever came to mind, wasn't she?

Poor thing, though, that Bitty. Not easy for a young woman in this business. Jenny hoped that Delle could find a way to support her. But these kinds of rivalries didn't tend to fix themselves, did they?

Maybe it could have been different, with her and Adria. She'd never know. She did have Adria to thank; she suspected, without having been told, that they had gone out to Adria first. And this was not the kind of production Adria did. Shot in Croatia to save money—close enough, they all told themselves, to the beaches of Greece. Cast and crew all staying together in a little hotel—charming staff, and Jenny had the biggest room. But still. Corners were cut. Worth it, to stay working, to stay active. She could only spend so much of her time feeding chickens.

She didn't want to become like Eleanor Quinn-Mitchell, a sort of apparition. Poor Eleanor had drifted through the festival, as if unsure why she was there. So much had changed since the last time Eleanor was working. To stop working was to lose the pulse, lose your currency. Even if they had to use computers to make you look younger, even if they swapped out your voice—you needed to keep going.

She looked out the window as the plane taxied. *Good-bye, mountains.* In a few months, she'd be back in Idaho, seeing the same peaks from the other side. This would be a nice quick flight, an easy landing. Yes, she'd cried, a little, on the way in, a physical response. But it had felt, too, like catharsis. A signal to let some old things shed away as she started this journey, one more time.

The flight attendant—Mark—made his way down the aisle.

"Empty glasses? Empties?" he said, just loud enough not to be drowned out by the jet engine.

Look at that—Jenny had drunk the whole thing. She handed it to Mark, remembering to look a bit abashed. *Look at how naughty we're being!* Taking pleasure in the indulgence of it all.

Mark leaned over the businessman to grab Jenny's glass, the flutter of his fingers against hers as subtle as a breeze. Jenny had to catch herself from reacting badly, from being startled, as he breathed into her ear, "Good luck."

She had collected her face by the time he pulled back. What a thing. What a wonderful thing.

Rooting for you, he mouthed, exaggerating the movement of his lips so she wouldn't miss it.

He was handsome, wasn't he—bad skin, he should have it looked at, but nice features. And a gentle manner, and sweet. She wondered if his parents had been good to him. She hoped he had love in his life. She sent all that was in her heart to him through her gaze, mouthed the words she'd be saying from a stage soon with all the feeling that it would take to make this a moment Mark would remember forever: *Thank you.*

He grinned, walked on to the next row and out of sight.

"What was that?" the businessman half-muttered. He took a slug of his coffee.

"I'm an—" Jenny began. No, not that. Not "I'm an actress." She began again. "It was just," she said, wistful already to be leaving this charmed trip to the mountains, "a kindness."

Adria Benedict,
Who Is Lisa Farmer?

"ADRIANA! SO GOOD TO SEE you."

Adria laughed, bringing her right hand, finally more or less healed, to her throat.

"Now that my parents are gone," she trilled, "you're the only person allowed to call me that."

"And I shall take full advantage," said Nancy. "Come here."

She stood up from the restaurant table, put her arms around Adria. She was dressed very nicely, trim slacks and silk blouse, simple pearl necklace. Adria herself was wearing a chunky turtleneck and dark jeans. They kind of looked like slacks, if you weren't looking closely. She tried not to think that this was likely the biggest event of Nancy's year.

"Your hand!" Nancy was staring right at it, smiling in relief. "It looks much better than you had led me to believe."

"Oh, it was worse," Adria said. Thanks to rigorous applications of lotion, she could say, thank goodness, that there would be no gloves at the awards. "I can tell you, I will certainly *not* be ordering a hot tea with my meal!"

The pair laughed, that simple and unadorned laughter that old friends use to communicate that a joke has been made, to acknowledge it and move on.

"How have you been?" Adria asked. "I have been so deeply looking forward to this."

"I have too," Nancy said, picking up a menu. "Oh, why am I looking at this, you know I get the same thing every year."

"Gorgonzola and pear salad, split the sea bass crudo to start!" Adria trilled.

"And you'll be having the Chinese chicken salad—"

"*No* wontons." Adria made herself the imperious actress, speaking in that peremptory, cruel tone she'd never really use with a waiter. Of course not.

"Never wontons!" said Nancy. "Should we . . ."

"Wine?" said Adria. "I shouldn't."

"Calorie counting! You need to fit into your dress soon."

"Oh, I don't know . . ."

"You'll be nominated," Nancy said. "You always are." A short pause, as if she were trying to find the words. "This movie is so special."

"Well, thank you." Adria rolled her eyes, but it did feel good to hear this, and she knew Nancy knew that. "You know, I might do a Caesar this time. With steak tips." She shrugged, cast her eyebrows up in a way she felt might look charmingly devil-may-care. "It feels like time to, oh, I don't know. Mix it up."

♦ ♦ ♦

ADRIA AND NANCY HAD KNOWN EACH OTHER FOR AS LONG AS Adria had been working onscreen, back when her calling card had been a couple of small, plum roles in theater in the Village. In their shared first movie, they'd played sisters fighting over the same man. That actor had tried to kiss them both offscreen, tried to do more with Nancy, but they'd made a game of evading him, and evading the director too. The actor had gone on to win every prize in the industry, most of them twice or more, was still working; the director had died three years ago. They'd toasted him with a "good riddance" at their lunch that year, laughed at the memory. What else was there to do?

Neither woman had lived in LA when they made that first movie, so they had pajama parties, made margaritas in Adria's motel room, laughed as the blender shorted out the power. Stayed friends as they went on working, cheered each other on as Nancy took a step back, and then another. And as Adria kept driving forward.

"God, remember when we were nominated together?" Nancy asked.

"And Eleanor won," Adria said. "Fair and square."

"Yes. I still need to see her new thing. Talk about a long break."

"Mm. Well, remember sitting together . . ."

"Buying our dresses at . . ."

Together they chanted the words "South Coast Plaza," both breaking into giggles at the memory.

"Now you get them picked out by a stylist, right?" Nancy asked.

"Oh, yes," Adria said. "It's a whole to-do. I try my best to make my voice heard, but it really . . . it has changed, Nancy, and not in good ways. I'd never complain, but I do miss just being able to buy a dress. Back then, it was enough for it to fit all right."

"We're not models." Nancy laughed mordantly. "Although you certainly still look like one!"

Adria nodded, accepting the compliment wordlessly and with only a slight eye-roll of self-deprecation.

"So," Nancy went on, "I'm thinking about going out on an audition soon."

It made Adria feel sorrow sometimes, thinking about Nancy; it was hard to talk, when they met for this special lunch once a year, about her own good fortune. So strange to keep meeting right in the run-up to the awards, when Adria was nominated most years. She didn't like that Nancy always had to congratulate her success, and that she had nothing comparable to say back. But it was hard to suggest changing the date: both women's birthdays were in January, and that was the point of it. Or they could meet more frequently, to remove the tie to awards season, but Adria was always somewhere, wasn't she?

"That's wonderful, Nancy!" Adria said. "An actress like you—they'd be lucky to have you. Oh, what's the project?"

"Do you know Davina Schwartz?"

"Wellllll." Adria drew out the word. "I haven't had the pleasure. But they say she's going to be . . . involved . . . in the awards this year."

"You've got to see her in this movie *Andronicus*," Nancy said. "It's a retelling of the Shakespeare play about the feud between a hero and a warrior queen, but it's from the queen's point of view. Seriously! It's, oh, it's the kind of role I always wished I could play. Nothing like me. So fierce. So fabulous. Ugh!" She tossed her head back.

"So, are you going to work with her on a movie?"

"Well, long story," Nancy went on. "Or, not long, but. Davina is on a TV show, it shoots here, and it's got one more season left. She plays a witch—it's period, you see. And they need a woman to come in for a four-episode arc as her mother. To show how she got the way she is."

"Are we that much . . ." Adria trailed off.

"Yes, Adria," Nancy said. "We could be Davina Schwartz's mothers."

Nancy grinned, letting the corners of her eyes just barely crinkle.

Adria knew that Nancy had invested a fair amount of money, over time, on injecting her face, and that face had begun to have a waxiness to it. Like the doll version of herself, meant to be collected by some person somewhere who wanted all of the women who'd been nominated in the 1980s up on a shelf. She looked all right, but it was certainly different.

"Well, you will get it," Adria said. "You must. And then we can toast you next time. We ought to be toasting you now."

"We'll see." Nancy looked as skeptical as, maybe, her face would allow. "They're saying it could even be more, depending on how things go. Maybe as many as six episodes."

"That's terrific," Adria said. "I'm so happy you're doing that. I'm thrilled, actually."

"It's just an audition. But thank you. It'd be special to meet Davina. She's a real talent, I mean it. And with Jeff and Matt off at college . . ."

"Our boys," intoned Adria, feeling herself lean forward and put her hands to her chest, demonstrating the sweetness of the emotion. "Our poor boys, with their actress mothers. Oh," she said, as the waiter approached. "Two iced teas? I think?"

"Yes," Nancy said. If she was disappointed not to get her lunchtime chardonnay, she didn't show it. "Thanks."

The waiter retreated with a nod, no attempts at ingratiation, no startlement at seeing Adria Benedict in real life; places like these, the nicer places over on the Westside, it was just as simple and seamless as that.

"And how are the Greenaway kids?" Nancy asked.

"Oh, just wonderful. Well, Jamey's wife—it's tricky. You'll see, someday, when Jeff and Matt find someone . . ."

"Jeff, yes," Nancy said. "Matt . . ." She wiggled her hand in the air.

It could feel so good to be a little bad! Adria laughed, covered her mouth.

"Oh, Nancy, no! Not that it's negative. But . . . how?"

"It's a recent thing. At Westlake, he played sports. Well, just tennis, but. You know. Still. But since he's been at Brown, he's gone out for drama, and . . . well, it's not just that. But it's an intuition I have. You know that feeling."

"And it is Brown." Adria felt a little mean joking like this. A gay son would have been easy in some ways—a little supplicant for her, no daughter-in-law to compete with—but, really, thank goodness Jamey had gotten into Harvard and Willy had chosen Bowdoin. "Lucky him, to have a mother in the arts!"

"Well, you'd think, but . . . I'm sure you can relate. He's not impressed by me—I'm just Mom. Want to know something awful? He loves Jenny." She paused to watch Adria's eyes grow round, her mouth open into the perfect little "O" of recognizing a cosmic irony. "Asks me all the time if I've met her."

"Of all people," Adria said. She knew where to take this next, knew the tone of relish that would be just cruel enough to not *really* be cruel. "But we know gay men love a tragic woman."

They both started laughing, really laughing, as the waiter returned.

"Oh, look," Adria said. "Our iced teas." She put her pinky up and pursed her lips in a grand imitation of primness as she took the glass, and both women dissolved. They sounded just like the women they'd been, sitting together in the front row, waiting to hear what their futures held.

♦ ♦ ♦

"MY LINDY," ADRIA BEGAN AS THE LAUGHS DIED DOWN, "SHE'S staying with us this weekend. Home from Northwestern."

"A graduate student! Can you believe . . ."

Adria made all the noises of protestation necessary to indicate that she could not.

"Why is she here?" asked Nancy.

"Oh, well, I convinced her to come watch me speak on a panel for the women in movies this year, but the dates got mixed up."

"Tell me it's not . . ."

Adria shrugged. "This was more important. We skip this lunch once, it won't come back. That's how it happens. Just the way of things."

"Well," Nancy said, "I'm honored."

"Don't be." Adria put lightness into her voice. "It's frankly wonderful to have a good excuse to miss out. The questions they ask at these things, you would not believe. You simply wouldn't. Now." She cleared her throat. "Have you gotten a look at my costar, Ms. Delle Deane?"

"That hair," Nancy said with a shudder. "In our day . . ."

"We are the dinosaurs," Adria said, "and Delle's generation is the asteroid."

Adria decided it was better not to get too much further into it. She'd beaten Delle, hadn't she? She would be a gracious winner.

"And Lindy's of that generation too. Just like your Matthew, I'm sure, everything I do is wrong. I couldn't believe she said yes, but I had thought it might be interesting for her to see me promoting the film, especially because she was a theater major too."

"Is that what she's in graduate school for?"

"No," Adria said. "I don't pretend to understand it myself." She gave Nancy a moment to understand the oddity, the surreality of something in the arts lying beyond even Adria Benedict's grasp. "It's called performance studies. Something about . . . oh, I don't know. Acting. The way we all do it. But in our lives offstage too."

"Huh." Nancy's mouth hung slightly open, her plump lips parted.

"And it's called sixty-five thousand dollars a year." Adria laughed. She needed to sound mirthful, to impress upon her friend that this was just a little joke. "But she has friends there, and that's all we want."

"I'm glad," Nancy said. "Because it's not like she'll meet a man there."

Oh, how wonderful it felt to laugh!

"Who else is it, then, this year?" Nancy asked.

"Oh, I don't know." Adria let out a puff of air. "No, I do. Jenny."

"She's back!" Nancy chuckled. "It's been—well, my boys would say, 'It's been a minute.' "

"Many minutes," Adria said. "This is awful. I can't."

"Say it."

Nancy had leaned forward, and the way the light hit her face only emphasized the work she'd had done. There was a funny little seam marking the spot that her lower lip began its perpendicular journey projecting outward from her face. Adria steeled herself not to avert her eyes, decided to go on, as she had known she would.

"I turned the movie down," Adria said. "It's Maria Callas, and I just figured—well, I'm not a singer. Not an opera singer. I do have a nice little voice, but." She paused. Kept going. "Not that that stopped Jenny. I hear she lip-syncs the arias."

"And what's the point of that?" Nancy said.

"Exactly." Adria squared her shoulders, bolstering herself a little. "We would never. Plus, it was filming far away, and Bill and I are finally able to enjoy each other's company these past few years."

"Well, we both wouldn't lip-sync," Nancy said.

Adria kept herself from wincing; it had been five or six of these lunches since Nancy had cried about Jeff and Matt's father. At least she'd gotten the house. The list of things that Adria had to keep from Nancy—it wasn't "far away," it was a free trip to Europe, and one that fortunate Adria hadn't felt like taking—kept growing.

"Anyway," Nancy began again, "you need to watch Davina's movie. It's special." She shifted back, out of the beam of light, casting her features back into the ambient dim of the restaurant. A relief. "Adria, she reminds me of you."

"I'm sure I'll love it," Adria said, her stomach lurching slightly. "Oh! Our crudo!"

The waiter silently placed a platter of chopped fish between them. It looked simply perfect. The elegance of a lunch like this. The whole world seemed coherent, seemed possible.

It would mean so much for Nancy to get to play this part. It had been so fun, back then, the two of them, but it had meant something too. There had been a sort of promise. Everyone, not just trivia collectors, had known Nancy's name then. She had a face that had been on billboards, and then in the corner of the screen, grinning and clapping, as the presenter said another woman's name. She'd been there.

"I have to ask you something," Adria said as she moved her fork toward the plate. Nancy was using her right hand to balance the slitheringly wet slice of fish against her own utensil. No need to be proper among friends, Adria supposed.

"Would you like me to . . ." Adria went on, ". . . is there anyone I could speak to? To put in a word?"

Nancy looked up from her project of moving the fish, seemed to attempt to furrow her brow. It was difficult to read an emotion into the smooth, flat screen of her forehead, but Adria knew in that moment that she'd made a mistake.

"A word? About what?"

Too late to go back now.

"I just thought... Oh, it's silly."

Play it like a joke. A bad joke. She tried to focus on the fish, but its slick and shimmering surface began to remind her of the way her burnt hand had looked, covered in petroleum jelly. She felt a throb, decided to put it out of her mind by pushing on.

"I thought how nice it'd be for you to get to do this."

"I know how to audition, Adria." Nancy's face was placid. But her eyes were burning. "I used to audition against you. Remember?"

"Well," Adria said. "Forgive me. And forget I mentioned it."

Nancy looked into her lap, made a show of adjusting her napkin. Her hair had fallen forward, shielding that unreadable face.

"Yum, yum. I love the way they do this crudo." Adria forced herself into a higher register as she waited for Nancy to be ready to resume their conversation. "Yum, yum, yum."

She had tried her best. She didn't see them except in her memories, but there was a whole population, Adria knew, of women from awards nights past, gone now. Sometimes it seemed like the only ones who remembered them were writers eager to make mention of this or that of her peers' fading fortunes with a touch of delight. Jamey, so brilliant, had set up the computer for her years ago, and then came the smartphone—she knew what they wrote. It'd be easier not to invite women at all, really, Adria often thought, pleased with her own contrarian streak. Better not to give them a moment at the party than to take it away.

And Adria had to keep going. What else could she do? If you skip any opportunity, it won't come back—that's how it happens. Just the way of things. Now Nancy was trying to find her way back in. She'd need more than luck. But, of course, everyone had their pride. Adria knew that as well as anyone.

"You know," Adria said, "I think I'll see if I received a screener of Davina's movie. That sounds fun, for Lindy and me to watch."

She waited for Nancy to reply, knew that—even though they alternated years, and it was Adria's turn to pay—Nancy would claw for the check. Even if Adria protested. So she would allow her to just take it, would cast her own face toward the floor as the card met the little leather folder, would distract herself by telling a story both would forget as it unfolded.

Adria always knew what to do, how to play it. And she knew this wasn't a scene she would want to remember. Not a moment she would want to repurpose for any role. Sometimes, she thought, it could be so painful to be so composed, to understand how to look away.

She could think about that on the way home. She could explain to Bill later that she'd just tried to help a friend out. She could distract herself with Lindy, if Lindy would deign to sit with her for a few hours, or however long this Davina Schwartz movie was. For now, though, Adriana Benedetta, as only Nancy was allowed to call her, sat staring forward, wondering how long it would be before her friend looked up.

Bitty Harbor,
Lyndon and Claudia

EVER SINCE BITTY WAS LITTLE, she'd liked to imagine a game show she called, to herself, *Which of Your Children*.

She could practically watch it, like it was on a television set whose corners brushed up against the boundaries of her mind. (Bitty had always, privately, felt that she was a very visual individual, a belief only enhanced by working with directors whose imaginations, she felt constrained from saying aloud, were scant next to her own.)

The host was a blurry male presence. He was wearing a suit—a gray one?—and that was where his role in things effectively ended. It was the contestant who mattered. In Bitty's first imaginings, she saw her mother as she was then, her hair teased the way she used to do it, and still auburn. Now, at twenty-eight, Bitty could see how youthful her mother had been. The contestant had a cigarette in her hand—she hadn't even tried to quit that for the first time yet. Nowadays, when Bitty played the game, her mother was hazy within it, shifting among past and recent weights and hairstyles, resting in the end in some undefined maternal betweenness.

The game had always been simple enough. The host asked Mom a series of questions: factual, then emotional, but the final question always stayed the same. Bitty had started playing it when she could no longer overlook how unreceptive the actual mother in front of her was at the end of the day. Fridays, Mom rallied with a rented VHS that they'd watch while she pulled Bitty's hair back into a braid, but for the rest of the week, Bitty was on her own. The girl only needed to be told so many times that no, sweetie, Mommy didn't know which of the three got kept inside at recess, and tattling wasn't a very nice thing to do anyway, plus it had been a really long shift, so could we go outside with Robby and Brendan? Or else play at being quiet for a while?

Bitty often chose the latter, staring at a wall of her bedroom, stroking her beloved stuffed rabbit, and thinking through the contours of her game. As a child, the questions Bitty made the host ask were prosaic, tied to the comings and goings of the student body at Waterville Elementary. When her mother didn't know, she was informed of the correct answer, and gave a sort of close-mouthed, contemplative smile of coming into greater knowledge of her brood.

Things began easy. "Which of your children," the host's voice would boom, "threw out their banana at lunch without eating it?" (Robby, of course. Why did she bother packing anything more than rolled-up turkey slices for him? Mom made a tsk-tsk face, lovingly concerned.)

". . . kissed Lauren Appleman at recess?" (Brendan, surprisingly. Bitty had him marked as a queer before this because of how inept he was on the soccer field, and she suspected her mother might have too. But Mom was good enough to simply look pleasantly scandalized at her son's bravado.)

". . . got to the third round of the spelling bee?" (Bitty herself, eventually knocked out after having mistaken "presence" for the thing

Santa brings on the night of the twenty-fourth. But she felt smug all the same at having beaten the infamous Lauren Appleman, who'd spurned Brendan the day after they were caught canoodling on the far edge of the blacktop. Mom beamed the way Bitty thought a mother ought to, the way she was sure her mother did on the inside. The way she would perform all the time, if she weren't working, or recovering from working.)

". . . do you love the most?" The object of it all was revealed here, and the answer was always correct. Bitty needed enough evidence to ensure, with no doubt, that the mother in her head would answer that it was her youngest, her lady, her Little Bit.

The game was meant to indicate to Bitty that her mother's refusal to answer this question, when she'd been posed it over and over twenty years ago, had simply been propriety talking. It was meant to show Bitty that all the time she'd spent listening to her mother chatter about Brendan's successful business and Robby's Alyssa and their baby Jordan was a sly motherly trick. Her seeming inability to be impressed by the work Bitty had been doing since dropping out—a bet that paid off, and wouldn't most mothers admire ingenuity?—was just a ruse. The game showed Bitty that even disconnected—even not speaking, as they hadn't been for some time now—there was, somewhere, a wellspring of fondness that Bitty would have to find by trust.

The game had never really gone away, though it receded from view a bit at times. Bitty probably only played it twice over five and a half semesters of college. In both cases, it was after the Christmas holidays, when she wanted to remind herself—or convince herself—of something. It came in a special kind of handy, though, on nights like tonight, when Bitty could really use someone to talk to but, from inside the aquarium of drink in which she'd hastily drowned her consciousness, even she knew that she was too far gone to avoid embarrassing herself on the phone.

"Which of your children," a male voice intoned in her mind, "is going to be on the cover of . . ."

Bitty's mother, who'd shown up to set tonight in one of the tracksuits she'd begun wearing over the past decade but with her 1990s hair, couldn't abide swearing, which was why it was good this wasn't a real game show.

"Which of your children," the voice started over, "is going to be in the *fucking* Movies Issue for the second time—maybe even on the cover again?" Mom got it right, and gave a way-to-go! thumbs-up.

"And which one is going to be speaking on a panel tomorrow with all the girls—all the women she's going to beat?" Two thumbs-ups this time.

"Which of your children asked to borrow ten thousand dollars from your daughter this time?"

Mom answered correctly (Robby), but with a look of reproach at the questioner. She seemed to be saying, without saying, *Let's keep things nice. We've all made our mistakes, haven't we?*

"Which of your children met Adria Benedict?" A knowing smirk—is this game *all* going to be questions about the brilliant career of Bitty Harbor? Well, okay!

"And which of your children is doing better than ever after not getting to work with Adria?" In the game, Mom didn't blink at "better than ever," and her quick response made it seem almost true.

Losing out on working with Adria, after they'd had what seemed like such an easy connection, after Bitty allowed herself in their meeting to be both the committed artist she was now and the fan she'd been in childhood, after she'd spoken about her process and her respect for Adria's legacy, had been an indignity she almost couldn't bear. Losing the part to Delle Deane erased the "almost." Which was why she was here, on this couch, with this glass, again.

Bitty sometimes imagined having a close friend to whom she could say, *I'm just having a hard time*. Maybe it could be Contessa—she was younger, yes, but they'd been working for about as long, probably had as many experiences, and they both knew Josh, so that was a start. When she said this, admitted to having a hard time, in her mind, she'd watch as the friend—as Contessa—began to realize how hard Bitty was working to understate things. Bitty would see the concern flash in Contessa's eyes and know in that instant that she was safe.

But there was Mom, telling her that it was all right, telling her that there would be a next time to work with Adria—or that Bitty would make her own "next time," would become her own kind of great actress. That a fictionalized version of her own mother, within a game Bitty herself had made up, thought she was doing well was a pretty thin justification for a reward, but Bitty took a long glug of her glass of vodka, tipping the glass back until the last unmelted sliver of ice on the bottom clicked against her teeth. She deserved it, because she'd overcome—well, better to let the game say it:

"Which of your children has overcome a lot in the past few years?"

As soon as the words reverberated inside Bitty's skull, she realized that she'd made a mistake, or several. The first had been allowing herself to work her way through this much of the bottle: not only was tomorrow going to suck on a now-predictable level of physical pain, but she was going to be onstage at the actress panel and she was scared of looking too puffy. Bitty mechanically got up and walked over to the bar cart again as she thought about how her body and face would look to the people watching her, if they'd think she was bloated or awkward or wrong.

It was time to switch back to wine.

The second of Bitty's mistakes had been in fucking up the game. She realized she'd done this when the host's voice, on "the past few years," shifted into Bitty's own. Tremulous and agonized and issuing forth from the blurred body of a medium-build, medium-height, medium-everything TV emcee: it wasn't meant to be so obvious that it was Bitty asking the questions. And it also spoiled the fun of watching fictional-Mom announce her love. The question had been too needy, too much. The response was fitting.

"All of them," Bitty's mother said. "All of my children have overcome a lot."

"Really?" asked the host, his voice (his own again) growing wheedling and soft. "All equally?"

"Well," Mom said, "no one wants to hang new drywall in this economy, and that's been difficult for Brendan. And— "

Enough. For now, enough. It wasn't worth—Bitty took a demure sip of her pinot, as if it were somehow to be her last of the night, so she ought to savor it—introducing a line of questioning about what "overcoming a lot" had really meant. It wasn't worth telling her mother, or "her mother," about the story of three years ago and the photoshoot with Delle. Why mother and daughter couldn't speak and why Bitty had almost quit the business. She would call her mom soon, once she got the nomination, and break the silence. She would be able to tell her, truthfully, that she had done a great job, that she'd made it. That the bet had worked.

Tonight she would drink a glass of water, drink two, before bed, and that way she wouldn't have a headache when she woke up. She would be clear. She would nail the panel. She and Contessa would have a good moment together. They'd start to become real friends after that. Josh would be watching from the audience, just like he'd promised her he would, and he would be so proud! She wouldn't smoke until after the awards—or maybe not ever again! Or, how about this, she'd smoke a final celebratory cigarette after she won, and know, in doing it then, that it was to be the last time.

She would wash her face tonight. She would finish this glass and get off of this topic, get out of the game. Bitty squeezed her eyes shut, hard, until they teared. She told herself, in a yogic, even tone whose origin she couldn't guess, that the tears were just a reaction to the physical sensation of clenching. She watched the studio lights come up and swallow her mother in blazing white.

Then she opened her eyes again, after what might have been minutes, to find that the room around her was blurrier than the vision she'd had of the *Which of Your Children* studio. Bitty got up, began shuffling toward the bar cart, so close and yet seemingly unreachable. Her feet refused to move the way she might have liked them to, even toward what she was now realizing was her favorite possession.

It wasn't just its utility on nights like these, holding Bitty's liquor even when she couldn't. The cart, silly and cheap though it was, felt to Bitty like the only thing in this home that was truly hers, and not part of a part she was trying to play. It was prosaic and a little quaint, with its perennially sticky glass and shameless faux gold. She'd surrounded it with little potted plants and dust-pink knickknacks—things, just things, that seemed like what someone studying for a role as a would-be Hollywood actress would surround herself with to prepare. In the movie of her life, the little plants and pots would belong to a pretender, but the bar cart was hers. God, maybe it was even Katie's.

Which of your children might not make it to bed, she thought, unsure if she was still thinking or if she was, inaudible to herself, murmuring it into the darkness. *Which of your children might still need one more.*

♦ ♦ ♦

"I MEAN, I GUESS I KIND OF DO IT EVERY NOW AND THEN," BITTY told Josh the next day.

She had left out the bad parts, the parts that made her look weak or dependent, but it was surprisingly easy to talk to him about the game. It made it seem like fun, like the kind of thing girls did—funny ones, tastefully artsy ones, enigmatic girls with things to say. But not too much. The right amount to say.

"You probably think it's weird."

"You are so nuts," Josh said, taking a long pull from his glass and exaggeratedly wincing as the bourbon traveled down his throat. "But you're my kind of nuts. I always wanted to be my mom's favorite too."

"Yeah?" Bitty tried to paint on a smirk. To be funny about all this. Maybe he got it! Maybe explaining this hadn't been a mistake at all.

"Yeah," Josh said, spinning his glass on the table, then moving his eyes up to meet Bitty's. "Every boy just wants to be loved by Mommy. And, believe it or not, I was the runt of the litter." A laugh, two: his, then hers. "But it's girls and their mothers, though—that's the real trouble."

Bitty took an appropriately, coquettishly small sip from her glass—smaller than she'd have liked, but she would be onstage soon. All of this was just to get over her nerves. And it had been nice of him to come to her dressing room to psych her up. Why had she told him all that, about the game? Well, why not! He was easy to talk to. Another little sip, down the hatch.

Amidst the glow of admiration for Josh and of the bourbon shedding new warmth inside her, Bitty remembered to overemphasize her own wince too, to match Josh, and to make it seem like she wasn't too big a drinker. Which she wasn't, really. This was all just for fun.

"Do you remember that day with Destiny and Sydnee—"

Josh picked up where she'd left off. "Those girls adored you. But the one day you had to talk to Miss Sydnee . . ."

Miss Sydnee! An inside joke. They just got each other.

"God, it was just like I really was her mom!"

Destiny had been a first-time actor, and her performance as Lyndon and Lady Bird's elder daughter Lynda was, everyone on set agreed, charmingly unforced. But Sydnee, who had worked on a couple of TV shows, could be a little terror. Bitty wouldn't let herself speak aloud the word she sometimes wanted to use for Sydnee. (Only sometimes! Other times, the girl was wonderful!) Sydnee knew exactly what she could get away with, and Bitty and Josh could both handle grouchy behavior, but it wasn't fair to waste your castmates' time by being late, unless you weren't feeling well. Things happen, everyone has their bad days—Bitty did, God knows!—but it's better to be punctual, to be focused. The two of them agreed that it'd be better if Bitty talked to her. It didn't really come naturally to Bitty to be an authority figure, but—well, Mom was the role she was supposed to play, right?

"You were great," Josh said. "But there was never any doubt about which of your children was the favorite."

Bitty tossed her head back, so that her hair—done this morning by someone the studio had hired to come to her house, someone whose knock woke Bitty from her position sprawled on the couch and who had the decency to wait for Bitty to grab a smoke and a quick shower—fell gloriously onto her shoulders, springy, soft, touchable curls conjured, somehow. All things considered, she felt pretty decent today; the bourbon was erasing the remnants of last night, so all that remained was a story. It was a story that illuminated for Josh all the humanity and the goodness within Bitty. She was making him remember what he already knew.

The door opened. As her publicist walked in, Bitty followed Leanna's eyes as she checked the level of Josh's bourbon bottle. It was an unfortunate little performance, classic Leanna: she focused first on the cap of the bottle, then cast her gaze down, down, down, moving south until she reached the line where the remaining liquid began. It was probably too low. No: it was certainly too low.

"Well, everyone's here," Leanna said. "The other actresses. And they're asking us to do last looks before you head to the stage." She now applied her up-and-down look-over to Bitty. "I do love that dress," she went on. "Red is truly your color—and Contessa's in this dark shade of pink, so it'll be nice and complementary for the two girls sitting in the middle."

She paused, shifted her face to look, Bitty thought, 10 percent less appraising. Bitty had passed the test.

"You look really good," Leanna said. "Are you good?"

"I'm great." Bitty grinned, exhaled slightly. "And that's cool about Contessa! I love that we'll be next to each other."

She resisted looking at Josh, even as she felt so sure that he wasn't thinking about Contessa. Josh and Contessa had worked together too, and it was hard not to feel competitive sometimes. Especially when Bitty knew that she was winning, for now.

"Honestly," she said, "I'm feeling really upbeat and, um, ready to promote the movie."

"Hell, yeah!" Josh yelled, slapping the table. "We need that energy! His and hers nominations, coming up."

He moved his hand to the bottle, ready to pour his and hers shots. In that moment, Bitty felt, in a flash so different from all their nights slaying their shared boredom together in Albuquerque, that she truly loved him. She knew she did, because she wanted to tell her mother about him.

Someday, soon.

"Josh, let's not derail our girl." Leanna let her voice get fluty and melodic in that way Bitty knew meant trouble. "And let's put this bottle away until after the panel."

Bitty's heart sank slightly—one more shot and she'd be perfect, so fluent, so on. But she was doing fine right now. Leanna was probably right. Oh well.

"Anyway," Josh said, "probably time for me to go find Rachel in the audience. She's so excited for you, Bit, and so am I." He stood up, seemed to consider taking the bottle, decided to leave it. "We'll do a quick one after you slay the panel. You can join if you want, Leanna."

He winked, then moved to the door and was gone.

"Thank you." Leanna was addressing his absence, drawing out the vowel sound for long seconds. She'd grown very preoccupied with tapping at her phone. When it was certain that Josh Jorgen was not present, she finally looked up. "What a card he is." Her voice was mirthless. She definitely didn't get it. "But I mean it." She walked over to where Josh had been sitting—opposite Bitty—and put her hands on the chair's back. "You really look great. And I mean what I asked. Are you . . . ?"

Ready? Okay? Still your favorite? All of the above?

"Yeah, I feel—I feel fine, honestly," Bitty said, thinking about the way Josh had left the room, how it had felt so strangely fast. She knew she wasn't losing track yet, hadn't had that much—but he'd been there and then not. It was so strange.

"I just . . . I don't know."

For the first time in a while, she walked to the dressing room mirror.

She'd been avoiding looking at her face, but it wasn't too bloated, it was fine. Josh wouldn't have hung around if her face was too bloated. Hair good, nice loose curls; red dress, pretty low-cut, but not too much. Too low for Bitty, but not too low for the part. It felt so capital-A Actress. So not the kind of thing she'd choose for herself. But the stylist had said it'd be right. Bitty figured she would know. It was just hard not to feel like you were miscast when you were wearing clothes you'd borrowed from someone else.

"I don't know," Bitty repeated. "I'm fine. I'm fine! I just feel like I look stupid." She paused, grasped. "You know. In this."

"I promise you, you don't," Leanna said. "It's a little skin. But it's not a bathrobe." They both did a sort of imitation of laughing. Thank God *that* day was over. "But we've got to make sure you're not so fifties Texas housewife. No more Lady Bird. You know, what I was trying to do with the men's magazine. Silly me."

Leanna reached out her hand slightly; for a crazy moment Bitty thought that she was going to push back one of her curls, but that was just the bourbon speaking, or some other substance within her, like hope. Leanna knew better than to mess with a professionally done hairstyle right before the panel.

"Bitty," she said. "I know you're going to make me proud up there."

Bitty knew, too. She would make Leanna proud. And Josh was there. And her mom would find out someday. And that would have to do, for today.

Selected messages about Contessa Lyle
submitted to a user-generated gossip
site from September to November

—contessa at book soup!

—in the drama section

—she left with a stack of books in her arms

—shakespeare mainly

—we stan a literate queen!

—

—saw contesa lyle at spin class (spin culture hollywood location)

—came in late and insisted on being center of attention

—instructor even played the nina theme song and she was cheesing all over the place

—good at spinning tho

—

—saw our fav girl nina out to dinner with her mom at my local italian place in santa monica

—(i think her mom)

—don't wanna say the resto name cause i don't want it to get mobbed

—she got the citrus and beet salad (my fav!!!)

—she looked sad so i didn't want to take a pic

—

—contessa lyle getting coffee to go!
—just off the strip
—she didn't even look up from her phone while she was ordering ☹
—her order is an oat milk vanilla capp with four splendas 😱

—

—ran into josh jorgen outside my gym and wanted intel for you guys
—asked him what it was like working with contessa
—he was so nice!
—he told me and i quote that she is "a genius"
—he was with some girl
—girlfriend i think? she looked annoyed
—please keep this anonymous

—

—randomly saw contessa lyle walking to her car outside a photo studio
—i know she was made up for the cameras but
—she's really pretty!

Contessa Lyle,
The Glass Menagerie

THE MAN WEPT AS HE looked at his wife in the hospital bed; she was holding the new baby she'd just delivered, pushed into the world as he sat shouting encouragements and words of love. Together, they left the hospital, got in the car, and drove, arriving at their baby's first day of kindergarten. They stepped out of the car together, took each other's hands, and watched as their adorable five-year-old, with a perfect little gap between her front teeth, looked back at them. They knew that they'd done a good job keeping her safe. The wife squeezed her husband's hand and looked at him, knowing that if either of them said a word, they'd both begin to cry.

There was nothing to do but get back into the car, where husband and wife drove to her mother's bedside. Together, the couple and their two children—their kindergartener now in high school, joined by a toddler brother who had just her same shade of light-brown skin and a gap-toothed smile of his own—smiled as they said good-bye. The children knew that their grandmother had lived a wonderful life, and had built the loving foundation for the family that they were all part of today, a family whose next car trip would take them to the daughter's first day of college.

On it went for ninety seconds, the sounds of family life covered by a bed of swelling orchestral music and the purr of the luxury car's engine. What a nice car this family had! The orchestra reached its apex as the former kindergartener, now a grown adult with a wife (yes!) of her own, handed her own baby daughter to her mother and mouthed *Thank you*. In a flash, the mother, now a grandmother, recalled that first day of school. In her mind's eye—and visible to the audience, watching the automotive ad for the first time just before the third quarter of the Super Bowl—the little girl, back in her plaid jumper, ribbons tied into her curls, looked right at her mother, right at the camera, and whispered:

"Life is the ride."

It was what had made Contessa famous, what some people, though thankfully fewer every year, still recognized her from. Newspapers had written articles about the phenomenon of people weeping as soon as they heard the first notes of the ad's music. The president had referenced the slogan at a press conference.

Today Contessa thought the whole thing was a bit juvenile and manipulative, and she remembered so little of the shoot. It felt strange to hear the music accompanying what was projected on the screen behind her, to know that her journey into a maturity she hadn't yet reached was playing out once again. The other women on the stage craned their heads to watch. Next to Contessa, Bitty sniffled. Contessa sat facing forward, forced by this choice to watch the audience watching her. It was the best of a bad set of options. But it'd be over soon.

There was her tiny voice, the four words, the applause that signaled it was over. The lights came back up.

"So." The moderator clapped his hands and leaned forward in his seat. "That was the first time the world saw Contessa Lyle."

"I know." Contessa was going to take it again. More brightly this time. "I know! Is everyone okay? Do we need tissues?" She laughed, tried to let the smile reach her eyes.

♦ ♦ ♦

EVERY ACTRESS HERE AT THE PANEL DISCUSSION (THE "TRIBUTE to Actresses" they held every year at the film festival in downtown LA) had some early clip from her career played, but it wasn't always so . . . stupid. They'd found a recording of Davina performing in her tap-dance musical in London—that was actually pretty cool, seeing her legs moving so rapidly as she belted to the rafters. It was hard to believe that the grave, awkward woman Contessa kept running into could do that. For Bitty, they played a clip from a raunchy comedy she'd been in when she was the age Contessa was now. Contessa hadn't seen it when it came out, had been too busy working to see many movies, but she knew it was about a group of girls on a disastrous spring break trip together.

Bitty had hid her face in her hands as, on the screen behind them, a six-years-younger version of her, in a straw hat and bikini, shouted, "Chicas, there are three things we're doing tonight—shots, hot boys, and more shots!"

"Hot boys" was rendered in a kind of slanty comic accent, both of the vowel sounds pivoting into unexpected angles, that made Contessa laugh despite herself. Bitty really could be funny. In character.

Jenny and Eleanor got to watch themselves in their signature roles: Jenny as the subject of a famous photograph, a woman living through the Great Depression, touching her cheekbone gingerly as she contemplated how she would ever feed her children. It was a strangely powerful moment, one that played without words, just a sustained swell of music that made Contessa feel as if the woman Jenny played would always be all right, because she believed in herself. Jenny's cheekbones really were incredible. She looked so regal then, and now too, bowing her head and clasping her hands, silently thanking the audience for their applause.

For Eleanor, they'd shown a clip of her big prize-winning movie, *The Education of Melody Hart*, in which she played a housemaid who taught every member of the white family for whom she worked lessons about togetherness and pride. Contessa had seen it as a kid; it was always on TV. The scene they'd chosen had Eleanor serving slices of coconut cake to two child actors, telling them that the sweetness of the coconut was extra-special because of how hard it was to open it, that effort and sacrifice are what make life worth living. Eleanor seemed uncomfortable as the lights came up. Normally Contessa might have wondered if anything could make that woman happy, but she kind of got it. That movie was so passé. They wouldn't make it like that now.

Just as Contessa wouldn't make a cheesy car ad now. But, she supposed, it had gotten her to *Nina in Charge*. Then to her first couple of movies and magazine covers. And now here, talking about her movie. Her and Eleanor's movie.

"You were so cute," Bitty exclaimed into her microphone, just a little too loudly. "Can I . . . can I just say that? Come on!" She gestured with her free hand, the universal symbol for *raise the roof*. "Give it up for that little girl!"

The other women onstage clapped. So did the man moderating their conversation.

"Bitty," Contessa said. "You are too sweet."

"Well, Contessa," the moderator said. "What do you think when you watch that back?"

"I think . . ." Contessa began. "Gosh. It was a really special day. My mom let me drink soda between takes. That was a big treat."

The audience laughed, kindly, Contessa thought.

"It's so incredible," Bitty said hazily. "To have come so far, so fast." She was looking at Contessa with a strange cast to her eyes. A sort of vacant intensity, as if Contessa were her only focus in the world. Then she looked out into the audience. "I mean, right?"

"It's all about," Contessa said, "choosing the right projects. Having taste. My mom helps me with that a lot."

She couldn't quite see the faces in the audience over the glare of the stage lights, but she hoped Melanie was smiling at that one.

"And having the right costars, I believe," the moderator cut in. "We are lucky enough to have both women from *The Glass Menagerie* here, and you are both competing to be nominated for the leading actress prize. What was it like to work together?"

What was it like to work with a woman who had taken the director's side in every dispute? Who just said "Mmm" the first time they met, after Contessa tried to explain how excited she was to build out their characters' relationship together, to collaborate? Who seemed completely blind to how hard Contessa worked, at home, every night, to master the sorts of movements her acting coach had walked her through during auditions? Who seemed to leave her trailer only to whisper with the director and glance Contessa's way? Who missed the times Jimmy, playing her brother, whispered to her, "You're fucking up," missed the time he tossed a lit cigarette and it "accidentally" landed just six inches shy of her, missed Josh asking to speak to Jimmy for a minute off set? Who Contessa knew, just knew, wasn't the lead actress of the film, because the lead would have been involved, would have cared, the way Contessa herself tried to?

"It was so incredible," Contessa said. "I learned so much from her."

"Yes," Eleanor said in her gnomic, unknowable way. She was at the far end of the stage, the last woman in the line, and Contessa resisted the urge to crane toward her to see her expression. "Contessa is a very, very smart girl."

"I do have to ask," said the moderator, fidgeting a bit in his navy suit. "Everyone on this stage is hoping for a best actress nomination. Did either of you ever consider going supporting?"

"Well—" both Contessa and Eleanor began at the same time.

Then Contessa laughed. "That's mothers and daughters for you!"

"Maybe Eleanor first." The moderator gave an awkward chuckle.

"If the performances are there," Eleanor said, "the voters will recognize them."

Oddly, then, a standing ovation from the audience. Maybe, Contessa thought, if you said anything trite with the appropriate amount of gravity, these people would get on their feet and applaud.

Once the crowd died down, Contessa chimed in.

"I think, well, we both worked really hard," she said, "and we both deserve a shot. I really hope we both make it in, equally, into the same category. It would honor the work that we both did."

Of course, Contessa had been pressured to go into the supporting race. The studio had told her team that it was a smaller part, and they were probably right about that by the numbers—minutes onscreen, lines on the page, years in the business. But they didn't know how much Contessa had done off-camera, how much she'd had to put into not just being someone other than Nina but being someone completely new. Becoming someone as scared of the world as Contessa was eager for experience.

Contessa's mom had gone to the studio and told them they'd keep quiet about Jimmy "creating a violent environment on set" for Contessa, they wouldn't talk about the tossed cigarette or the time the star May Or May Not have felt that the director went a little too far in moving her body around when blocking Laura's movements. Her mom had only known about that because Contessa broke down and told her just before the end of shooting. She didn't know that Josh had intervened in his days on set. And that was okay too. In the end, Melanie had handled everything. Almost everything. Always had, from the beginning. And that was why Contessa had gotten as far as she had.

Ultimately, it was decided that it would be a fun publicity hook to have both women in the best actress race!

"Well, the voters will judge for themselves," said Eleanor.

A moment's silence, broken by Jenny.

"Hear, hear," she added, a little tepidly.

Jenny was second from the end, and seemed to reach her hand out as if to grasp Eleanor's, before realizing their chairs were too widely spaced for an intimacy like that.

"Yes, the voters will decide!" said the moderator. "But costars are so important. The trust you build."

He seemed to grasp at the air. Contessa's team had insisted that no questions about Jimmy be asked at all, as a condition of her participation.

"I'd just like to say," Davina jumped in, "that Contessa and Eleanor made some real magic together. And take it from me: it takes a lot of maturity to play Laura Wingfield." The crowd erupted again. "I tried it!" she said over the din. "On the West End. Canceled in previews. Contessa . . ." Davina mimed shifting the brim of a cap. "Hats off."

She could be so randomly nice!

"Thank you, Davina," the moderator said. "Now. Costars. So. On set, you two worked with Josh Jorgen—he plays the Gentleman Caller, who your characters believe is wooing Laura. Of course, he's not really interested. Josh also took time off from playing Scubaman to take on the role of Lyndon Johnson, opposite Bitty."

The crowd applauded; Eleanor sat motionless; Contessa made herself beam; Bitty appeared, oddly, to well up with tears. Maybe it was just that Contessa was sitting next to her, but Bitty seemed to be emitting waves of tension that the whole room might eventually feel.

"Bitty," the moderator said. "Can you talk about the level of trust that goes into building a portrait of a marriage?"

"Wow," Bitty said. "So. It was scary! It was definitely scary. Sorry." She dabbed at her eye, sniffled once again. "There was just this real responsibility, because, wow—I just respect Lady Bird Johnson so much. And so it felt really, um, powerful, to have Josh there, helping me out." She leaned forward, in the manner of someone conveying a secret, one she was sharing with all twelve hundred audience members. "He's actually here today."

"Talk about supportive!" the moderator roared. "That's terrific!"

Contessa's face burned. How awful. How rude. How disgusting. How obvious that she'd been missing something. Josh hadn't texted her after her cover shoot. He hadn't been texting at all. She'd done something, said something. She hadn't been right, hadn't been perfect. Not that Bitty was. But maybe she was for him.

Didn't he also, still, have a girlfriend? So there Contessa was—not just losing. In third place.

"Let's bring the house lights up!" the moderator said. "Josh? Josh Jorgen? Fly him a mic."

Contessa could see, eventually, that she wouldn't have been able to find him even once the dazzling stage lights came down. After some moments of confusion, a stagehand determined that Josh was five rows back, wearing a pulled-down baseball cap, and ran toward him with a microphone, "flying it in." A little dramatic, but Contessa supposed she had heard the phrase a million times by now. Despite how angry she was—the indecency of his showing up to support Bitty, without even telling her—she felt a surge of love. It was so decent of him not to be demanding attention. And it sucked for him that, despite that, he got dragged into things. That Bitty dragged him in. That she couldn't be cool about it.

"Hello, ladies," Josh said.

He got maybe the loudest applause of the panel so far. Finally, Contessa thought, they all got what they really wanted. To cheer for a dude. But this was uncharitable, because, inside, she did want them to be cheering for him. She just wanted them to be cheering as he geared up to say nice things about *her*.

"Josh Jorgen," the moderator said. "We'll move on to your work in *The Glass Menagerie* momentarily. But your lead role, as Lyndon Johnson. This creative marriage. What was it like working with Bitty Harbor?"

Josh tilted his head, rubbed his chin. From the stage, with the lights up, Contessa could see that he was playing to some invisible camera. Playing to Bitty. Contessa shot her eyes over, watched Bitty hold her left hand balled into a fist and keep her right hand wrapped around it. Bitty propped both under her chin as she sat, eyes glued to Josh. Contessa worried a fingernail against her thumb, careful not to make any movement that would read in any direction. She thought—hoped—that her face looked pleasantly neutral.

"To any casting directors in this audience," Josh said. "Cast. This. Woman."

The crowd erupted once more. Bitty shook a little, like she was holding back some cataclysmic burst. Maybe imperceptible to the audience, but Contessa could see.

"She was just incredible. She put every bit of herself into Lady Bird, every bit," Josh said.

"Thank you, Lyndon!" Bitty shouted, not using her mic, then caught herself, repeated it more calmly, only a little more calmly, into the device. "Thank you to my Lyndon. My husband."

"Anything for Bitty," Josh called back. "Because she gave everything to our movie."

"Wow," the moderator said.

Jenny, silent for so long, raised her hands above her head to applaud, then brought her mic down and said, "It takes one hell of a man to show up for a woman."

The crowd whooped again, so loud that Contessa thought that they might never stop, that she might break the fingernail she was pressing into her thumb, or break the skin, bleed out all over the stage. Soon, she knew, they'd ask him to talk about his couple of days on set with her, and what she gave of herself to her part. Because he was the only person who had thought she deserved to be in that movie. And he had seen it. He had. Why else was he still in her life? If he really was.

The house lights were still shining, obnoxiously, and Contessa looked into the front row. Her mother was sitting there, the bottom half of her face twisted into a rictus. As Contessa caught her eye, her mother pointed to her mouth. Kept on glaring but kept her lips upturned. Silently spoke the word *Smile.*

Contessa knew how to perform; she'd been trained well. Soon enough, she'd be in the car, traveling on to whatever was the next obligation, the next campaign stop—away from Bitty, and Josh, and Eleanor, and toward the time when they'd all be watching her hold a trophy. Life really was the ride. So. Until then. *Smile.* That's exactly what she did.

She felt the expression seep in, convince her to do more than play at being happy. Before this panel ended, there would, eventually, be a story Josh would share with this crowd about her talent. After it, he would text her, or even just glance her way. Give her something that she could clutch on to. But for now, she smiled at the pleasure of proving, if only to herself, her skills. For she knew in that moment that she was the most gifted actress on that stage.

Davina Schwartz, *Andronicus*

"To be loved is the journey of a lifetime."

No, that wasn't right. Davina looked away from the traffic outside the car window and back down at her phone. She'd never had trouble memorizing her lines. She was just distracted.

"To love, and to be loved," she repeated, reading from her manager's email, "is the adventure of a lifetime."

Adventure. The *adventure* of a lifetime. It certainly made sense. The fragrance was called L'Avventura. Italian for—well, one knew what it was Italian for. But the contract for her to be in its next ad campaign, speaking a line about love while, she had been told, a computer-generated image of a dove would fly into her very real hand, had come together head-spinningly quickly—so much so that she hadn't even sampled the thing. She assumed the perfume smelled fine; it was all the same to her, really. But it had felt a little rushed. Just a little.

"There's that saying," her manager back in London, a man Davina hadn't called too frequently before the past few months, had said, "about when one ought to strike the iron, isn't there?"

Hopefully L'Avventura, in its slim-necked little bottle that Davina would hold at the end of the advertisement, didn't smell like hot metal. But she supposed that was also the smell of money.

The commercial would bring some cash in. That was good, because the rest of the work that Davina had been doing lately was for free. At least the studio was paying for her clothes, and for the car taking her away from the panel. That group of women had been torture—it was good to be leaving them.

"The adventure of a lifetime," she read aloud once more, to try to clear her head.

It didn't quite work. She looked at Rory, sitting next to her, for a few moments.

"To be loved, you mean?" Rory smirked, after letting the silence hang for a few beats.

"To love *and* to be loved," Davina corrected her. "I think I got the order right . . . yes! Just as it says in the email."

She clapped her hands slightly, tucked them under her face as she leaned back toward Rory.

"They're lucky to have you," Rory said. "So am I. The whole production is. You were so good on that panel. I loved that they played that clip of you dancing. And you were so cute watching it." Rory grinned. "I think people are seeing it. That you're nothing like Tamora."

"Nothing, eh? So you don't think I'm fierce?"

Davina considered growling, a little joke, but deemed it probably too much.

"I mean that you're sweet. Not jaded. This stuff means something to you. That counts for a lot."

"Maybe it means too much. Faking nice for ninety minutes was tough." They both laughed. "I could use a drink."

Rory smirked again, her eyes unreadable behind mirrored aviators. "As Bitty Harbor once said."

"Oh, stop, you," Davina said, slapping Rory's knee like a schoolteacher, one from another era, dealing with the class clown. She smiled too, tried to keep her lips from curling into the smirk Rory kept making. It was sexy on Rory, but Davina couldn't pull it off. "But, really, Bitty was just awful back there," Davina went on, feeling a small dart of guilt. No matter—it was just them talking. "American women," she concluded, shrugging exaggeratedly.

"We're not all bad." Rory slapped her knee right back.

Enough time had passed for her to forget it, so time to test herself. In her mind, Davina began again: *To be loved*...

♦ ♦ ♦

THE CAR WAS INCHING ALONG, BACK TOWARD DAVINA'S. HER fridge was empty—well, that was nothing new, but she hoped Rory was in the mood for takeout. She wasn't really sure what Rory liked; the director had been good, at least, about Davina being a vegetarian. It had been kind of her to come to the panel, better still of her to sit in the back. If anyone wondered why she was there, well, she was just supporting her leading lady. Just as Josh Jorgen had done for Bitty and Contessa—completely innocent. But still. Better not to call attention to anything but the work.

The work! It was time to get back to work. The commercial shoot was set for tomorrow! Then, in two weeks, she'd be flying to New York for *Staying Up*—they'd just started running promotions for it on television, her name in next to that of a pop star she'd never heard of.

Her manager had told her to watch a bit of the show to know what she was in for: lots of costume changes and new characters, the host onstage basically the entire time but for the musical performances. She'd found an episode from a couple of years ago hosted by Contessa, who was stunning but a bit nervous throughout, just as she'd seemed to be today. (She'd chosen the episode for reasons that were obvious enough to her, but she had considered, for a moment, watching Bitty's, from five years back. It just seemed too painful to watch Bitty in a live setting, though. Davina had just lived through a bit of what that felt like.)

In Contessa's monologue, she had taken a series of increasingly invasive questions from a deranged gay—Davina assumed this was the idea?—fan, who kept calling the host an "iconic mama." Apparently, this was one of the signature characters of the show. No accounting for taste. But the bit did, at least, allow Contessa to seem game and charming as she played along.

She eventually closed her monologue by shouting back, "That's a little bit iconic!" and grinning, the tip of her tongue between her teeth—a real smile, or a brilliant performance of one. She hadn't told any jokes, but she had done that, and that was enough. Maybe a smile like that was what made a star something different, or something more, than just a theater actor.

Didn't seem like the kind of thing that Davina could do, although the costume changes and the characters—that much would be fun, like being back doing plays at uni. And the musician: maybe he was someone that Jeremy's generation would like. Maybe her son would think that it was cool that she'd met him. They could take a picture together; the singer could sign it. It would be a little bit iconic. Or something like that.

She idly scrolled through her phone, trying to find the email from her manager listing the details of how she'd be getting to New York. She'd been booked first-class, which still felt special, although Davina still wasn't quite used to the brusqueness of American air hostesses. There were a couple of emails from Beth, both with photo attachments; and then a contract for her to look over, about an endorsement deal for a line of hotels; then another for her to exclusively wear a certain brand of jewelry for the rest of the season. More money coming in. A note from her manager saying that Broadway producers wanted to meet with her about a new play from the perspective of Hamlet's mother, Gertrude—a bit repetitive after what she'd just done with *Andronicus*, but she'd take the meeting. An email with a PDF of a script she'd only skimmed through, a comedy about a high school for aspiring superheroes. She'd play the headmistress. Still more money, and—Davina stopped herself, almost, from contemplating how it might actually be a fun experience, if Contessa were cast as the girl with the power to bend her limbs in any direction.

God, she'd been a bright spot at that panel, at least at first. Nerves and all—she was a real person. Shame about how quickly she rushed out at the end. Whatever negative energy there had been between Eleanor and Contessa, Davina felt compelled to take Contessa's side, and not merely because of her beauty. It was an older performer's job to uplift younger actors. To welcome them along. Just as she'd tried to do, a bit, in that funny joint interview they did. And Contessa had helped her in return.

It was something she had too rarely experienced herself when she was emerging. On *Virginia Woolf*, for instance. Her costar had immediately sensed she was too green. He was an old Welshman, resentful of the girl who was trying, so prodigiously, to do everything too fast. And the way he averted his eyes when they crossed paths backstage before performances wasn't his way of staying in character. It was his way of impugning hers.

"Eleanor Quinn-Mitchell seems awful, doesn't she?" Davina mused.

"I don't know," Rory said. "Directors talk, just like everyone, and that sounds like it was a pretty tough set. Lots of blame to go around, especially when momagers get involved." She glanced out the window. "Not quite as bad as what happened with *Lisa Farmer*—sorry, I know you idolize Adria—but not good."

"Hmm." Davina didn't know how to respond to that. "What do directors say about our set?"

"That I'm the ultimate professional. And so are you." Rory stuck her hand into Davina's lap, stroked the inside of her thigh. "And that's why we support each other so well."

"I'll miss you, in New York." Davina let her voice lower to a purr.

"I know," Rory said. "I think there's going to be a lot of time we're missing each other. All these offers of yours."

"Yes. I'm lucky, I know. But it's a little too much."

Rory raised an eyebrow.

"Well, there's one more season of *Salem*, and then . . ." Davina said. "I could stay here. Or try to go to Broadway. Or . . ."

"Or."

Davina wondered what Beth and Jeremy were up to right now. She'd lost track of time—wasn't wearing a wristwatch, too deep into the backseat of this SUV to see the car's digital clock, felt gauche looking at her phone. Even after so many years of doing the conversion in her head, she'd forgotten how many hours she'd have to add to get to London time. She never did this, never forgot a line, never lost the time. Just distracted, that's all.

"Where you should go after this, I cannot tell you," Rory said.

"Well," Davina said, "I just thought—maybe you could give me advice. I need some friendly advice. About what to choose." She gestured at her phone. "From these projects."

♦ ♦ ♦

THEY INCHED ALONG. RORY HAD BEGGED OFF HELPING HER DEcide, told her that she had enough to worry about setting up her own next thing. Besides, Davina had time—why not just try to get through this season? Why rush things? This, Davina thought, was why it was hard with younger women, women who didn't know that if you chose to take a pause, you'd fall away.

A companionable silence had fallen. Davina knew that once they got home, they'd have sex, and the anticipation blanketed them both, less like nervous tension than like comfort and familiarity. Something that could be mistaken for home. Rory sang along quietly to a song playing still more quietly on the radio, a duet of two unobtrusive voices. Davina could see Rory's lips more clearly than she could hear the song.

Davina was scrolling through emails again—maybe it'd be worth just saying yes to the superhero headmistress, no one who mattered to her would see it—when a new message came in, with the sender's name reading only AB. She opened it.

dear davina schwartz, it read, in uncapitalized text.

i was fortunate enough to watch your performance in andronicus with my husband bill and daughter lindy recently. the three of us agreed that you were a performer of uncommon grace and tenacity, and that your future is very bright. i look forward to sharing my congratulations with you in person. best of luck to you, and my best wishes always.

sincerely yours,
Adria Benedict

These last two words, the first ones properly capitalized throughout.

"Rory. Rory, guess what?" Davina wanted, for a moment, to rip Rory's sunglasses off, to see in her eyes how much this would mean to her too—Davina having achieved a dream that she didn't know she'd had. She wondered how soon she would get to meet Adria, to absorb her praise. It was all coming together: This email, meeting Adria, Broadway in the fall, back to finish *Salem* in the spring. Back west for garden-salad lunches with Adria, finding the roles they'd play opposite each other, that first project in which Adria would welcome her encouragingly into the fold. Davina would still, somehow, be the younger performer—still capable of learning. The recipient of Adria's best wishes. Always.

But first, the perfume shoot tomorrow. How full of conviction her voice would be, how right her performance would feel, even in this unusual place in which she'd found herself. She'd memorize her line eventually, once she adjusted to being somewhere she never thought she'd be, somewhere she might never want to leave. Those who watched her, once the ad was shot and edited, once everyone in the world knew her, would be able to smell the fragrance through their television screens. And it would smell like falling in love. She would practically sing out, tomorrow, as she told the world the truth: that being loved—and, yes, loving, don't forget that—was the experience of a lifetime.

Jenny Van Meer, *The Diva*

JENNY WOULD HAVE PREFERRED IF they'd shown a different clip—one that maybe, just maybe, showed that she did have a sense of humor? Well, there was nothing like that in *The Migrant Mother*, nor should there have been. It was a very worthy film. But, goodness, Jenny wasn't always gazing into the middle distance. Sometimes she even spoke!

She just had to pick up the handbag she'd left in her dressing room, and then she'd be on her way. Doing this herself, in a season of being tended to, was her attempt to remain sane, remain human, reclaim a moment. Her publicist was waiting in the front to meet her, and they'd be driven back together to Jenny's hotel, where Jenny would have to change ahead of a cocktail party honoring *The Diva* tonight. That party would be in West Hollywood, a couple of miles of traffic-choked boulevards from where she was staying in Beverly Hills. "Tastemakers" would be there, the publicist had told her. So would voters. She would have to look smart. Perk herself up. Lots of riding in cars, being driven around. It didn't feel natural, after these past few years at the ranch.

Funny to feel so wrung-out, so unevenly distributed, by the

perpetual flattery, Jenny thought. Almost like she was less the honoree than the prize, being passed out handclasp by handclasp, cheek-kiss by cheek-kiss, to any hanger-on who could claim a piece of her. No. This wasn't fair. It would be a great honor to eventually win. A legacy. A place in history. It just never used to feel like this.

Backstage, the lineup of doors, a little warren of dressing rooms. Each woman had been in her respective corner until the panel. (It hadn't been that bad, in the end, although one wondered what was bothering Eleanor so.) Jenny was fairly certain she'd left her bag behind the second door to the left.

Nope! She'd only opened the heavy door a crack when she heard sobbing—gentle, somehow, as if someone was choking back a louder outburst, desperate to be quiet. She took a step back and did a calculation. How likely was it that her opening the door had been detected by whoever was inside? She made a move toward the second door to the *right*. Surely it had been that one.

Damn, damn. Too late. The first door Jenny had touched opened.

"Hey," came a tremulous voice, one that didn't need to be ornamented with a surprisingly solid, movie-ready Texas accent for Jenny to recognize it. "Is that you?"

Bitty, looking pallid and red-rimmed, her hair deflating, sized Jenny up.

"Oh." She caught herself. "Jenny. I thought everyone was . . ."

"Just . . ." Jenny trailed off.

In a fluid sequence of steps—Jenny felt a sudden gratitude for her movement and dance classes when she was first starting out—she pivoted to her proper dressing room (yes, that was the one), whisked the door open, scissored her right arm into the handles of her bag, extricated it, returned to face Bitty.

"Apologies," Jenny said. It would be best to be breezy with her. "The memory goes, with how many dressing rooms I've seen these past months. I was sure your room was mine."

Bitty barely seemed to register this. "Oh, it's fine, it's fine. Sorry. I thought you were—uh, well. Great panel." She looked down at Jenny's bag, seemed to jut her head back in shock. "Wow. A Birkin."

"It came to me recently," Jenny said. A treat, to get her through the endless rooms she'd walk through. Something bolstering, its soft nubbed leather a kind of armor to help her endure these days, emerge unscathed. "I am not really one for material things, but you must remember, I just finished playing one of the great divas of all time. And so . . ."

She laughed a bit, signaling that it was okay to join in at poking fun—gentle fun, of course—at an old lady's vanity.

"Yeah." Bitty didn't volley a laugh back. "I don't really pay attention to fashion besides what they give me, but even I know a Birkin."

A heavy silence. Bitty appeared so strange to Jenny, so delicate. She'd seen her, in passing, at events these past months. The way Bitty seemed to glow, seemed practically to levitate, when Josh Jorgen stood up in the audience—well, maybe that was acting. It could just be to sell the movie. But the way the vowels in the second repetition of "Birkin" seemed to slide out of her mouth, weak-ankled on the ice rink of her elocution, gave Jenny pause. It would be a long season for Bitty. For them both.

"I know," Jenny offered, "that these things are hard work. But, Bitty, you shouldn't let your makeup run." With a simple, elegant movement—who else but Jenny could do all this with such élan?—she produced a tissue from, yes, her Birkin. Placed it in Bitty's hand. Squeezed, very gently.

Just then, she remembered what Delle had told her about Bitty, back in Colorado.

"She's an excuse-maker," Delle had said, glass of wine in hand. "I own my shit, for better or worse. But she'll find any excuse to moan and complain and not do the job. Or cut people off. Or pretend to be heartbroken. It's exhausting. An energy vampire." She'd finished the wine in one go, made a little *Another?* gesture to the waiter. "Be grateful you don't have a reason to deal with her."

Well, now Jenny did, as she'd figured then that she eventually would. She couldn't speak to what had passed between Bitty and Delle. But Bitty didn't seem to be pretending much.

"Thank you," Bitty sniffled. "It really means . . ."

"Don't worry." She gave Bitty a wink. "I get allergies too."

Something more needed to be said. For a wild and strange moment, Jenny considered asking Bitty to her own party, but—well, wouldn't that be strange, an actress stopping by a campaign event for the competition? No matter how lonely she was. How lonely either of them were. There could always be a dinner, down the road, when they were both here in town, but . . . Who could account for where Bitty, or where Jenny, would be called, in service of the glory of winning? She settled on solace, in lieu of an invitation.

"I worry for you youngsters. There's just so"—she gestured around herself, at the wall of doors that had only just housed them both, Contessa, Davina, Eleanor—"much now. So much."

"I'm doing okay! It's honestly, it's honestly, I would say that, you know, it's great." Jenny perceived that Bitty was convincing herself, watched her nod forcefully, with her curls coming undone bobbing in syncopated time with her head.

"I'm glad you feel that way, my dear." Jenny felt herself struggle to mean it.

Jenny didn't need her own powers of perception to figure that Bitty was crying over Josh. Back at the panel, she'd tried to emphasize that their bond was clearly special, that Josh showing up meant something for Bitty. A mistake, she could see now. But it had also been a rare chance to jump in and say anything at all. It had been a little maddening that the panel had forced them all to speak about themselves in parallel. Anytime one woman had tried to praise another, the moderator had forced a next question. Jenny had eventually stopped trying. Maybe this could be another chance.

"You're just wonderful as Lady Bird," she said. "The way you love those two little girls. It's the heart of it all, isn't it."

"Thank you!" Bitty seemed practically to gush. "I meant to talk about them! I'm . . . so glad to hear you say that. I was worried people wouldn't see how important that was to the performance. Claudia as a mom, and trying to balance that. . . ."

"To hear you call her Claudia." Jenny tilted her head back. "Heaven! Of course she isn't Lady Bird to you. She's the woman, not the persona."

"Well," Bitty said, "thank you. That really means—I mean, it's just. It's a lot. So, wow. And you're . . . you're, well, you're you."

"For better or worse, my dear." Jenny knew it was time to go. "And I truly do hope our paths cross again."

Bitty nodded, dabbed at her eye again with the tissue, embarrassed yet somehow thriving in her embarrassment. Jenny had wanted to make this easy, to avoid giving Bitty anything more to feel shame about. To make her feel like there was a future in this field, beyond one day, or one race.

"Thank you, Jenny." Bitty spoke now a bit more clearly. Jenny felt herself exhale slightly. "It's just unbelievable. I can't express . . ."

"The pleasure is mine." Jenny cleared her throat. "Now, really, I must—but I do know that one way or another, we'll meet again." She had felt her voice begin to grow thick and grand with self-regard.

A vibration in her purse. Jenny hated what phones had done to interactions with her peers as a general matter, but it was probably time to break this moment. She extracted her phone, read a text from her publicist saying that Ceridwen Darby had been in attendance and wanted to say hi before they left, and could Jenny make her way to the front so they could beat traffic to the hotel? She maneuvered her phone back into the handbag, trying not to think about the clawlike posture it took to hold the massive thing, wished that she could find a way to hide her hands. The columnists had mocked her when she'd worn gloves, the last time she had attended the awards. So no more gloves. Maybe the Birkin was a better vehicle for that vanity of hers. It was built to contain it.

Bitty was just watching Jenny, her mouth hanging open a bit, as if Jenny herself had just stepped off a movie screen, as if she were a miracle.

"Before I go—it's an honor to meet you. Come here," Jenny said, gathering Bitty into an embrace.

Bitty smelled so strongly of a freshly smoked cigarette that Jenny couldn't pick up anything else.

What a relief, Jenny thought, to have something to go to tonight. Despite it all, despite how scraped-out she was coming to feel. There was a next thing to do, a reason to stay dressed up. A reason to keep trying, to keep showing the world the ways that she was winning. She hoped for Bitty that there was something for her like that too. That she wasn't on her own.

She'd had this hope, too, for Adria, who never came to these things at all, never put herself out there, didn't need to. It was silly, Adria had a family, but just think of how oddly she'd behaved in Colorado. How alone she had seemed. Jenny hoped that there was something in Adria's life to put the work into perspective. To give her a place to be.

As she held Bitty in her arms, just before she broke her grip and went to meet the famous editor before getting in the car that would take her to change clothes for a party in her honor, Jenny let her mind tick. There were points she needed to remember. Things she needed to say. Maria Callas, she thought, was a strong woman, ahead of her time. And though she suffered bad luck, she persevered. That's what *The Diva* celebrated. And Jenny knew—as she'd say to those strangers lining up to see and hear her, to take a memory of her as a relic—that she had done this incredible woman justice.

An email from Eleanor Quinn-Mitchell's publicist to Ceridwen Darby, November

Hi again!

Circling back on our pitch for Eleanor Quinn-Mitchell for one of your covers during the nomination voting period. I know it's a tight squeeze time-wise and an incredibly competitive piece of real estate (and that there are other contenders from Eleanor's own movie!), but the whole team here really thinks that this could be a special opportunity for a legendary star who reinvented herself this season!

Eleanor is doing very select press this cycle (as you're surely aware!), and (as you're similarly likely aware!) is coming out of an early retirement, during which she was caring for her late husband, the director Walter Mitchell. Their partnership in the years before his death gave rise to some of Eleanor's best work—work that many now believe is worthy of reappraisal, making Eleanor, well, overdue for recognition!

Wouldn't personally use the word "comeback," but Eleanor's return to the screen as the lead actress of *The Glass Menagerie* is an instant-classic turn—proof that even as trends come and go, talent doesn't fade. It's the capper on a long and distinguished career, and a story that deserves to be told.

I'm obviously biased, but her history-making journey through Hollywood would make for an amazing interview, and she's as wry and as passionate about moviemaking as she was in her early days with films like *Melody Hart*. (Also, sidebar: Have you seen *Melody Hart* lately? It was on cable last week and I got sucked in—as moving as the day they made it! Tears. Serious tears!) Anyway, Eleanor is totally game to give time for an opportunity that would present her and her powerful narrative in the right light.

Please let me know if this would be a possibility or if we can find time to talk on the phone this week! Crossing every finger that we can make something work out for Eleanor!

PS: Probably goes without saying! But we are considering solo cover opportunities only at this time.

Eleanor Quinn-Mitchell,
The Glass Menagerie

"AND WE ARE ROLLING," PERRY said.

Eleanor hadn't wanted to do this. It seemed silly, and unnecessary, and like tempting fate. It wasn't that she didn't want the nomination, and eventually the award—of course she did. (Was it greed motivating her toward this second prize? Well, maybe if the newspapers had printed that you only beat Adria Benedict and Nancy McCord because the voters felt bad that they'd never awarded a Black woman, you might get greedy too.) She had always wanted it—she felt the twinge every year when the list was announced, even these past years, when she hadn't been making movies at all.

"The shot looks great," May said. "You look great. We're just going to hold like this with you and the TV both in frame, so that we can get your reaction. What are you thinking, EQM?"

"That I can't believe it," Eleanor said levelly, holding May's gaze so as not to look at the muted television set, rushing through the last bits of local news before the announcement, or back out her window, where the grim darkness of February and of 5 a.m. awaited. "And that it's good to be with you."

She really couldn't believe that she'd agreed to do this, but her second statement was adjacent to the truth too. May was a kind soul, and certainly a hard worker. It had been her idea to tape Eleanor reacting to the nomination announcement, and she'd put her back into convincing Eleanor to say yes. Eleanor didn't really know why she'd agreed; it was one more thing, one more little piece of her life offered up for public view. (She'd won, the first time, after doing just a few magazine interviews and the one late-night show that existed back then. Just to get a one-page profile inside the Movies Issue this year, she'd had to get on the phone and tell some college student about all the movies her late husband had directed, and avoid his repeated requests that she tell him which of her past leading men she'd like to have married or slept with. *Enough*.)

But there was a certain thrill to being in the mix, even as the manner of doing business had changed. It had become a full-time job—welcome enough. Eleanor needed the distraction. May's dispatches about how well Eleanor had been doing were heartening. Magazine covers had been hard to come by—Eleanor had her own theories about why—but she made the most of what she'd been given. She aced a late-night TV karaoke performance of a pop song she'd spent the day and a half prior learning, had shaken more hands than Contessa at every cocktail party for *The Glass Menagerie*. It was tiring. But it made her feel as if she hadn't been forgotten.

"Eleanor," May had told her, "you are a Hollywood legend. And people want, so badly, to see you win. If you show them this moment of real joy, people are going to share it."

Eleanor understood that the "legend" framing was meant to flatter her into giving something more of herself, but she was fine falling for it all the same. It had the benefit of being true—the voters had made her the First. And she also understood that the want, in this case, was May's, to keep Eleanor—only in her early seventies! early!—from becoming any more removed from the heart of things than she already was. So she had decided to trust May.

Besides, thinking about what to wear for this video and how to properly calibrate her reaction gave her something to consider beyond the possibility that she might not be nominated.

The mere fact of May's having planned this all out put Eleanor at ease: they wouldn't be making this video if the nomination wasn't happening. May knew this whole world better than Eleanor could have, after five years of caring for Walter and two sorting out his estate, or trying to. She could hardly have done better, after having been without representation the past half-decade or so. Kevin, her publicist before Walter died, had retired to Palm Springs and fallen out of touch aside from a Christmas card each year, addressed lovingly to "Ellie"—a nickname she would tolerate only from him. It was, at least, different from the clinical "EQM," which she felt made her sound like a disease. She allowed "EQM" with, she thought, a touch of equanimity, because May was under forty, and who knew how that generation spoke to one another. Maybe it was a sign of respect.

Respect, from a young person. Imagine that!

Now, now. Contessa might—might!—be nominated too.

♦ ♦ ♦

MAY HAD, ABOUT AN HOUR BEFORE, INTRODUCED ELEANOR TO Perry, the fellow the PR firm had contracted to set up the camera.

Eleanor took a liking to him easily, and not merely because he was the one responsible for transmitting to the world her moment of triumph, the moment she'd be named one of five, for the months before she'd be named one of one. Perry had an easy manner, as though this sort of thing was a common and welcome part of his job, a worthy way to put his expertise to use. It helped her believe that this was not an exercise in vanity, in chasing a dream. He was also appropriately discreet and apologetic when it came time to mic her; May and Eleanor had decided together that it made no sense for Eleanor to be in "full glam," and so she wore a nice silk pajama set she'd had someone from May's office go out and buy two days prior, providing the perfect lapel onto which Perry could clip a mic while looking away.

Eleanor had, though, put on some makeup and fixed her hair. This new kind of campaign demanded she let people into her home, but she wasn't about to look like she'd just woken up. She'd barely slept anyway, and approached the impending announcement—three minutes now, if her watch had it right—with a funny feeling of flying.

She watched with an alien sort of pleasure as Perry moved furniture around to get the perfect shot. The chair she'd spent so many nights in these past years, watching old movies, was now positioned practically perpendicular to the television, so that her face could be in three-quarter profile as she watched good news about herself from the corner of her eye.

"One last thing!" May had said as Perry finished, and asked Eleanor to go get her old award and place it on the end table next to her, as if the golden being, shaped like a man but the size of an infant, were watching the nomination announcement with her.

On another morning, or at another time of day, Eleanor might have protested—the gaucheness of flaunting her past good fortune to the world seemed too much, and she didn't want anyone to seriously think she sat with her best actress trophy next to her at all times. (The family prizes lived, very tastefully, next to her wedding photos with Walter, at the center of her mantelpiece in the great room.)

But May knew what to do. She knew what Eleanor couldn't possibly about how the world's expectations had changed, how much more of her was needed now. And so Eleanor went down the hall and into that grand, high-ceilinged room, the one she and Walter had once used for entertaining, and picked the prize off the shelf, where it had been placed between the two Walter had won. Right in the middle, and pushed slightly forward. Walter had given her that—pride of place. She didn't let herself hold it practically ever (what would be more sad, and more painfully symbolic, than a trophy tarnished from too many sweaty hands grasping it over the years?). She brought it down off the shelf, holding it tightly by the narrow pillar above the base, pointing its head toward the floor.

The first thing that had struck her was its weight. Had it felt that way on the night? She was younger then—stronger, surely, at least in some ways. But it was the sort of weight one couldn't avoid noticing, the kind that alters the way you move, that demands you take a special sort of care. Then, in the maroon silk of her nightshirt, Eleanor noticed the bounce of a golden shadow, as if the thing were not merely reflecting light but generating it. An energy source.

Eleanor could have found the mirror in this room with her eyes closed, given how carefully she'd tried to avoid it in those first days without Walter, when she turned away all his moviemaking colleagues who had wanted to come pay tribute to her widowhood. Now she walked over to it on her way out of the great room unaccompanied. She looked at herself: Presentable. Camera-ready. May had a certain kind of mad persuasiveness. Eleanor never, but never, would have thought she'd agree to appear on-camera in her pajamas, even ones newly purchased for the purpose.

She liked the way she looked right now, after everything: Relaxed, if only because the obliterating force of sleeplessness forced all but immediate needs out of her head. Happy. Bouncing with that golden light from the object she clutched. She knew May was waiting for her, but she also knew that she had to bring herself back to a place she hadn't been for so long, maybe not since the night she'd won, before the mornings when she'd had to read in the newspapers that she'd stolen something.

She summoned . . . Why deny it? She summoned Contessa. That self-indulgence, that sense of being owed success. And she pointed her trophy upward, clutched it to her chest, and grinned, as if she'd just won it for the very first time.

♦ ♦ ♦

THIS HAD HELPED. IT HAD PREPARED ELEANOR TO EXAGGERATE emotion, and to really feel it. She'd been surprised at what had coursed through her as she held the prize, as she channeled her costar. She had always felt at a remove from Contessa—perhaps this was what helped their performances, made it really work when Amanda Wingfield wondered why her daughter couldn't just get her head out of the clouds. Of course, in Contessa's case, it was wanting her head out of her phone, or out of their costar's derriere. Say this much: Eleanor felt grateful, if nothing else, that there was room for her at all, after her years away, after Contessa's generation had taken over.

If Eleanor was being generous, or fair, she'd concede that Contessa gave a creditable performance: somehow, through some work Eleanor never saw her do, she carried across Laura's sadness and her physical maladies. But the things the director told Eleanor, in their occasional huddles! My, my, the things he told her.

Eleanor knew how to speak director. She knew their language. She'd known she was falling in love with Walter when, on their first blind date, he bluntly told her *Melody Hart* hadn't worked, that it had been a fantasy to make white people feel better about themselves. "But you were . . ." he'd told her, appraising her so closely that she flushed, in a way she hadn't realized she still wanted to. "You found your way there, I suppose." He smiled guilelessly, knowing he had shown her the respect it took not to kiss her ass.

No wonder they were married six months later. And that her post-award career doldrums began to melt away. They spent fifteen years—not nearly long enough—coming up with ideas for projects they could make together, projects that looked different than what a Black woman rounding the bend into deep middle age might have gotten without a famous director as her dogged advocate. Some of these projects had even gotten made. Walter wanted so badly to show different sides of Eleanor than the flat, sunshiny Melody Hart: he had pushed her to play grief, to play joy. Thrillingly, he pushed her to oscillate between the two in *The Discovery*, where she played an oncological researcher on the verge of a major scientific breakthrough while battling cancer herself. Eleanor knew after Walter died that she'd never again watch the movies they'd done together, but the irony of this one was more than she could even bear to think about. And making it had been such a thrill. It was a script he'd found on a pile, which they'd workshopped together, adding notes of Eleanor's own stubbornness, her own unwillingness to accept familiar limits. She should have been nominated for that. But after spending years losing out on parts she wanted, that she could have played, to Adria and sometimes to Jenny, the fact of the movie was enough.

The prize was that Walter had trusted her with that, and she'd trusted him to be honest with her. To get the most out of a director, one had to be open, willing to hear something other than flattery. To push forward together. Maybe that's why she hadn't worked for so long. Because she hadn't been ready to talk to a director the way that she'd need to in order to do her job right. Or she hadn't trusted that whoever her next director was would treat her with frankness and honesty. As something other than a widow.

The *Glass Menagerie* director hadn't been collaborative, exactly. The script was the script—"What the great man wrote!" he chortled on the first day. But he was utterly open with Eleanor. And he told her that he couldn't be that way with Contessa. He told Eleanor that he had felt compelled to hire the girl because she was famous, and not for her accomplishments, like Eleanor or Jimmy. (Eleanor, it seemed, was no longer enough to guarantee a film's funding. But that went unsaid. And she knew it had always been an uphill climb anyway.) He had to fight to keep her pushy mother off the set—a white woman at that. Little wonder Contessa had no home training. And he said what Eleanor could clearly see: that Contessa was totally unwilling to take part in the spirit of play that a good set required. Eleanor knew Jimmy could be a bit intense—some would have called it "Method," even as Walter had always derided the imprecise use of the term—but she'd worked with some of the greats, and fought them to a draw. Jimmy was easy. And she could see for herself how immature Contessa was, how immersed she was in finding someone else to do her battles for her. That girl emerged from her trailer each day ready for the camera, but little else.

Eleanor could not imagine having a daughter like Contessa. Her poor, awful mother. It had been too late for her and Walter, and he had his grown children already anyway, but she imagined she'd have done better. She did better onscreen, showing Amanda's frustrations and the best of her intentions, the human inside her, stymied by her children's faults and lost in memories of what she'd once thought she would have. She and the director had worked that out together.

But that was what a good director allowed you to do. The worst thing that Eleanor could say of Contessa was that Walter would have hated her. He respected strength, in men and women both. Giving as good as you got, no matter how delicate you seemed. And this, to Eleanor, was a special kind of fairness, one Contessa would never understand.

And so, she let Contessa fill her: The aloofness, the entitlement. But she knew that, in her case, it had the benefit of being earned.

♦ ♦ ♦

"DELLE DEANE," THE ANNOUNCER'S VOICE SAID, "FOR *WHO IS LISA Farmer?*"

"She is a lock to win," May said.

"Excuse me," Perry said, "but we need this footage as clean as possible."

"Sorry, sorry!" May said, "EQ—"

"I'm all right," Eleanor said.

Eleanor had a glass of fizzy water, Walter's old brand, before her, but she knew that if she reached for it, she'd fumble, spill it down her front.

"Just," Perry said, "stay really, exactly as you are. The shot is perfect. I promise."

She missed the rest of the supporting actress nominees, but of course she knew Contessa wasn't among them; the studio had agreed they were both the leads. In a situation where neither she nor the woman who'd brought Contessa into the world would accede, it seemed like the only option. And Eleanor thought that beating Contessa fair and square would have a certain poetry to it.

"We're coming up soon," May said. "Just sit tight."

Eleanor worked to structure her face in a way that suggested calm. She shifted her left arm, putting her index finger to her chin, so as to feel the pajama sleeve brush down her forearm like a comforting whisper. Reminders of Christmas mornings in the good times, ski trips. Moments that came as a break from working on something together, or coming just before diving into a new script, a new chance to drum up funding. Happy, cheerful times marking a blessed respite from the wearying joy of the work they did together; times when she had put in the effort; times when there was someone to notice.

A warmth emerged, glowing within like her trophy. She'd been in this business long enough to know that costumes really did help.

♦ ♦ ♦

MINUTES PASSED LIKE THAT, UNTIL . . .

"And now," said the announcer—the president of the group that gave out the awards, jolly and rotund in his suit—"the nominees for the best actress prize."

"That's right, Tom," said the young woman he'd been paired with. Eleanor thought she recognized her from the *Scubaman* installment she'd watched to try to figure Josh out, before she'd given up. This actress had helped prevent the destruction of the land of Aquaria before being torn apart by a shark; this morning she was in some sort of businesswoman drag, wearing a white oxford shirt, open one button too low, and a high-waisted pencil skirt. It was funny, Eleanor thought, to spend as much money as this woman's team surely had, all in order to look so classless.

"Without any further ado," the man said. "Adria Benedict, for *Who Is Lisa Farmer?*"

Eleanor knew that the initial of her surname meant that she would be in the latter half of the group. And she had known that Adria would be nominated, because she was Adria. It was hard to begrudge her. Adria had been kind enough to her. Kinder than she'd needed to. She'd sent flowers for Walter. They'd met about Eleanor taking a supporting role in a movie or two of Adria's before that, but nothing connected. As she got older, Eleanor had to count on Walter to make things happen for herself. But then, she'd known that since they met.

Adria had seemed so strange in Colorado, wild-eyed and lost, and Eleanor knew Adria hadn't been sure what to say to her, could sense the vanity in Adria batting against the instinct not to make Eleanor's loss all about Adria herself.

But then, Eleanor had been frightened too. It was no small thing to try to walk back into the party. Maybe Adria's true genius was in knowing never to leave. There was a shamelessness to her that Eleanor couldn't help but admire: *Who Is Lisa Farmer?* was perfectly nice, and Eleanor had been envious that Adria could get those kinds of roles at their age without it being a stunt or a comeback. But it was Delle Deane's movie.

If only Contessa had an ounce of that young woman's work ethic!

Eleanor worried that these roiling, busy thoughts, racing within her in the moments between names, were playing across her face. She struck the smallest look at May, who was grinning, effortfully and hard, at her. Perry was nodding in a slow rhythm, as if wishing the next name forward, urging it to be Eleanor's. The room on television was eerily silent between the names as the two hosts, standing before unseen journalists waiting to write about Eleanor's triumph, took longer to get things moving than they strictly ought to. Eleanor knew this morning broadcast was always an awkward affair, but . . .

The pause ended abruptly.

"There we go," the woman said. "Teleprompter problems. Whew!" She mimed wiping her brow, then went on, "Anyway, Bitty Harbor, for *Lyndon and Claudia*."

"Contessa Lyle," the man said. "For *The Glass Menagerie*."

Eleanor nodded and smiled as she'd been coached to if this should happen.

"Good girl!" she said, in an ad lib.

But she suddenly felt the floor sucking out from under her as she spoke. Felt for the first time as though she might not . . . let alone not *win*, which had always been a possibility, but might not . . .

"We're . . . still struggling with the teleprompter here, folks," the man said, a bit of frustration entering his voice. "We'll work this all out before the show, promise."

As she waited, Eleanor turned and looked openly at May. She felt herself saying, "I'm nervous!"

She knew as the words left her mouth that this was a breach of the sort of dignity that she was meant to possess in every moment of her life in public, but especially moments where vanity and awards might be concerned. She knew, too, that she had placed just enough real feeling into this confession that viewers would understand what this moment meant. Not a comeback to Hollywood; she was secure enough that her name would live on. But emerging from the house after these years. Shaking hands with people who weren't new attorneys; planning a strategy directed at securing new glory, not just taking what was rightfully hers, what had been willed to her, from the clutches of Walter's greedy children. Being seen for what she could still do, not just for what she'd done, or for what she'd been for too long unable to imagine doing again. Putting on a pajama set from a nice department store, instead of just wearing Walter's old slippers and sweaters until they nearly fell apart. Worrying just a bit less about feeling close to him, because she realized now that the closest she could ever get was on a working movie set—no matter who her director was, who her costars were. As long as she was finding her way there.

She was nervous. And the world would feel for her. Feel her.

"Davina Schwartz," the woman said. "For *Andronicus*."

A whoop went up in the room on television; a surprise. Some part of Eleanor's brain, remote from the sting she felt at realizing that, of course, "S" comes after "Q," and her journey had ended, reminded her that she and Walter had watched Davina in an old television series from the UK in those last months; his attention, after so many years giving so much of himself to movies, had finally dwindled, and a few six-episode British seasons, fifty minutes at a time, felt only just manageable. He'd said, watching her play a cop investigating crimes outside Glasgow, that Davina would make a great lead for a future film of his, an idea that felt, for him, still too close to share. He'd said that she had an intensity that couldn't be matched.

She'd known Walter was beyond making films at this point, and of course he'd known it too. His praise for Davina seemed sweet in retrospect. He knew that Eleanor's prickliness around his complimenting other actresses had faded a bit in the years she'd spent caring for him.

It was Eleanor whose intensity onscreen couldn't be matched—no, not even by Davina. But of course Walter didn't want to think about the performances Eleanor had given onscreen, even in his movies; she was trying so hard to be present, in whatever time together they had left, as herself. It was a final compliment, if Eleanor looked at it the right way. Davina could take Walter's final film, a film they both knew he would never make. Eleanor was the leading lady of something greater. Grief and joy, oscillating between the two, those last days. The performance of a lifetime.

But they hadn't been able to see that work. Hadn't read into Amanda Wingfield the loneliness and disappointment she brought to it from these past years. All her late memories with Walter, rooted in this business—the work he didn't get to do as his health failed, or the work she chose not to do to be with him: this morning revealed that she hadn't had a story worth telling, or one that she was able to tell well enough. Leaving years of disappointment behind, emerging only to be met with more of it—that was her narrative. And it hadn't been good enough. Not like Contessa's.

"And Jenny Van Meer," the man said. "For—"

May plunged her head into her phone. "Of course we're going to have to congratulate C. We'll get something up on your social channels."

Eleanor had never touched or even seen those. May had hired someone to make them for her. And Eleanor had thought she might look for the first time this morning, to see what people said on Instagram, to see if people understood what this meant, what she'd tried to share with the world in her video. A thumping, pounding sound filled Eleanor's ears; she realized that someone had muted the television, but it was all too believable that she'd suddenly lost her hearing. Without thinking, she reached for the trophy on the end table, simultaneously wanting to clutch it to her once again and to hide it in a place where no one would ever find it, to make sure that it could not somehow be taken away. It felt exposed, sitting here where anyone could see it, where foolish May could steal it from Eleanor like she'd stolen her pride.

"Of course we have to," Eleanor said, a robot. "What a wonderful experience for her."

"She's following," Perry began. "She's following in yo—"

"Eleanor," May said. "Should we get you out of . . ."

She didn't feel surprised then, or even angry, or sad, although she had the painful pinch of anticipation that these feelings would come in time. It was silly, disgraceful, really, to think this, but Eleanor had chosen this line of work for the reason that it allowed you to be silly and disgraceful, when you were in character. And she had kept herself bottled up too long. Now, after months of strange and wild hope, she was the lonely widow once more. And when she emerged from this day that was only just dawning, she'd grieve again.

"I think," Eleanor said, unclipping her own mic from her lapel, "that I am going back to bed. Please figure out a way to give my best to Contessa."

There was a silence in the room, deep and profound, the kind of silence Eleanor felt she could practically swim through to get to the other side. When she arrived there, she could allow herself to cry. She could take off the department-store finery and put Walter's ratty cashmere sweater back on. To get there, she needed to endure the seconds it would take her to cross back to the great room, to put her award back on the shelf. She had to be sure not to drop it. She kept her gaze focused on the television set, where some fellow had come on to analyze the nominations. Through the blurring of water, she saw the words "Adria" and "Jenny" in the chyron at the bottom of the screen. She stared a moment longer and thought she saw the word "snub," before looking away.

"We're not still rolling, are we?" May said.

Eleanor didn't want to wait for an answer. She turned to Perry—a filmmaker whose future lay before him, and a boy who'd spent his morning watching an old woman fail.

"Before I go to bed," she said, "stop the tape. And delete it."

A button clicked, then another. Eleanor's morning, in what she knew would be the only solace when she allowed herself to consider it in the future, was erased.

Adria Benedict, *Who Is Lisa Farmer?*

IT WAS A SILLY THING. To be this excited, after this many times. But really. To be in the game. So consistently. And always as the lead actress. It meant something. It was a legacy of sorts.

That made it feel all right to attend the nominations luncheon solo. All of the nominees, from actresses to film editors, were gathered for a special luncheon so that everyone could applaud everyone else. No hierarchy.

The event had grown, of course—everything had gotten more massive, more bloated, since Adria's early days. Now journalists came, and candid photographs of the nominees talking together were released and run online. Well, let them see how happy she was for others' success, how eagerly and avidly she'd chat up her seatmates, whatever screenwriters or makeup artists they paired her with. Everything had changed. They used to serve the best food too—hearty things like beef Wellington or even just a nice piece of salmon, an indulgent pause to enjoy oneself, after the months one had already spent dieting. But the past few years it had been "plant-based," little salads and couscous dishes. All the better, Adria supposed—who wanted to be photographed diving headfirst into a chicken pot pie?

The SUV pulled up to the curb of the hotel and Adria thanked her driver with a warm and wordless nod. A phalanx of cameramen right at the entrance, certainly not the kind of photojournalists who would be allowed into the room, all men, all clicking away at her as she strode into the lobby. This was why she kept her sunglasses on until she was indoors. This was why she gave so little when not certain of who was clicking the camera, who was asking the questions. It was her own image to give, or to keep. There was only so much of her.

A mill of people, a churn, as Adria walked up to the registration table. Everyone seemed just to be standing around, waiting for someone else to go ahead of them and check in first. But if one walked with purpose, it was easy to see the opening.

"Benedict?" Adria murmured, amused at the humility she could conjure up for a young woman with a lanyard. "Under 'B.' "

Ms. Lanyard, an employee of the awards, looked appropriately stricken, still more so when Adria took off her sunglasses, folded them, seamlessly placed them within their case and the case within her handbag. This was another reason she kept her sunglasses on until she was indoors—to give some lucky person the experience of meeting her eyes anew. The lanyard woman looked appropriately awed. How gratifying.

"Of—of course," she stammered. "I have two tickets here?"

"No need. I apologize for leaving an empty seat, but today it's just me."

♦ ♦ ♦

BILL NEVER CAME TO THINGS LIKE THIS, OF COURSE. HE ONLY came to the awards, in the years when Adria was nominated, because even he knew how bad it would look if she were sitting there utterly without support. They loved each other for reasons beyond show business, Adria reminded herself—for the things that were really true. And that was enough. She hoped he was enjoying his golf foursome.

She'd considered asking Lindy to fly back out again—but no. Lindy had been put out when Adria backed out of the panel discussion, seemed to know that it was not just about a conflict with a lunch with Nancy that could, really, have been moved anytime. When Adria came home from lunch, Lindy was flopped on the couch, reading a magazine with Jenny on the cover. How petty of her daughter. How small.

After an afternoon spent in their respective corners, Adria had suggested in the early evening that they all watch *Andronicus* together, at Nancy's suggestion. It turned out Adria had a screener in her pile. Bill had fallen asleep twenty minutes in, his snoring drowning out Davina's words until Adria shook him, sent him to bed. And Lindy had interjected with so many questions—didn't it feel, frankly, a little trite to just reverse the perspective of Shakespeare's play without interrogating what he was actually saying about the female capability for brutality, and so on, and so on—that Adria finally announced that she was enjoying the film, and that those who weren't could leave. Lindy flew back to Chicago the next morning, catching a ride from a friend to the airport. Didn't touch the quiche Adria had ordered and left in the fridge for her. It used to be her favorite.

She was looking too thin, Adria thought. Didn't suit those thick features of hers to be all skin and bone. A mother worries.

Ticket acquired, and on into the ballroom. Always funny to be reminded, year after year, that this was just an ordinary space. What made it extraordinary were the feelings one brought to it. But the tables, the chairs, the hors d'oeuvres—ah, there he was, the young man with the little toothpicked dollops of polenta topped with roasted wild mushrooms, and Adria gave the smallest shake of her head to indicate she wasn't interested—well, there was only so fancy a hotel ballroom could be made to look. It was on par with a relatively nice wedding in the end, wasn't it? The only difference was that they didn't know who the bride was yet.

She scanned the room. Ah, the set decorator she'd been paired with at this lunch three years ago—charming woman. Adria put up a hand. How nice that she was nominated again, that they both were. The connections you make at these things. She kept looking. No Jenny, yet. There by the bar were Bitty Harbor and Josh Jorgen, both from the Lyndon Johnson movie. Adria found the thing a crushing bore—but then, she'd lived it. As a child, but still. Not exactly untrod ground, and a shame for the woman's part to be written just as the supportive wife. Bitty brought something to it, didn't she—she was certainly a live wire onscreen. She was written to submit to Lyndon, but one could sense how badly she wanted to prove herself his equal. It was as if she were pushing up against the limits of the role, as if she were ultimately too modern to be able to subsume herself into the person of a woman who was only there to say yes.

Adria, generally speaking, hated period pieces for this reason. It seemed like they were all that Jenny knew how to do, too. Couldn't step into her own moment, the moment of strong women onscreen that Adria, with precious little help from her peers, had worked to carve out.

Although *Andronicus* was different, and—ah! There she was. Over in a far corner, speaking with Contessa Lyle. Lovely girl, wasn't she? She walked toward the pair, gently turning down a vegetarian "fig in a blanket" topped with cashew chèvre crema and mouthing *How are you?* to the costume designer for a film she'd made years prior. They'd catch up, once she was done speaking with Davina.

"Oh, wow," Contessa said as Adria walked up. "It is . . ."

"The honor is all mine." Adria bowed her head. "Eleanor is an old friend of mine, Contessa, and you matched her beat for beat."

"Jeez . . ." Contessa seemed startled. "I . . . My mom's over there"—she gestured hazily with her left hand, out into the broad expanse of the ballroom. "She won't believe you said that."

"Maybe I'll get the chance to tell her myself." Adria smiled in what she thought was an appropriately maternal manner. "You don't yet have any idea, do you, how long these luncheons can go."

"I guess not," said Contessa.

She was wearing a navy sundress with a little white cardigan over it—too girlish by half, Adria thought. Contessa was among adult women, wasn't she? Look at Davina: in a strange periwinkle tuxedo, but at least she was dressed. Maybe, eventually, Adria could teach her how to outfit herself for these things. Contessa should have known better, but Davina—Adria found it odd and moving that she was so unsuited. The theater actress was only just beginning to figure this game out. For Davina, maybe, it still was about the work.

A photographer walked up, gestured wordlessly with his hands that the women ought to spread their little triangle into a straight line. They broke apart and reassembled without comment, and he clicked and walked away.

"Make us look good," Davina called out to his back.

"Contessa," Adria said, "you're clearly a student of theater. Playing Laura Wingfield."

"I don't know about all that." Contessa looked a little abashed. "I wanted to do a good job, so I did some research. Like, for instance—"

"I can't think of a better education in theater than speaking to Davina here," Adria cut in. "The things she did in *Andronicus*. Have you watched it, Contessa?"

"I have!" Contessa said. "It's so great! It's a shame only one of us can win."

"Hear, hear!" Davina spoke a bit too emphatically. "Would that we could all share."

"Mmm," said Adria. "Now, Davina. How are you?"

It was a phrasing that Adria had perfected over time, the emphasized "are" becoming a sort of exhalation after the near-whispered "How," inviting the listener to exhale too, to unload.

"I'm—oh my," Davina said. "Look at this food coming our way."

She grabbed a skewer even before the server had announced it was tempeh satay; the other two women demurred with slight raises of their hands.

"Oh, delicious." Davina assayed the stick in her hand, its pointy end resembling a weapon. "It's a relief that they're so accommodating for vegetarians." She took a bite, slightly too big, had to shift the food in her mouth for a beat before speaking. "Mmm. No, apologies, I'm starved. But otherwise, I'm really quite well. Lots of opportunities."

"Davina is going to be on *Staying Up*!" Contessa trilled. "I still need to give you some pointers. Paul Ardman is really funny, but he can be a little . . ."

She manipulated her fingers like a marionette artist.

"I don't watch it much," Adria said, "but my kids used to love it. I think that'll be wonderful for you, Davina. People can get to know you."

"It's certainly going to be a tight squeeze." Davina raised her eyebrows. How refreshing to meet a woman Davina's age, not so very much younger than Adria, who could still do that. "I have to be back here Sunday night."

She was booked, she went on, the Friday night before they were all to convene at a smaller awards ceremony, a sort of rehearsal for the big show.

"You've hosted it, Adria?" Davina seemed almost nervous saying the older woman's name.

"They ask, they ask." Adria waved her right hand in the air. "Oh, I don't know. It just seems like a young person's game now. I don't really stay up very late anymore."

They did ask, dutifully, every time she had a new movie. Adria hardly needed it—certainly didn't need to take the risk. But for a woman like Davina: well, how wonderful it could be. To really be seen. With luck they wouldn't do anything too stupid with her. She could just show off her shrewdness. Find her light.

Davina turned to Contessa, smiled gently. "I have something I'd love to tell Adria—just between us."

"Okay!" Contessa said. "I'm going to go find my mom."

Adria's eyes followed Contessa as she walked, practically skipped, into the morass, not slowing down or even seeming to acknowledge Jimmy, nominated for best actor for playing her brother. Well, another one of those stories of what happens between men and women on sets, perhaps.

"I wanted to thank you," Davina said. "For the email you sent."

"Oh." Adria knew it would be best to play at being flustered. But, really, she hadn't expected to hear about this again. Davina really didn't understand the ways of women in their position, the way gestures could be passed without making a scene, did she. "It was . . . well, it was nothing."

It was something, Adria knew. It was a fantasy she'd told herself, about being able to appreciate art with her own family, getting to share the experience of something she loved. Having that moment. Davina got to give that to her. Without even realizing she'd done so.

"I can't tell you," Davina went on, "what a thing like that means."

"I'll be brief," Adria said, "because I know we're supposed to circulate. But I just wanted you to know that when I was starting out—well, I never felt like I had the encouragement I wanted. I needed. From my elders. I did everything alone, hacking my way through."

"Your parents . . . ?" Davina began.

"Didn't begin to understand why I couldn't marry a nice butcher from around the way. Old-line Italians, first-generation. You know 'Benedict' is made up. Anglicized. Made me more acceptable, for all the parts of me that weren't." Now was the time for Adria to laugh, and so she did. "Anyway. They didn't understand that either."

"Mine were sure that I was wasting an Oxford education." Davina laughed too—mordantly.

"Exactly. They lived in New York, but wouldn't come see me on Broadway. And then my movies . . ."

Adria felt herself growing sonorous, her voice like a bell, a timbre she knew she'd taken and polished and repurposed from her own mother's monologues about the sacrifices she'd made for an ungrateful daughter. Adria made it cleaner, made it better, keeping the sense of drama and the knowledge of the power her own words held. But she redirected it outward, toward praise, not self-pity.

Maybe there would be something in this exchange that Davina could remember, something they shared that the younger woman could take with her and hold. Maybe seeing inspiration and gratitude continue to swell in Davina's eyes would give Adria something worth holding on to as well.

"I just wanted to give you that encouragement," Adria said. "That I didn't always feel. It's a tough town. A tough business. But you have the talent. You must know that."

"I'm beginning to feel as if I do."

"Do you have a support system?" Adria asked. "My Bill isn't in the industry. And that makes all the difference. Keeps me grounded. Somewhat."

She laughed once more. See! She was approachable. She could joke about herself.

"Ehm. I do. I truly do. I have a full life."

Davina paused, seemed for a moment penned in, an odd darting expression entering her eyes, as if, for the first time, she was not viewing this conversation as a privilege. But then she went on.

"My goodness. So. Adria. I'll see you again. . . ."

"You will, after your triumph on *Staying Up*." Adria winked. "Don't be afraid to show off that dry British wit." She presented her hand, took Davina's, gave it a squeeze. "I'll be watching," she murmured.

It felt so good. To have her insight mean something to someone. She wished that Lindy could watch *Andronicus*, to understand why it moved her. To be able to be moved herself.

Davina stammered some kind words, ones Adria took to heart but had indeed heard before, and then Adria was off. She meandered away, half-thinking that on this high, she'd find Contessa, introduce herself to the young woman's mother, say some more nice things. She had goodwill to spare today. (No cajoling from Howard needed. See how magnanimous, how *good* she could be?) For this room was one that she knew how to operate.

She cast her eyes about as subtly as she could, looking for Contessa. Wishing she hadn't removed her sunglasses—although how egotistical would she look with them on? Across the room, she spotted Jenny and Delle, laughing as they extracted rice crackers topped with broccolini tartare off a server's plate. The black-vested server was laughing too. It was so easy for Jenny to have the common touch, wasn't it. Delle too.

Shifting herself around moment by moment to find a way to please whomever she was speaking to. Delle met Adria's eye, gestured toward Jenny, mouthed something that appeared to be the word *Look*. Adria turned away.

Her good luck never failed, in the end: a server came up to Adria just then. An unoccupied woman, an easy mark to unload some loose vegetables.

"Fire-roasted carrots with pepita salsa?" the server asked.

Nauseating. Adria was more of a carnivore than she'd ever had occasion to realize. This yearslong craze for vegan party food had made every gathering into a festival of gnawing and gnashing.

"I . . ." She held up her hand, then noticed that the tray had been rushed by a paunchy fellow, in a decent but somewhat threadbare tan suit. Wearing loafers, not dress shoes.

"Oof, I'll take it," the man said. "Not enough real food at this thing, but . . ." He glanced at her, took a second, realized. "I am *so* sorry."

Emphasis on the "so." Adria's presence demanded intensifiers. Always had.

"Oh, don't be." Adria considered a touch on the shoulder, decided against. He would likely feel ashamed about the grainy feeling of his suit jacket beneath her palm. "We're all nominees together, aren't we? I'm Adria. An actress."

"I'm Ben—Benjamin." The fellow eyed the toothpicked carrot he'd grabbed. "Documentary shorts."

"Oh! Please, go ahead, take a bite. I will too." Adria reached for a quivering carrot, sweating off green effluence. "And what's your film about?"

Benjamin wasn't Davina. Not close. But, she realized as she bit into her carrot—not nearly as noxious as it appeared, suffused with the wholesomeness of something that had come from the earth and hadn't been needlessly altered—there was a warm glow that could come at these things, anytime. The feeling of allowing yourself to admire, and, yes, to be admired. As Benjamin spoke, she saw a photographer approaching, hoped there wasn't carrot between her teeth for the photo she and Benjamin would take together. A photo that would prove, once again, that Adria Benedict was no snob.

Her voice went into that register again; she had the feeling of singing out from deeper in her diaphragm, to make sure that she was really heard.

"Documentaries are so important, I find. The truths they tell."

It was a bit of puffery, but it wasn't a lie. Everyone knew the kind of work Ben did mattered, at least in principle. But there was a reason so many people in this room were called the creatives, while Adria and her peers—or, at least, Adria and the women nominated alongside her—were called the talent. Documentarians were important. But so, as proven by every eye that followed Adria as she moved through the room, were actresses.

Bitty Harbor, *Lyndon and Claudia*

BITTY HAD MADE IT THROUGH the red carpet. Not a small thing, given that she and Leanna had gotten into an argument in the car on the way there. It wasn't worth dwelling on, just one of those things—Leanna didn't think Bitty should have had some wine while getting dressed. But this was the fun awards show, the rehearsal for the Big Night, the one where everyone drank champagne at big tables. And how else was she supposed to calm her nerves, be coherent and present? She was going to be interviewed on the carpet; she was presenting an award with Josh; she was waiting to find out if she'd won.

It wasn't as meaningful as the big award—the five women nominated for that were split up tonight, with Jenny over in the musical or comedy field. (Eleanor had taken her place among the drama actresses, and tonight would be the end of the road for her.) But still. She'd been nervous about this show for weeks. She would either win or lose, and both had their pitfalls: losing was, well, losing. And if she won, she'd have to give a speech, and have to figure out in the moment how to convey her emotional connection to Lady Bird Johnson and her sense of herself as a performer who worked really hard to tell the truth, all in a way that would be intelligible to her family. Somehow. She'd been trying to work on it, even sitting down with a pen and paper three nights in a row, but she always ended up in the wilderness. She would, first, draft a speech that would take ten minutes to deliver and right every wrong that she'd ever suffered. Then, on her next attempt, she would stall out after "Thank you so much."

So why was Leanna making things worse? It was hard to understand as anything other than obtuseness, but, thankfully, at least it was over. Leanna wouldn't fight with her in the presence of cameras. As she walked away from the red-carpet interviewer who'd asked her, in front of millions of viewers, who designed her dress (isn't it amazing?) and why she'd wanted to play Lady Bird (she was a strong woman!), she grabbed Leanna's hand, and Leanna didn't push her away. Bitty felt boosted. It wasn't just the wine (and, okay, a sneaky vodka in the kitchen between makeup and hair). It was the fact of landing where she knew she belonged. Bitty held Leanna's grip in her left hand, then reached her right hand up and waved at the crowd of fans, safely behind a barrier and watching as she and her peers—her peers!—strutted into the awards. They roared.

This was where Bitty was meant to be.

"Do you think Josh will be here soon?" she whispered to Leanna as they began walking up the steps into the theater.

Clip-clop, clip-clop, she said inside her head, reminding herself that she needed to step with intention and care and to make sure each footfall came directly and squarely onto a stair.

"I'm not sure," Leanna said. "I've been trying his team all day. No one is happy with the language they used for you two yesterday at the rehearsal."

When Bitty and Josh had shown up yesterday to practice presenting best original score, which had been so much fun, the host had introduced them with "Here to tell us all about scoring—she's itty-Bitty, and he's one big Johnson! Together, they're a perfect fit." Bitty had found it titillating, and Josh had laughed really hard when he heard it! She certainly didn't mind the implication that she was skinny. Leanna ought to have been happy with that, in fact.

"I think it's fine," Bitty said as they reached the top of the staircase.

"Well, I don't," Leanna said. "There's a bit of a sensitivity issue there. Bitty, Josh is in a relationship, and—"

Bitty didn't need to respond. Because right in front of her was Contessa—Bitty had to stop short to avoid walking on the train of her gown. It was a rich, deep emerald, studded with occasional clusters of crystals, and it seemed to have been perfectly arranged behind her, not bunching, not clumping. On Bitty, she felt sure, the train would have by now gotten caught in something, or she'd have tripped on it by now. *Clip-clop, clip-clop. Move forward.*

"Contessa!" Bitty yelped, louder than she meant to.

"Ah!" Contessa seemed startled.

She turned around and tapped her mother on the shoulder to stop her. Bitty was worth a stop; how nice. Contessa's face settled into a small smile, slightly hard to read, but—well, she seemed happy to see Bitty. Why complicate things. They were both happy.

"Hi, lady," Contessa said.

"You look incredible!"

Bitty wasn't lying. She was surprised at how breathless she felt. Getting up the stairs shouldn't be that hard. The dress, jewels, hair . . . she was just carrying a lot. She'd compose herself at the table.

"Aw, thanks." Contessa beamed. "It took forever. But, you know, worth it, right?"

"Me—uh, me too," Bitty said. "Took forever. And I'm not really sure if my dress is right. Do I look like I'm going to a funeral?"

"You look cute!" Contessa said. "And I heard you're presenting too?"

"Yeah, with Josh." Bitty paused. "It's nice. Feels like kind of a last hurrah for us—for our movie. Us presenting as a duo."

"Well, there's still one more show after this one," Contessa said. "But have fun. I better go get seated."

Was this all Bitty was going to get? Contessa was the one person here who felt like a potential friend. Besides Josh. Which was a whole different thing.

"Meet you at the bar at the first commercial break?" Bitty asked.

"Oh, I don't know," Contessa said. "I don't want it to go to my head—you know, in case I have to . . ."

"So smart." Bitty nodded. "You're so right."

She could feel Leanna next to her, feel her eyes shooting into her side, so she chose to stay focused on Contessa. She looked her fellow nominee up and down, trying to be surreptitious, probably failing. She was so curious about Contessa. The calmness with which she operated. The fact of her mother, right there, watching Bitty with a serene expression, waiting for this conversation to be done so Contessa could go claim her destiny. When all Bitty had was Leanna waiting to pick at her.

"Anyway," Contessa said. "Good luck! In our category. *Our category*. How crazy." She smiled.

"Good luck!" Bitty called after Contessa as she began to turn away.

Contessa smiled again, put her left hand next to her sharp jawline and waggled the fingers, turned around so that all Bitty could see was a pulled-tight hairstyle with little crystals woven into it somehow, and then her shoulder blades jutting out of her dress's open back. Bitty had wanted to do something special with her hair, but there was never any time.

Bitty felt overawed by Contessa. She felt as though the conversation was owed some kind of grace note. She wanted Contessa to know the real Bitty: friendly, kind. Special.

To the jewel-woven crown of Contessa's head, retreating from her as she stood there with her unspeaking publicist, Bitty shouted, "Hope you win!"

♦ ♦ ♦

"STILL NO WORD FROM JOSH, RIGHT?"

"Bitty, have I been on my phone at all?" Leanna asked as they walked into the auditorium. "I think his team is focused on him, not on you two arriving together. And I haven't had a minute to look." She sighed. "Just supervising you."

"I'm sorry," Bitty said. "I thought maybe you looked. *I* was focused on my friend Contessa Lyle. My fellow nominee."

She stuck out her tongue at Leanna.

"Keep doing that and you'll fuck up your lipstick," said Leanna. "Come on. We're up close to the stage."

They were wading through the tables toward the back, the ones where the nominees from TV shows were seated. Bitty felt for them, felt herself swelling up. It was so good of her, in her fortune, to be able to understand how frustrating it might be not to get to sit close to the stage.

"Oh!" came a voice from a table to Bitty's left.

She was hesitant to stop. She had good momentum going, and she was remembering to kick the grand tulle skirt of her dress out as she stepped so as not to trip, but she recognized the voice. Even at a single syllable, she heard the unplaceable accent, and sensed the assumption that an "Oh!" would stop an actress on the biggest night of her life so far dead in her tracks and command her attention.

As she turned her head, she remembered.

"Bitty!" Ceridwen Darby called from her seat. "I have some news for you."

"Ceridwen, hi," Leanna said.

Bitty had instinctively reached out, and Ceridwen clutched at her greedily. She remained seated while the two women stood over her, Bitty trapped by Ceridwen's claim on her hand. Bitty hoped that her palm wasn't as sweaty as it felt. This room was too hot. She could get to the bar really quickly before the show started. Maybe she'd need to tell Leanna that she was going to the bathroom.

"Leanna," Ceridwen said. "I'm sorry for the radio silence. I go into the decision-making place I go, and I'm just—I'm Hamlet, I really am. But I've made my choice."

"Can we do this tomorrow?" Leanna asked tightly. "I can set up a call."

"I'd like to break the news to Bitty now, if you don't mind, so that I can see her face. Making dreams come true is, I've found, a particularly delicious fringe benefit of this new gig." Ceridwen chuckled juicily.

Her voice was thick, a porterhouse of self-conscious melodrama. Bitty wondered if she'd had a little to drink too. Or if, somehow, some people just found this much pleasure and richness from daily life.

Actors, many of them people Bitty recognized, were attempting to pass around Leanna, Bitty, and Ceridwen. This odd little trio was holding everything up. But Bitty couldn't move. Not before she saw . . .

"This," Ceridwen said, "is the front cover of the Movies Issue. Out next week."

Ceridwen held out her phone and showed Bitty the image: On the far left, Contessa, smirking with her arms crossed, waiting for her destiny to arrive. On the far right, Davina, reclining on a chaise, her forearm over her head as if she'd been stricken with a glamorous wasting illness. And right in the middle, Bitty herself.

Bitty saw her carefully made-up face just hiding the sleeplessness in the corners of her eyes—something that hadn't been edited out, maybe couldn't be. She saw the deeply, regally violet gown whose velvet sheen was a memory that she could feel even now, just as she could feel the scratchiness of the damn cotton robe. It looked like something else, someone else—on her face, a look of almost romantic contentment that Bitty had often seen on her own mother's face after the end of a Friday shift, when her brothers were facedown in ice cream bowls and Parliament smoke fought lemon dish soap and oily daffodil petals for dominion of the kitchen air.

Which of your children, she thought, *looks just like you.*

"Bitty!" Ceridwen said. "No, don't—I'm sorry. Is this not what you want?"

"No," Bitty said, wishing she had something to use to dab at her eyes, her nose. Suddenly, the smell of the cigarette she'd smoked just before getting in the car with Leanna seemed all over her. "It's—it's great. It looks like me. And it looks like that day." She looked up from the phone, directed it back to Ceridwen, who was perched on her seat expectantly. "Thank you, Ms. Darby. It's perfect."

♦ ♦ ♦

"THAT'S REALLY WONDERFUL NEWS." LEANNA DIDN'T LOOK BACK at Bitty as they continued moving. "You have worked so hard for this. Forget all the other stuff I said today."

She smirked.

"You didn't mean it, right?" Bitty asked, knowing the answer she'd get, not minding the insincerity she anticipated.

"All I want is to look out for you," Leanna said. "But no, I didn't mean all of it."

"How much time do we have?"

"Maybe twenty minutes."

"I'll be super quick. But I need to step out."

Bitty didn't wait for an answer. She'd presented at this show before, knew where the smoking patio was, knew she could find her way back to her seat before the show began. She heard Leanna exclaim her name in a sharp whisper to her back, but—look. She wouldn't be able to give a coherent speech when she won, unless she cleaned out her mind right now.

This was redemption. She had found it. Her last time on the Movies Issue cover—what could she even say? It was a nightmare. Literally. She only remembered flashes of the day they'd shot it, with the skipping-around half-logic of a dream. Leanna telling her that she knew they'd agreed on swimsuits, but the photographer was a legend, and he just wanted to try something fun and a little different. It was a big deal that they'd asked her to do this after just a few movies, but they thought she had something. Bitty saying okay, but only if she could talk to Delle first. Delle producing a bottle of vodka in her dressing room, along with two juice glasses. The photographer barging in with the editor, two men in their sixties, clapping their hands and telling Bitty and Delle how gorgeous they were, how lucky the magazine was to have them.

The photographer's hands, repositioning Bitty's ass so that her labia wouldn't show on-camera, pressing her front into the velvet sleeve of an actor's tuxedo. Both women laughing afterward, on the car ride to a nightcap, laughing about how strange the photographer's commands had been, mocking his European accent. Trying to excite each other into believing it really was all cool—or maybe Delle *had* believed it. Bitty driving, changing lanes without a signal, knowing that she was immortal because the cover would live forever, and she'd always be twenty-five and beautiful. One of the two actors, the one Bitty had been draped across, showing up at the bar; Delle winkingly confessing she'd texted him. All of them heading back to Bitty's old house, the one in Studio City with the sweet little yard and without any of the accretions of pink potted plants that she'd bought to stage a life. One more drink, together. Bitty laughing unstoppably as she toasted to "The future! My future!" Hands everywhere. Silence.

She rehearsed all of that as her body moved, as automatically as if she'd known the way from the minute she'd been born, to the smoking patio. It was pleasantly empty.

Bitty would be in her seat by showtime. She would. She dug into her purse, found her pack, lit up. What a relief. To know that she'd be on the cover. And to have a minute for herself. She blew smoke into the air indulgently, knowing that no one was watching her. The patio had a few little café tables with ashtrays, but Bitty knew that if she sat without someone to help her back up in her dress, she'd never get out of the chair. So she stood, hunched over one of the tables, making sure hot ash didn't touch her dress. This felt appropriately penitent, and she spent a few moments that way, enjoying the feeling of being punished, or punishing herself, in the silence of the night.

Of course it would be interrupted.

"Hi," came a voice that Bitty recognized more easily than Ceridwen's. The flat affect, the carelessness, the lack of an attempt to seem excited or curious or any of those things that someone ought to be when starting a conversation.

"Hi, Delle," Bitty said, straightening up.

She would have to be careful with her ash. She looked Delle up and down. Delle had dyed her hair a single color now, pitch-black, and she was in a red dress that, contrasted with it, made her look like the Queen of Hearts. The dress was oddly romantic, with dreamy draped tulle layers floating beneath Delle's waistline. Bitty tried not to feel envious. Her black dress was the only one, out of the options provided by her stylist, that she'd woken up not hating.

"I just wanted to say—you know, I heard, and I was sorry about your mom."

Delle held a cigarette to her lips, ignited it. Bitty was silent.

"You know, I'm friends with Josh's girlfriend Rachel. And, look, sorry, word gets out. I know you opened up to him." Delle laughed. "Rachel's pretty freaked out about it, but I think it's sweet you had him there in Texas."

Delle would never change.

"Albuquerque, actually," Bitty said, clenching her jaw.

"I think my point stands," Delle said impatiently. "And I want you to know that I forgive you."

"You what?"

"I think we both . . ." Delle said. "Look. I also heard you're on the Movies Issue cover, and I think we both regret the way things went down last time. I don't recall being the one who kept ordering more drinks. But I think what I'd say is—"

Bitty drew on her cigarette, wishing it would vaporize in its entirety into her lungs instantly, even as she saw she had about two minutes' worth left, and that's if she smoked rapidly. She didn't want to bend down and ash on the low table again, so she daringly tapped it with her pointer finger, as far away from her body as she could.

"You're mad," Delle said. "And that's okay. But I feel like we'd be more powerful as friends. You won't believe this, but I really look up to you. You totally own your movie. Meanwhile, psycho Adria stole mine out from under me."

Bitty had been curious about this. She had to admire the use of a tactical intimacy to try to resolve things, not least because it was a story that really did intrigue her.

"Was it a tough shoot?"

"Impossible. Adria is a complete dickhead. She won't try anything outside her comfort zone; she's always the same. It's just her being threatened, which is weird, because she's the one who took over this movie where she was just playing the therapist and changed things all around."

Bitty felt a rush of affection for Delle. A small one.

"And that was just during the shoot. In Colorado . . . you already know this, I'm sure. But lawyers almost had to get involved." She paused. "We should get together sometime. But not for drinks." She raised her left arm, shimmying her wrist. There it was, glinting in the light: a chip on a little gold chain so fine that it looked like a strand of Bitty's own golden hair.

"Sixty days this time," Delle said. "You're the first of my, I guess, colleagues to see it. But I'm wearing it tonight. And I really hope I'll be wearing it in a month when we meet for the next one."

"Cool." Bitty knew that it was time to go, probably. She was almost done with her cigarette. Close enough to done. "Hey, I forgive you too, I think."

"Really?" Delle asked. "Why?"

"Because I'm really tired," Bitty said. "And because you were nice about my mom. And honestly, because, no offense, the fact that you went through the program and took from it that you're supposed to ask other people to apologize to you is kind of amazing."

Delle laughed, a real one.

"Look," she said, "we both fucked up. You cool?"

"Yeah. Day by day."

This, Bitty knew then, was the part she'd bring to Leanna, if the publicist heard Bitty and Delle had spoken, if she asked.

"Cool," said Delle, shoving her hand through her hair. "Maybe we could . . ."

She stuck out her hand and pumped Bitty's with a forceful motion, but her grip was soft and loose. Bitty wished for a hug, but she accepted this for what it was, tried to focus on the chip dangling from Delle's wrist so as not to meet her eye.

"And hey," Delle began. A halting tone of caution had entered her voice. "If you ever want to come to a meeting . . ."

"That's not really my thing," Bitty said. "And the next month is going to be really busy."

♦ ♦ ♦

DELLE HAD GONE BACK INSIDE, AND BITTY PROMISED SHE'D BE right behind. A piped-in voice from a speaker proclaimed that it was time for everyone to take their seats. Bitty badly wished she'd gotten a drink at the bar on the way out, but it was always so thronged. She'd just have to live in the itch for a minute longer.

She took her phone out of her purse, swiped away a few texts from Leanna. She noticed there was nothing from Josh, but their presentation was forty-five minutes into the ceremony. He'd be there. She pulled up "Mom Home" in her contacts. She thought about Josh again, how good it would be to see him, how she hoped she didn't mispronounce the name of whatever composer won the award they were presenting together, but how maybe it would be cute and funny to recover from that if she did. It came as a surprise when she heard her brother's voice.

"It's you."

"Hi, Robby."

"It's Brendan."

She winced. It had sounded just like Robby.

"You guys sound more and more alike each day!"

"I'm fucking with you. It's really Robby. You do stay gullible."

Enough of this.

"Hey, how's Mom?" she asked.

Robby sighed.

"You need to either do this way more often, or not at all. It only confuses her now."

"I've been busy," said Bitty. "I haven't stopped working for months. I met Jenny Van Meer." A pause. A lie. "We might be working together soon."

"Yeah." The voice on the phone had turned sour. "It's funny, Bitty, no matter what he's doing, even our dad makes time to check in, every Sunday morning, rain or shine. Hungover or still drunk. He brings his new girlfriend." Robby paused. "You'd hate her."

Despite herself, Bitty chuckled.

"And Alyssa saw you on late night," Robby said. "She said you were laughing weird and being kind of insane, but she wants to see the movie. Who is it, Jackie Kennedy?"

"It's Lady Bird Johnson," Bitty said. "I'm glad she wants to see it. She should text me, if she wants."

"I think things are good where they are," Robby said. "And I really don't want you to fuck with Mom. At least it's not two in the morning this time. But every six months you call her, and you cry, and she cries, and she gets confused."

"Robby," said Bitty, "I just lent you ten grand last year. I'm trying, and I don't think you get to order me around. I'm calling from an awards show. Because this is important to me."

"The movie star appears," Robby spat. "And has she done any photoshoots lately?"

"Actually, yes," Bitty said. "But—"

"I don't want to fucking hear it from you." Bitty worried for a moment Robby would hang up. "Good, I'm sure my buddies won't stop sending me pictures of your tits for the next year. Here, I'll get Mom. Thanks for your generosity, Miss Celebrity. Great to hear from the next Adria Benedict."

A long silence. Bitty had such a long night ahead of her. She was so far from home.

"Hello," came a sweet, tired-sounding voice. "Who is this?"

"Mom, it's Bitty."

"Who?"

Bitty envisioned a face she hadn't seen, even in fantasy, in too long: her mother's real face, weary and worn but released from all of life's pressures, existing in a prematurely delivered kind of peace.

"Mom, it's Katie."

"I knew a Katie once. She was my friend. We called her Bitty."

"That's me, Mom. Katie."

"That's nice."

Bitty began to shake, thought about hanging up. Might as well keep moving forward, toward the end of tonight. She'd waited for so long to revise the conversation she'd had with her mother once the nude cover appeared in grocery store aisles, the one where her mother had called her names so awful that Bitty wouldn't use them for an enemy. She'd never used profanity before—maybe that was the first sign something was wrong. By the time Bitty was ready to talk again, her mother was already losing words. To his credit, Robby had taken the lead at home—Brendan was as bad as their dad. Bitty tried to check in, but she worried that what her mother remembered of her made her ashamed. Or, as she'd told Josh after the hardest day on set, after she'd broken down and Destiny and Sydnee got sent home early, she worried that her mother was better off forgetting.

This movie, this cover, this change in Bitty's life had happened too late.

But it had happened.

"You sound sad," her mom said. "Are you sad?"

"It's happy tears," Bitty said. "Mom, guess what?"

A pause, the sound of a throat clearing, a softness and gentleness Bitty had never known in childhood in her mother's reply.

"Who is this?"

"Mom," Bitty pushed ahead, "guess which—guess who got to do a big magazine cover?"

She considered breaking it down into pieces, explaining each part of that sentence. But she decided to simply go on faith that somehow, the tone of her voice and the care she took would send meaning her mother's way, would lend the story some clarity. She knew that after this call she'd walk back into the awards and sit there laughing at the foot of the stage. She would show the world that she'd achieved her dream. It didn't matter that the dream didn't work—she could still feel the heat of the spotlight on her skin. Later she could get to work on finding a familiar way to obliterate herself, her selves.

"Please take your seats," the voice on the loudspeaker said. "The show is about to begin."

Soon enough, Bitty would be back there. Josh would be right next to her. And they'd clink glasses, and she'd drink at the appropriate pace, and they'd talk about how the banter that had been written for them was so funny. But they'd be way funnier together than an awards-show joke writer could ever be. And then she'd win, and beat Adria. But first, she had to finish the call. She had to say it.

"Who is this, dear? I'm sorry," her mother said. "Do I know you?"

"It's me," she said. "It's Bitty. It's Katie. And I'm going to be on TV soon—tonight. I'm going to be holding a trophy." She paused, and let out a sob that became, somehow, a laugh, as it shook her body, all the way down to her unsteady ribs. The silence on the patio was so perfect that Bitty no longer knew if her mother was on the line. But she was out there somewhere. "I'm on the cover. And I did it. By myself. Just me."

Contessa Lyle, *The Glass Menagerie*

"AND COMING UP NEXT—BEST ACTRESS in a drama!"

Contessa and Melanie were the only people left sitting at the *Glass Menagerie* table as the announcer spoke. They were close enough to the front of the ballroom that Contessa still thought she might win. Or, at least, that she could be seen being a really good sport clapping for Eleanor. These awards would help determine how the season would end. Contessa had already stood up and whooped for Jenny, when she won best actress in a musical or comedy; had clasped her hand to her mouth as if holding in a gasp while Jenny talked about what the support for her shoestring movie about a great woman had meant; had raised a glass when Jenny asked for a toast to "La Divina." Whatever that meant. Anyway. Contessa was proving she had it.

Maybe she would prove it to the people who had vacated her table too. As soon as the cameras had gone down for a five-minute commercial break, Jimmy and the director exchanged a nod and headed for the bar together. Eleanor muttered something about the ladies' room, and got up with her own publicist and left. They weren't the only ones—celebrities were blocking every aisle as they milled about, tuxedoed servers gently elbowing their way past to clear away empty dishes. Contessa watched Eleanor engage in something of a standoff with one server, neither sure who should let the other pass first. At least the server had somewhere to go.

Poor Eleanor. She seemed like a ghost here, even more than she usually did—she'd gotten this nomination, for this precursor awards show, but that would be all for her. This was the end of her season. Maybe Eleanor should have been nicer—maybe then she'd have had a shot. And the fourth member of the cast, the Gentleman Caller, Josh—well, he was at the *Lyndon and Claudia* table, of course. Why wouldn't he be? He was just a small supporting player in this cast. In Contessa's life.

"Is there anyone you want to say hi to?"

"The minute I stand up, this skirt will get all screwed up. It looks perfect right now," Contessa said.

She was wearing a massive train, attached to the kind of dress that she hoped announced her as a winner. She really ought not get too caught up in this stuff, but she had looked, of course she had looked, and @BestOfContessa had already posted about the dress. A whole carousel of pictures. And another of close-ups of her hair, with the crystals woven into it. Getting that done had hurt, and so had the 5 a.m. wake-up. But it had been worth it, for this.

"I think we could arrange your dress back," Melanie whispered.

She had dressed simply, as she always did. Long black dress setting off her pale skin, no jewelry but a small chain with a cross on it. She looked lovely in a completely neutral way, which meant that she would make a plain and easily blurred-out backdrop for Contessa. She shuffled herself in her seat, glaring at Contessa.

"You haven't said a word to anyone all night."

"Well." Contessa leaned in, lowered her voice. "They haven't said a word to me."

"I really regret not being on that set," Melanie said. "I would have whipped them into shape."

"Why are we discussing this right now? I don't want to be upset five minutes before the award." The director had, on the first day of shooting, pulled Contessa aside and told her, director to star, that he didn't like entourages on his set, that it distracted from the work. And Contessa got that. She agreed, and sent her mom home. Because it was time to be an actress. A grown-up.

"I would have." Melanie either didn't notice that Contessa was getting upset at the memory, or didn't care. Which was worse?

"No," Contessa said firmly, her voice rising in emotion. "You would not have. Because they didn't respect me, because I was a kid actor. And that's not a problem you solve by bringing in your momager." She took a long sip from the champagne flute in front of her plate. "Okay?"

"I thought you said you wanted a clear head for your speech," Melanie said.

"It's two sips of champagne."

"Twenty-two years old and a seasoned drinker. My God," Melanie exclaimed. "What about Josh? He helped you. You should go say hi."

Contessa shot her eyes over to the *Lyndon* table. Josh didn't usually bring Rachel to these things—in interviews, he said he liked to "keep my personal life personal." He hadn't discussed her with Contessa at all. Back when they used to keep up, when they used to text. But there she was, sitting upright between Josh and Bitty. Bitty was listing slightly forward, hunched in a way that emphasized the narrowness of her collarbones. There was a hazy look in her eyes; a woman on her other side whispered intensely into her ear. Rachel was straight as a lighthouse, a beacon of discomfort. She fiddled with a ring on her right hand, looking into the middle distance while Josh shook hands and chatted with Adria. Apparently she had come by to pay tribute.

"I will after," Contessa said. "After the speech. Whoever it is. Can we just . . ."

Melanie glanced at Contessa, looked up at her hair, sparkling. Resplendent.

"They really did a nice job. Getting you ready. We'll have the team send a card."

"Flowers." Contessa nodded. "We should send flowers."

"We've got to find your next movie to pay for all of this," Melanie said. "Studio got the dress and hair, but flowers? That's on the Visa."

Time to change the subject again.

"Do you really think we should say no to *Staying Up*? It'd be after the awards are all over. It could be, like, a victory lap." Contessa was jinxing it.

"Did you somehow miss what they did to Davina two nights ago?" Melanie said. "Making her mock Adria like that? I notice Davina won't even show her face here tonight."

"That's Davina." Contessa had the futile sense that this was one exchange she would not win. "She's so awkward. Doesn't know how to stick up for herself. I'm me." Contessa tried her best to look utterly guileless, like the girl from the car commercial, the girl her mom had plied with treats and rewards that day. "And I have you."

Melanie didn't fall for it. As Contessa had known she wouldn't.

"No. You need to stay here in LA, pick up another movie. Maybe try not to alienate everyone this time."

"Mom, *stop*. Stop it now. They alienated me."

"Whichever way it went. You were on the set of a movie and now the director isn't talking to you. Neither are the other actors. So."

They'd already been speaking in a low register, and now Melanie leaned forward even farther, her voice so quiet that it felt more tactile than audible, something that could only be detected from the hissing movements in the air Contessa breathed.

"It can't always be," Melanie whispered, "the excuse that you were a child star, and they don't respect you. Make them respect you."

Melanie took a long moment, long enough that Contessa heard another loudspeaker announcement for the crowd to take their seats. She looked away from her mom, saw Josh let go of Adria's hand, saw him catch her own eye. It was like a cloud passing in front of the sun. Josh smiled, but it was not the kind of smile Contessa would give a friend. He mouthed a *Hi* with his lips turned flatly up, nodded, turned back to Rachel. His smile shifted—lips opened, forehead relaxed, eyes came to life. His smile, for Rachel, became something like real. Rachel clicked back in, turned toward him with a matching grin, fully turned away from Bitty.

"*That's* your advice?" Contessa was practically spitting. It would take her a while to come back to herself. She hoped they had long enough before the cameras went up. Whatever. She'd find a way. "Your advice is to 'make them respect me'? Maybe a good first step would be having real representation. Not my mother."

"You need to stop before you say something you can't take back," Melanie said.

"Maybe you need to stop taking fifteen percent of everything until you can actually fucking help. With anything." There it was. She wasn't Nina. Wasn't Laura. But was, at last, her mother's daughter. The mother who showed this side, Contessa knew, when Contessa wasn't there.

Who fought these battles for her, all so that she could spend her time being as unbothered and airy as her fans needed her to be.

They weren't done fighting. And they didn't need to be. Contessa was suddenly ready to dig in. To kick her mother out of their table. To call her car and go home herself if Melanie wouldn't leave.

"You worked with Josh Jorgen, and you managed to screw that up," Melanie said. "Biggest star in the industry, no respect for you."

"I didn't—"

"Contessa, I know more than you think. I went looking for a mint in your bag at the cover shoot. After you thought I didn't see you stick it in some drawer. And if this"—she pointed her finger at Contessa, thank God cameras were still down for the commercial break—"is the person you think any director ought to be respecting," Melanie said, rearing back and shifting into a slightly more audible register, "then I've made a lot of mistakes."

How could she explain it? How Josh had been the only one there for her. The research she'd done, the movements she'd practiced, all tossed out the window when the director told her, on the second day, that he wasn't in the business of leading an acting school for kiddie-TV wash-ups. The way he couldn't have known how shooting forty episodes of television a year for five years had made her an expert at controlling her body, at knowing how things would read. He didn't want to know. The time the director apologized, on the fourth day, and asked if he could give her some coaching between takes in her trailer. The funny feeling that made her decide to say no—maybe it had just been her belief that she didn't need to be singled out. Maybe something more.

And the feeling that she ought to have kept her mom on the set from the beginning, insisted on it, but now she couldn't, now she'd said no like the director wanted, and things had turned. The whispers between Eleanor and Jimmy and the director. Jimmy muttering at her, over and over, a word she stopped trying to make out once she figured out how to read his lips. Josh, with his few days of making everything bright and fun, and their rebuilding Laura Wingfield together. The way that Josh's admiration was the only prize she could have taken from the experience of being mocked for wanting to do something beautiful.

The way she'd really looked up to Eleanor. Before.

She'd fire her mom. Eventually. She'd have to, to move forward. But maybe they could get there over time. After her mom helped her pick out one more movie. Melanie wasn't wrong. They did need the money.

"I made mistakes too." Contessa sniffled a bit, hoping her mother heard. "I think—I think you should have been there."

"No, don't. Look. Don't. You'll mess up . . ." Melanie grabbed Contessa's wrist. "Constance Teresa Lyle. Do *not* cry right now."

Contessa squeezed the muscles of her neck, shifted her head from side to side, sipped her water. She felt herself regain control. God. It was that easy. If you were built different.

"Someday." Melanie's tone hadn't softened. But she was being careful to speak quietly. "Someday you will understand the sacrifices I made. Your father."

"I know," snapped Contessa. "I'm trying not to cry. Remember? What you just said?" She hadn't touched her eyes again, for fear of dislodging a glued-on eyelash. She'd just made herself stop.

"I am too," Melanie said. "So I'll just say that I chose you. This life you told me that you wanted. And you'll understand that someday. When you have a daughter of your own. If you ever figure yourself out. If I ever stop wanting this for you more than you want it for yourself."

"You wanted it too!" Contessa was worried people were staring.

She wouldn't let herself cry again, especially given that she knew now that it wouldn't help her get what she wanted.

"I want," Melanie said, "for you to be happy. And if that's not happening, maybe it's time to walk away."

The director and Jimmy swayed back to the table. Somehow they'd all found each other, and Eleanor was leaning on Jimmy's arm, although it was hard to know who was supporting whom.

"Hiya, Mom. Hi, C," the director said, suddenly charming after a night of stony silence. He was mad he hadn't been nominated, Contessa figured, but he still had to be there, to support his stars. Well, to support Jimmy and Eleanor. He seemed to lurch toward Contessa and Melanie in his final step toward the table. How much time had elapsed; how much liquor could one drink in five minutes? Sometimes Contessa realized how much there still was left for her to learn.

"What's the hot gossip?" the director asked.

"Mother-daughter things," Melanie said. "She's been so quiet tonight."

"I think," the director slurred slightly as he sank into his seat, "that Contessa has the whole game figured out."

He glanced at Contessa, tilted his head. Dared her to respond.

"I—" Contessa began.

"Not quite," Melanie said. "She's not good at dealing with assholes." She took a sip of her champagne, untouched until now, and then looked straight at the director. "On the other hand, I am. Thanks for saying hi on your fourth trip back from the bar."

"All right." The director held up his hands, palms out. "All right."

Jimmy glowered, straightened his tie. His category would be called after Contessa's. He had longer to wait. Contessa tensed the muscles of her neck again, looked at Eleanor. The older woman's eyes were fixed on

Melanie, with a strange expression Contessa had never seen in Eleanor before. It looked almost like respect.

"Whoever wins," Eleanor suddenly announced, "I think this whole table should clap."

"All right," Jimmy muttered, echoing the director. For his part, the director blurted a stream of syllables that sounded a lot like "of course" placed on loop, repeated and blurred beyond recognition.

The music started, and the host came back onstage to introduce the presenters who would decide Contessa's fate, at least for the next few hours, before everyone's attention turned to the real show in a month.

Contessa didn't believe in superstitions, not really. But she just didn't want to be disappointed. So she hadn't thought much about what she'd say at the podium, if she won. She knew she would find some combination of words and a certain underpinning depth of feeling to convince the world—who was she kidding, to convince Josh—that she was special. She wondered if what she was wearing would finally trick people at home into thinking that she was sufficiently grown-up, if they'd bring up Nina. If the train that followed her, regally, would finally sweep up all the other associations that dragged behind her. As the presenters walked onto the stage, she wondered how grown-up she really was.

It would be impossible, she thought, to keep going like this. She needed to have experiences, wanted so desperately to have experiences, to give her work some grounding, to make her life into something worthy of art. She couldn't just keep playing characters who were as lonely and cut-off as she was. And she didn't want to be Nina forever. Yet the more successful she got, the less life was available to her. No one was even speaking to her. Who ever would? Bitty, maybe. Maybe she ought to have given Bitty a little more of herself.

She thought that she might use her speech, the one she'd give in just a few moments, to blow things up—thank Josh for protecting her from Jimmy, thank the director and Eleanor for nothing, tell Josh she loved him from the stage, even though the one thing she was confident of right now was that she didn't. She wondered if he'd feel bad for her if she lost, and if that would be better, somehow. But she'd win. And she knew she'd end up crying, thank her mom. She would mean it—she loved her, she did—but it would be part of the costume too. It would complete the pose that convinced people, even convinced Contessa most days, that Hollywood was a place worth dreaming about.

Contessa inclined her head to her mother, and Melanie leaned toward her. She didn't look angry with her. Not anymore.

"Mommy," Contessa began. She'd give Melanie that, and give it to herself. The feeling of being Melanie's baby for one night longer. Regardless of what was ahead. "I still really want this." She paused. "All of this."

Melanie looked back at her. Shook her head slightly. Touched the chain around her neck. Even after twenty-two years together, Contessa wasn't sure how to read her. Maybe growing up meant realizing that her mom knew how to keep things in reserve. That she was an actress too.

And maybe Contessa had gotten that from her mother. Because she knew she was a good actress—a great one. For so many reasons. And one of them—oh, they were saying her name as one of the nominees, time to look abashed and dip her head and squeeze her mom's hand in the moment the camera would capture. But one of them was that she wasn't Laura Wingfield. She wasn't. Because she wasn't pathetic. She got to make her own choices. They could even be brave ones.

A rip of an envelope, the rustle of paper, showily loud, as if amplified to please the cameras, and to rattle the women who were waiting.

"Wow," the male presenter said.

The woman by his side leaned down, looked at the envelope, gasped.

Contessa, with the last remnants of unblinked tears woven into the corners of her eyes like the crystals crowning her head, looked at Melanie. And she smiled. It might only be for the cameras, but she knew she'd get a response. She knew, even before she saw it happen, that her manager, her mother, the first person to choose her, but surely not the last—she knew that Melanie would smile back.

From Ceridwen Darby's editor's letter
in the Movies Issue, February

In this issue, we annually fête the stars who make the town glitter—and this year, my second running this magazine, we've chosen to spotlight the women of the season. Loath though I am to admit a mistake, I have come to think such a tribute is likely a year overdue.

Consider the only of these cover subjects I'd seen before—though we'd never interacted. On my annual theater trip with my two best girlfriends from my graduate-student years in Cambridge, I saw Davina Schwartz in *Who's Afraid of Virginia Woolf?* She was a notably young Martha—probably, going strictly by the numbers, better-suited for the role of Honey, the innocent wife who's naïve to all the destruction around her. But Davina Schwartz was made to play the destroyer. Her Martha was so perfect that I didn't even hold against her that she was an Oxonian.

To say that this gentle, thoughtful woman was nothing like Edward Albee's greatest monster is to state the obvious. As TV viewers across America are coming to know from Davina's new presence on talk shows and the awards circuit, she is a gracious, reserved figure. (She resides alone in Los Angeles, but, she told me, jets back to London to visit with friends when not shooting. She and I compared notes on the Victoria and Albert Museum and—her favorite—the National Portrait Gallery. No surprise that this expert crafter of character is drawn in by artistic representations of great women.)

And her trademark humility—even now, after emerging as a television star (most recently in the horror series *The Screaming at Salem*) and as a nominee this year for her role in *Andronicus*—was in full effect on set. After I enthused to her about her work onstage, she clutched my hand, thanked me, and told me she'd play Martha differently today. "Less anger," she said of this woman realizing the brokenness of her marriage. "More sorrow."

Hindsight is a too-rare quality. So is reflectiveness. And Davina's ability to run through years-old stage work and reimagine the decisions she made up there treading the boards is the sign of an active, ticking creative mind—the sort that's distinguished artists from the dawn of the cinema up to Davina's clearest antecedent today, Adria Benedict. Davina's closer, in talent and temperament, to Adria the Great than she may realize—she blushed when I put the comparison to her. But I'll just abandon objectivity and admit it: Speaking as a fan, I think Davina Schwartz is doing just about everything right.

Our next cover star is Contessa Lyle. . . .

Davina Schwartz, *Andronicus*

"CAN WE SAY THAT'S A little bit iconic?"

Davina's head, buried in her phone for the past she didn't know how long, jerked up as she heard the man's voice coming out of the television. Instinct made her glance at the screen to confirm that, yes, it was a shot of herself as she'd stood next to that awful comedian on Friday night. She was surprised to note that she seemed, in the shot, genuinely flattered at his praise for her; she could still manage to astonish herself at just how adept a performer she could be.

"That's Davina Schwartz and Paul Ardman on Friday night's *Staying Up*," a female voice butted in over footage of Davina and—right, his name was Paul—standing together onstage during her monologue.

(Really, more of a dialogue, Davina thought, seeing as how the man hijacked it. Or *his* monologue.)

"Hey!" squeaked the escort from the airline, a slightly built man Davina forgot was watching her carry-on luggage in the moments when he wasn't speaking. (Her three checked suitcases were somewhere within an endlessly delayed plane that had been scheduled to leave New York hours ago, one that had been rebooked after her first flight out was outright canceled.) Unobtrusiveness was the point of him, perhaps, but here he was, obtruding. "That's you!"

Davina flicked her eyes the airline employee's way, said nothing.

"I'm glad you think I'm a—what's the word you used?—an icon," Davina-inside-the-TV said. "But, really, I'm just a working actress, and it's simply an honor to be here. That's 'honour' with a 'u.' "

"Okay, it's giving humble British legend, mama!" Paul snapped his fingers as the audience roared.

The anchor's voice butted in once again over mute footage of Paul and Davina clasping hands and taking a bow. This, she'd been told, was his style of comedy, his whole thing—fawning over actresses in a way that felt, to her, quite close to mockery. But the news anchor's voice burbled with amusement.

Davina listened as the voice told her what she already knew, what events of her professional life were somehow no longer just novel but news. She had hosted *Staying Up* to promote her role in the film *Andronicus* ("scary stuff!" the anchor's voice said, which struck Davina as both objectively true and a bit unnecessary), and she was "expected to appear at tonight's" awards—a smaller-scale version of the most important show, a month from now—which might give a sense of who would "take home the big prize" at the end of the season.

All true, Davina thought, but what was going unreported was that the expectation she would appear would soon go unfulfilled. She'd been stuck in New York for a day and a half. Today's airport journey was a last-ditch attempt, coordinated with the studio, to see if she could somehow get into Los Angeles in time to show up at the awards tonight, at least in time for her category. Now the ceremony was an hour from starting, and she was still in the airport lounge, watching entertainment news on TV. So much had gone wrong that it was time for a stroke of luck, so she allowed herself to hope that this would be the end of the segment.

"And Davina made waves on Friday's broadcast with her impersonation—"

Davina bolted out of her seat.

"I'd like a walk. Can you—"

"I'll just stay here with your stuff!" the airline rep called after her.

It had been a doubly bad idea to do *Staying Up*, Davina thought as she walked toward nothing in particular. She had felt out of place when she showed up Monday morning to begin the hurried planning of her episode. She'd been part of an improv troupe at university, along with her musical theater studies. This all ought to have been easy, ought to have been fun. But there was something sinister in the air from the moment Paul introduced himself, told her that "Davina Schwartz" was a strange name for a British actress to have, said he would have expected her to be called "Dame Phyllida Crumpetbottom."

"Well, Britain has Jews too." Davina had made her voice bright and quippy, and he'd laughed. A beat too long. To someone else, someone she trusted, she might have quipped, "More's the pity," and while she hardly thought this Paul was an anti-Semite—he didn't seem the type—she didn't trust him to know what was a joke.

He broke the silence that followed, asking her to tell the funniest joke she could come up with about the other nominees.

"I think we ought to go easy on Bitty," he said, miming glugging from a bottle, making the noise, *glug, glug, glug*. (A bit much, really.) "But what's your best joke about Ms. Eggs Benedict?"

Responding to Paul had been some of the only improvisation Davina got to do. (She'd told him, without explaining why, that his plan to end the monologue by shouting "Mother!" at her made her a little uncomfortable, and he'd honored that, at least.) In the first couple of days of planning, material was thrown at her by writers who didn't seem terribly interested in her input. Didn't seem interested at all. Davina suspected, in retrospect, that the game might have been to attempt to win them over, rather than to suggest ideas of her own.

Where was she going? Well, she might as well find a tea, or something hot. She sat down at the bar, empty but for one red-nosed gentleman at the end nursing something brown over a magazine. Wiser travelers had decided to try their luck tomorrow—all that remained were the foolhardy or the truly desperate.

The bartender sauntered over.

"Grim out there," he said. "What'll it be?"

"How about," Davina said, eager suddenly for some erasure, "a hot toddy. With bourbon, please."

"Coming up." As he turned to face the wall of bottles, he asked, "Where you headed?"

"It was to be Los Angeles," Davina said. "Now I'm not so sure."

♦ ♦ ♦

SHE HAD SUGGESTED, IN CONVERSATION WITH ONE OF THE writers, that they play off Tamora's monologue to her sons in some way, tie into American politics as she'd been told they liked to do—they were the experts on all that, weren't they? In the movie, she urges her sons to carry out a vengeance plot on her behalf, "or be ye not henceforth my children." Maybe there was something there?

"Oh," the writer said. "That'd be fun! But I worry that not everyone at home would get that it's a reference to the movie. I did English at Dartmouth and I barely got it!"

Some hours later, another writer told her that Paul "had a few ideas," that Davina was in good hands: "He totally loves his divas."

Davina's other idea, to have a singing monologue—leveraging her training and the still-lovely voice she so rarely got to use—was nixed too.

"We have hosts sing when we don't trust that they can really tell a joke," Paul told her. "And you seem really game to play."

She hadn't gotten out of the show whatever she was meant to, that was certain. Davina had already been wishing she could pull out of the show when her publicist told her that she shouldn't worry, but there was a small chance New York might get snowed in. As Davina had left the studio early Saturday morning, the fat flakes falling on her eyelashes had felt like the final insult. She had hoped she might just leave this experience behind, but now here she was, still stuck in it.

Since *Andronicus* had played at film festivals, Davina had never stopped traveling, never retained a sense of what time it ought to be. She was meant to be accepting an award to rehearse accepting a bigger award—when did it end? It was hard to feel grateful for the unexpected break in the action when she was suddenly so assured in the knowledge that she was supposed to be somewhere else. And now she had too much time to stew.

Her publicist, calling Saturday morning, had told her, "Davina, you've never done this before. People are going to think this was funny, and think that it's cool that you were game. Everyone knows this wasn't your idea."

The toddy arrived. Davina took a sip—ah. This was what one, or one's studio, paid for when getting first-class lounge access. Perfectly spiced, warming deep within. Davina exhaled. Looked around. To her left, an empty expanse all the way to the lounge's picture window, beyond which planes sat, grounded; to her right, the gentleman with his brown drink continued flipping pages. He picked up the magazine, and Davina could see its cover: a headline in gold letters reading "Awards Season Heats Up!" Smaller text, in deep red, said: "Adria and Jenny Face Off!"

The art was bizarre—photos of Adria Benedict and Jenny Van Meer had been placed atop the bodies of slender plastic dolls who were posed as if they were about to break into a fight, with Adria's open palm about to connect with Jenny's smiling jaw. Jenny's smile, surely from some event earlier this year, the woman happily unaware that soon enough this same face would be placed so close to peril, even if imagined. *Probably even worse than what we did to Adria last night,* Davina thought, *but at least we were clear that we were joking.*

What a waste! What a dumb waste. She could have created an episode memorable as an introduction to who she really was—her ambition and her talent—not just whatever the writers wanted from her. In one of the less degrading sketches, she played a pupil at a cat boarding school, licking her fur and coughing up hairballs. She hacked with the best of them, but was *this* the way America would meet the real her?

Why did everything have to be like this? On set, onstage, Davina loved conflict. It made things better. When she'd first met Beth, putting on a university production of *Into the Woods,* their arguments had improved the show: Beth had been the director, and Davina the young wife who got lost in the forest. (For all that her later television career didn't suit her, Davina had to admit it felt more comfortable having aged into the role of the witch.) Beth had thought that the wife's big final number should be played, at least a little, for laughs—that the whole tone of the show was to be outsized and a little loony, they were in the realm of the Grimm Brothers, were they not? And Davina argued, just as forcefully, that there was a poignancy to playing it straight.

They'd compromised, then; Davina's song came through clearly and plainly, with all the yearning that the actress wanted. Even she had to acknowledge that the occasional pulled face or exaggerated shrug at key moments made the crowd—studded with her friends, but still—roar. They'd always been able to compromise together, she and Beth. That was what they did. That was why she was able to be here, and how she'd gotten to the work that had gotten her here. Beth had walked away from the stage, had kept things going in London. All so that, someday, Davina could return, having achieved whatever it was she wanted out of all of this, out of her work.

Compromise was what made things happen: On *Salem*, sure, she was a hired gun, but the directors on that show came and went. It was her vision of the character, such as it was, that won out. Could she ever have guessed, back in her university days, that she'd want to perform a role as outsized as possible? That she'd hunger for attention that she, nearing an age her own mother never saw, no longer got just by singing simply and sweetly?

On *Andronicus*, she'd fought to be more richly and elaborately grotesque—why shouldn't she, for instance, wear a necklace made up of body parts of enemies she'd slain?—even as Rory, the director, insisted that Tamora's great tragedy was not that she was born mad, but that she'd been pushed to madness by what she'd suffered. The mania came in flashes, ones Tamora ought to be seen trying, and failing, to repress.

Rory was right. Yet it had been great fun, fighting it all out, great fun making her case. Davina rarely got to vary her performance on *Salem*; with Rory, she got to play.

"Do you do this with Titus too?" Davina had asked, toward the end of one of their early marathon sessions, arguing over how Tamora ought to first announce herself.

"Well, sure," Rory had said, shoving her left hand through her bleached-blond hair so that the various bangles on her wrist clattered, obscuring her face at just the moment Davina was most curious to see it. "But"—a pause, the hand returning to Rory's lap, the expression on her face glimmering into legibility for Davina—"you've got my attention right now." There was a plainness to the way she spoke, so unlike the gentility to which Davina was accustomed. "So does Tamora."

Strange to want to hear from her wife right now. But only Beth could reassure her that Davina had been the right kind of mean on *Staying Up*. Been a kind of mean that, like Tamora, she'd been pushed to by circumstance. That the real Davina, the one with whom Beth had been working things out their entire adult lives, still shone through.

"Thanks for the drink." Davina slipped a ten-dollar bill under the glass. Best to stop at one. Best to have a clear head. No need to call Beth crying. She looked at her phone as she walked back to the attendant. Still nothing from Rory, but Davina allowed herself the thought that one of Rory's many positive qualities was that she did not watch shows like *Staying Up*. Then a text Davina had missed: bravo! bravo! next time i host, i hope to be brave enough to do it just like you with five red-rose emojis and a dancing-lady emoji, followed by this is bitty harbor btw and a :). Too sad to contemplate.

She mechanically opened her email once more, mechanically reopened the wound that had been festering since she woke up after the show.

Dear Davina, she read. I'm sorry you think so little of me.

She stopped walking long enough to absorb the familiar waves of agony within her as she read, once more, the signature:

Adria Benedict.

♦ ♦ ♦

[Scene: Four minutes past midnight. A red carpet, familiar to viewers of any awards ceremony. This has all the trappings: a lineup of cameras and reporters, a printed backdrop with the name of the ceremony, logos of the sponsors. This red carpet, though, is indoors, and leading nowhere. Indeed, it's the setting for a comedy sketch starring **Davina Schwartz**, award-nominated actor, and **Helena Hart** and **Paul Ardman**, two of the cast members of *Staying Up*.]

Paul, as the tuxedoed red-carpet host: Welcome to the Eighty-Fifth Annual [redacted] Awards! The stars are *out* tonight, mama! Look at that—first down the carpet is Adria Benedict, the top-billed star of a movie where her character's name is *not* the one in the title! Give it up for the queen of cinema larceny!

Davina [*dressed in a standard-issue Adria-style cream ballgown, with a diamond necklace of just the right level of ostentation around her throat*]: Hello, and welcome to *my* awards. I'm so pleased to be the host and executive producer of this ceremony, as well as the recipient of *all* the trophies.

Paul: Well, not so fast! You're one of five nominees tonight, including the formidable Jenny Van Meer, who played Maria Callas! Talk about the ultimate icon, mama!

Davina [*barely breaking character, only allowing herself the slightest sidelong glance at Paul*]: Well, I believe my record speaks for itself.

Paul: You mean the fact that you've won countless awards, and that Jenny might someday get the participation trophy?

Davina [*with a dollop of Adria-tic self-deprecation about which she was, in the moment, proud*]: We-e-ell, there is that. But no—the *record*. Lindy?

Helena [*dressed in a black, almost gothy dress and stilettos that make her instantly recognizable to true diehards as Adria's daughter, Lindy, the way she'd looked the last time she came to the awards*]: Hi, Mom. [*She kisses Adria on the cheek.*]

Davina: Hi, honey. And to think people are always wondering why you look so unhappy on-camera with me. Did you bring the record?

Helena [*smirking*]: Here it is. *Adria Benedict Sings Maria Callas*. Great job, Mom. [*She hands over, from where she'd hidden it behind her back, a vinyl record with Davina's image, dressed in khakis and a cream sweater and extending her arms outward theatrically, on the sleeve.*]

Davina: You see, just as I am the star of *Who Is Lisa Farmer?*, I also spent years training as an opera singer before the release of *The Diva*. So, really, if she wins, it's my trophy after all.

Paul: Wow! What are your other hidden talents?

Davina: Well, you've heard of *The Glass Menagerie*—Lindy, show them what I spent last summer working on.

Helena: [*opens purse to reveal a collection of fine blown-glass ornaments*]

Davina: That's right! I apprenticed as a glassblower in Italy. So, really, who put in more work—me, or the girl from the kids' show?

Paul: Now, don't tell me you also studied to become Lady Bird Johnson.

Davina [*in perfect Texas accent*]: Studied, darlin'? She was one a' my closest friends back in Austin! Ah built a time machine to go back and meet 'er!

Paul: Okay, okay—so you aren't just the lead of *Who Is Lisa Farmer?*, you're also more prepared than Jenny Van Meer, Contessa Lyle, *and* Bitty Harbor for their roles. That's four out of five. What can you do better than Davina Schwartz?

Davina [*speaking once again in crystalline East Coast elocution*]: . . . Who? Just like everyone watching, I have no idea who that is.

Paul [*only barely beating out the laughter that's engulfed the three performers onstage*]: Okay, can we say: That's a little bit iconic, mama! Our time is up, Adria, and Jenny Van Meer is about to walk down the carpet. . . .

Davina: No! Wait! Give me a few more minutes! Lindy, hand me my juggling balls! [*She grabs a second purse from Helena and whips out three tennis balls, which she begins expertly juggling.*] Keep the camera on me! And get me my unicycle!

[A look of mania takes over Davina-as-Adria's face as she keeps all three balls in the air. As the camera pans back to reveal the boundaries of the set before the show goes to commercial, audience members whoop in admiration and Paul rushes in to give Davina a hug, which predictably causes all three balls to fall. Davina is disappointed—she had wanted to see how long it could go, even if it meant running past the end of the sketch, missing the planned second half of the show—simply staying in the spotlight for just as long as she could keep it all aloft.]

♦ ♦ ♦

SHE WAS PROUD OF THE JUGGLING, DESPITE EVERYTHING. AND didn't it seem like she was in on the joke? The meanest punchline of the thing was the one she'd directed at herself, that Davina was unknown. Shouldn't Adria understand that the joke being told about her was that she was almost too admirable? That she was precise and prepared, a woman who outdid others by force of talent and will.

That had been Davina's idea. Her intention. How could she explain to Adria that she'd been the one to pitch it to the writers? Paul had made it clear that he wanted something, anything on the race. If the joke was about Adria's remarkable preparedness and capability—well, that wouldn't be so bad.

But it transformed, somewhere in the process, going through rewrites while Davina was handling photoshoots, and costume fittings, and testing different wigs. And she didn't feel certain how to tell the writers, or Paul, that suddenly it seemed like the joke was Adria's ego. And her vanity. And, a little bit, her relationships with her kids, about which Davina knew nothing. (She'd tried to convince herself, as the sketch began, that the joke was that her daughter was quite helpful?) That much had been too far. She herself would have hated to be known for who her parents were, and they weren't really anybody, just the pharmacist and his wife in their little corner of Norwich. Only Jewish family in the neighborhood, so back then she was known less as Davina than as a Schwartz—all three of them with dark hair and a record of permanent absence at church. But no one had gone on television to point her out. Including the daughter had been a mistake. The writers' mistake, but Davina ought to have caught it. She knew better.

And she would have caught it. If she'd had a moment to think. Just a moment.

Maybe it would all pass. Her publicist had told her that, anyway, the biggest hit of the night had been "Catsworth Academy." Up to three million views online within a day. Three million people had watched her cough up hairballs. Well. That's the business she was in now.

"Hello again, Ms. Schwartz!" the luggage attendant said.

"I think I am going to change my plan. If we can get all of my things back to my hotel, I'll check back in and spend the night there, and then fly to London."

The studio would figure it out, wouldn't they.

"Sounds great," the attendant agreed. And why wouldn't it? "Let's get you to a car."

This was how elegantly one could move through the world. How simple it was to have everything done for you—how much Davina, even now, knew that she would someday miss it. As the attendant slung Davina's garment bag, with the dress she'd been meant to wear tonight, over his shoulder, she looked back at her phone, at the draft she'd begun writing last night, after some wine.

Hello Adria,

It is good to hear from you, under regrettable circumstances.

I expect I shall not see you tomorrow, as I am presently stuck in New York City due to the snowy weather.

Perhaps I would be wiser to avoid further inflaming what are rightly hurt feelings. But I have had much time to think.

Please know that you are one of my idols. I need not tell you more about my life story than you would care to hear, but acting was an escape. And your films were among the ones that showed me how much was possible. Excuses are useless, but, I suppose, led astray in my attempt to be helpful and friendly to some hostile comedy writers, my intention was to try to convey how impressive you are to all of us fans watching you at home. You seem able to do anything. While I can't even get through a comedy show without hopelessly bollocksing things up.

I hope that we are able to speak before the end of the season, so that I can convey what your work has meant to me.

xDavina

Davina sent it later that night, from her new hotel room in New York, after she'd called Beth and woken her up, told Beth the news that she was heading back to London for a week, absorbed Beth's anger. (What did Beth mean that Davina was using their family as a fallback plan? Wasn't one's family the place into which one could always fall, always come back?) She sent the email after she'd changed her mind, waited for a commercial break in the awards show she'd been forced to watch on television, called Rory and told her she was coming back to LA as soon as she could, something Rory had never had any reason to doubt. Davina just had to say it. She sent the email after watching the awards' host, in his monologue, say that with the pantsuits Davina always wore, her movie should have been called *Androgynous*.

Ouch. Davina had earned that one, karmically, hadn't she.

She watched enough of the awards show to see that Adria seemed fine, just like she always was, smiling through the blurry distancing effect of superstardom from the front of the audience. But it was striking that she was in bright pink, not her usual creams or beiges or eggshells. Maybe it was a rebuke. Maybe it meant nothing.

She could barely look at Contessa on the screen—how unfair, not to be seated near her, absorbing her energy—nor at Bitty, who seemed to be forcing herself to smile in every reaction shot.

Davina sent the email to Adria just after Jenny won best actress in a musical or comedy, but a few minutes before the presenters announced that Davina herself had won the best actress in a drama prize. And it was a good thing she did too, because suddenly her phone was unusable, flooded with congratulations and well-wishes.

How had Paul Ardman gotten her number? And why did he text I think this is a little iconic, mama!—did he ever drop the bit?

Eventually the texts began to die down, as everyone in Los Angeles moved into the evening, off to whatever parties where they'd toast all the winners but one. Davina, three hours deeper into what she already knew would be a sleepless night, had not heard back from Adria. As she knew she wouldn't. She refreshed her inbox, did so again, moved to her camera roll. She clicked on a video. She'd handed her phone to a network page to record it—a gift she'd present to her son. When the time was right.

"His name is Jeremy," she heard herself say. There she stood, in the Adria Benedict costume she hadn't changed out of after a rehearsal, with her arm around a famous singer whose name, whose songs, she hadn't known.

"Hi, Jeremy," the musician said. "Your mom is really cool. She can't wait to see you."

Tomorrow she would send it to Beth. For now, she let it loop one more time. "His name is Jeremy," she heard herself say, dressed in the clothes of another woman, more glamorous than herself, but speaking, just for the moment, in Davina's own accent, her own voice.

Jenny Van Meer, *The Diva*

JENNY FELT FOR DAVINA. SHE really did—it was too easy to be talked into something that one knew better than to do. Talk about a misguided target too: Adria could really hold a grudge.

But concern for a peer only went so far. It felt nice (Jenny could admit it!) to have one less winner at this party. With the best actress in a drama winner taken off the board, the best actress in a musical or comedy winner was all the more—well. Not important, exactly. Nothing about tonight was important. Not truly. But all the more celebrated. An object of still more fascination and awe. It could feel good to be objectified.

The first ones to come over to the lovely overstuffed couch on which she'd perched at the after-party had been Contessa and her mother. Nice girl, Contessa, and it took a talent to make a small insincerity like Contessa's praise for her feel real, feel nourishing. A touch of the child actor had entered Contessa's voice when she snapped her fingers and said, "I'll get 'em next time!" but—well, what could one expect. There she was with her mother, whose jaw was set so intensely. Losing was hard—hard on the family, the whole team. Jenny knew this. She'd let everyone down before too. Several times. Six, in fact.

This would be the seventh, and seven could be lucky—Jenny remembered that from when she was a schoolgirl, counting hops in hopscotch. Lucky number seven. And tonight had gone well. She'd spoken about Maria. About what the music meant to her. She had more she wanted to say, about Pup, and about what caring for him those last years had meant. About how he didn't need to be ashamed that he'd needed to lean on her. That she was happy to do it, proud to be his daughter. About her mother, and how she'd encouraged her. Even after those first couple of losses to Adria. How hard it had been to keep on going. How unwanted she had felt.

Well, she wouldn't say that last part. But the rest, about her parents, about how it was all a tribute to them—that last part deserved to be declared from the grandest stage. She'd trust the voters to understand, to intuit, that she was keeping something of herself in reserve.

Delle had sat with them for a while, but ended up leaving after only half an hour or so; her speech for her best supporting actress win, in which she thanked Adria so profusely for being "the best partner a girl could hope for," had taken it out of her.

"It's hard, you know?" She'd put her arm around Jenny's shoulders before heading for her car. "Being perceived. Awful. Exhausting." She gave one more congratulations—"I really mean it, you did good"—and was off.

Jenny had understood what Delle meant, kind of. But being perceived didn't feel so bad right now.

The flattery hadn't stopped. Josh Jorgen and his girlfriend had sent her a drink from the bar. A silly thing to do, when the liquor was free. But looking at all the length of Josh winking and mouthing *Congrats* to her—well, she supposed she could understand why he was on top of the world right now. Why Bitty had thrilled to his praise, cried at his absence. And why that young woman next to him seemed to be holding his hand like it was something precious she was scared she might lose.

The director of *Andronicus*, a striking woman with an intense stare, came over to talk to her, told her that she would love the chance to cast Jenny in a project she was putting together. How flattering! How kind. What a reminder of what this was all really about—the work.

Each new person who came over insulated Jenny further and further from her director and castmates at the table; none of the others had won a prize after all. Eventually they began to peel off—and, saying good-bye to the actor who'd played her Onassis, Jenny caught Bitty's eye, found herself hoping the young woman would sit down.

Bitty was standing alone but for her publicist, who seemed absorbed in her phone, tapping away with no small amount of fury. Bitty held Jenny's gaze, smiled a little, looked away. Maybe she was a bit chastened by the way they'd last met. How teary she'd been. Jenny tried to gesture to her to sit down—to send Bitty, with her eyes, a signal. That it was okay. These days really were long. Losing wasn't fun. And even when you won, as Jenny was finally primed to, it was a sacrifice, spending this much time talking about a competition among artists instead of making art. She thought all of this, for and toward Bitty. She hoped that the woman who'd been so intuitive, so natural, as the mother of Lynda and Luci would feel it in the air. Bitty took a sip of a near-empty drink, started moving for the door, her publicist following, as perceptible as a shadow in twilight.

Who else was there to talk to? Jenny didn't have a date, anything like that. After Mom died, she never knew whom to bring to these things. Others had more luck in love than she, but that was all right. It felt all right, at least, now that she was working again, had a focus. Her own publicist was at the bar, recruiting more directors to come talk to Jenny. Her next job, then the one after that, and the one after that. Incredible. All because of a movie she'd done for the union minimum pay rate, and a bed in which to sleep for five weeks in Croatia.

"May I sit here?"

There she was. Jenny hadn't been monitoring the room closely. She'd wanted to keep her focus on whichever person was coming to pay tribute next, to make their three or five or seven—lucky seven!—minutes together meaningful. So she had barely registered that Adria was even at the after-party.

"Yes. It's wonderful to see you."

"Oh," Adria said, touching her hand to her throat. "Oh, you. Thank you." She exhaled loudly, making a *phew!* sound, as she gathered her skirt in her hands and prepared to sit. She was wearing electric pink—a bit flashy, Jenny thought, for a woman of their age. But one could say this much: she certainly didn't look the way she usually did.

"Jenny Van Meer," she said. "A winner at last. Congratulations."

Jenny chuckled a bit, said nothing. She had channeled a little of Maria Callas as Adria settled into her chair. A little of Adria too. A woman in charge.

"Well." Adria looked levelly at Jenny, tilted her head, seemed to chuckle at herself. As if she were puncturing her own vanity, or the years of silence between them. *"Hello."* She laughed outright.

"Hi, Adria."

"It's just, oh, I don't know," Adria murmured. "It's wonderful for you. Having this."

"Thank you," Jenny said. "That means a lot, coming from you."

"Hmm." Adria seemed, briefly, as if she couldn't go on, gathered herself. "I don't . . . I don't know." Some of her hauteur was melting away, like makeup when one wept. Coming off of her in streaks.

"I'll admit," Adria went on, "I'm feeling a little vulnerable tonight. I don't know if you've watched television this weekend . . ."

"I saw."

"You did." Adria shook her head. "Davina Schwartz has a pair of balls on her." She looked at the ceiling, down again at her lap, where she was pulling at her left index finger with her right hand, as if to pull it off. "And I never speak like that."

"Well, you know how TV is. The things they make you say," Jenny said. "We've probably both said things we regret." Right now, oddly enough, Jenny couldn't think of one. "I thought what Delle said about you was lovely."

"Oh, Delle. We fight, we do, but it's like mothers and daughters," Adria rattled off distractedly. Even she couldn't make it seem as if her heart was in it. "She left, didn't she? Let me guess, with *Bitsy*."

Jenny glanced at her reprovingly.

"No, no, I know Bitty's name," Adria said. "Give me a break. And I don't know if you've had the pleasure of speaking with Josh Jorgen. But he makes the men of our generation look like theoretical physicists. And *that's* their standard-bearer." She sighed. "Oh, Jenny. When did we get old?"

"Speak for yourself!" Jenny tried to seem stern for a moment, then smiled, despite herself.

"I'm glad we can laugh," Adria said. "You know, Jenny, I do wish things had been different between us."

"You do." This wasn't quite a question.

"Oh, Jenny, it's just, it's awful, these things." Adria was staring into the middle distance, speaking hurriedly. Like the words weren't connecting, like she wasn't quite off-book on the script she'd written. "I always felt such a sense of competition, from both of us. And, you know, it isn't easy, being the one in my position. The press practically had it that I was choosing to beat you, choosing to . . ." She scoffed. "Goodness. To make you my victim or something."

They were strangely, perfectly alone together. In the middle of this crowded room.

"You know, I regret that you never won. I do. But—Jenny, you have to understand, neither of us have it easy."

Jenny just looked at her quizzically. Wondering where the two of them would be taken next. Adria wasn't getting out of tonight, it seemed, without giving a speech.

"It's funny, isn't it," Adria said. "Time passing. You realize it at these things." She laughed, a *hoo-woo!* exhalation that seemed to Jenny more of an Adria character than the woman herself, whoever that was. "You know, Jenny, I've had a bit of a grudge against you, all of these years."

"I've noticed."

"Well, I'm not always proud of the way I act," Adria said. "It's the . . . God, I shouldn't say this. The Italian in me, isn't it. Hot-blooded. But, Jenny, the first time I won—you remember."

"We were both nominated—both of our first times."

"So you do remember."

"Yes."

"Jenny—when I won . . . you didn't clap."

All Jenny remembered now of the moment Adria first won was a thudding sense of confirmation, an early premonition that this was the way things would go, for as long as they were to go on.

"I'm sure of it, Jenny. I've watched it—oh, this is silly, but the speeches are all online now. And I've watched it. You moved your hands. No one could say you didn't literally *clap*." Adria took a breath, seemed to commit to going on. "But you . . . it was all over your face. You were just crushed. As if I had taken something from you. Feel how you like, but it would have been good to have that support. To have supported each other."

"I don't recall this at all," Jenny said. "But I'm human. Am I supposed to hide how I feel?"

"Well." Adria inhaled sharply. She looked, for once, squarely into Jenny's eyes. "Isn't that our job?"

"I think there are a lot of things we could say to each other right now," Jenny began, realizing she didn't know where else to go. And she meant it. About the way Adria hoarded roles, always had—committed to films she'd never have the time to make, so that no other woman their age could play a part. About the way she'd made such a show of never speaking to Jenny, had created this narrative that they were rivals, had forced Jenny to be a character in a real-life soap opera before she was an artist on film. About what it would have meant to have a friend, a real friend, in this business, in the early days. She thought about all of this. Tried to send it Adria's way.

"Maybe," she said, "we could meet, when all of this is over."

If Jenny's emotions entered Adria's consciousness, she batted them away with ease.

"Well, Jenny, really. I go into production as soon as awards season is over. And then this summer, I'm heading up the jury at—"

She stopped, mercifully, smiled with a shade of what looked like embarrassment.

"And I should say hello to more guests," Adria said. "I just wanted to clear the air. And say congratulations. And now I have."

"We could have been so much better together," Jenny said. "We still could. This—this campaign. It could have been different. Our careers could have."

"Aren't you happy, tonight of all nights, with how your career is going?" Adria appeared to stop herself before she could go further. She issued a dry laugh. "Here we are. And isn't it wonderful to have even this."

Jenny felt something, a catharsis, just beyond her grasp.

"Adria," she said. "You know, it's funny. No one has ever asked me this. So I'll ask you. Why did you want this?"

"Well." Adria gestured toward the party just beyond the sphere the two women occupied. "Isn't it obvious? It feels good. To be celebrated. To honor the films." She tented her hands, leaned forward slightly.

"No," Jenny said. "To be an actress. Why did you want to?"

"Well." Adria drew out the word, seemed to savor it. "Why did you?"

"It sounds silly to say it to you now, but—to tell stories."

Adria nodded, took this in, seemed to shift her eyes out of focus. When she spoke, her voice lacked the richness it'd had to that point. It sounded smaller.

"To become someone else."

Jenny nodded. "I should let you enjoy the party," she said.

Maria in Jenny's voice again; Adria there again too. This was not an offer. It was a command. Their time together had ended.

"Thanks for saying hello to me," Jenny added. "And congratulations on everything you've achieved."

She stood; Adria did too, and turned away. An embrace would have been silly. Soon Adria would be absorbed back into the party.

Delle was half right. Being perceived wasn't awful. But it was exhausting. Just one more thing to say, and then she could go back to the hotel. Just a month left.

"And, Adria?"

The woman who'd defined so much of Jenny's work and life turned back to face her, an expression of bemusement—no, of curiosity—in her eyes.

"Go easy on Delle Deane," Jenny said. She allowed her smile, the one moviegoers knew, the one that would win her the top prize at last, to break across her face. "We were where she is now, once."

Adria Benedict,
Who Is Lisa Farmer?

"I KEEP SAYING IT, BECAUSE I mean it." Delle was speaking into the microphone held by a particularly avid red-carpet reporter. The one they all were forced to talk to, on-camera, on big nights. And tonight was the biggest. "Working with Adria taught me so much. It changed my life."

"Goodness," Adria said, holding a hand to her collarbone. "Delle, sweetheart."

"Would you say the same, Adria?" the interviewer—the same man who always did these, with his tangerine-rind tan and the shellacked look to his hair and glassy eyes—asked.

"I—you know, I would," Adria said. "I certainly would. Delle is a truly dynamic performer."

There. Those were the words. This was the last time she'd discuss her. The second-to-last time. Adria would thank her in her speech tonight, wouldn't she.

They had agreed that Adria and Delle would do this interview together; for some reason, Delle had asked for that.

"Wouldn't it be better to be separate?" Adria had asked Howard, on their most recent call. "For her. To give her a moment all her own."

"It seems that she feels as if being next to you confers some status. Some dignity." He chuckled. "And who could deny that?"

Adria felt herself swelling a bit. She knew she was too easily won.

"Take it as a compliment," Howard said. "You'll do the red carpet alone next time."

"Or I won't," Adria said. "You know I hate these interviews. I would skip them all if I could."

"Now, now. No need to get a reputation."

So there she was, a woman soon to enter her seventies, standing with a microphone thrust phallically into her face. She tried not to mind, to remember that she was almost finished. She was practically vibrating. She was so close to breaking the record. To being done with questions and photoshoots and all of the things that people needed from her to prove that she was real. Or that she was better than real.

"Any fun stories from the set you two can share?" the man asked.

Delle and Adria looked at each other, and Adria felt a flashing certainty that they had the same idea at the same time. They could get through this if they made it a joke, a game. They both laughed conspiratorially, as if there were something they were on the inside of that the interviewer wasn't. Adria hoped that it would seem intriguing. Maybe get some people to click on the movie. Or however it worked on a streamer.

Delle brushed an invisible hair off her forehead. "It wasn't really that kind of movie." She laughed again, charmingly unknowable. "You know, we were telling a really serious story." Her face became, suddenly, grave. "But I think it was incredible, the way we could support each other through this."

"And I want to say," Adria added, "that our director ought to be here with us. Because he got the thing made. And he did a terrific job. It isn't easy, wrangling us girls. Right?"

She made as if to elbow Delle, who got the memo. Laughed again.

This was the final stop on the carpet before the long, long staircase into the theater. Delle and Adria had created a small backlog. Right behind them, waiting just off-camera, were Josh Jorgen and a woman Adria believed was his girlfriend, and behind them Davina, in some awful turquoise thing with big slits revealing both of her legs. Adria had experimented with color recently, but that dress? Well, it belonged on a woman twenty-five years younger than Davina. On Contessa, perhaps. Davina stood with the woman who'd directed her. Leave it to Davina to be so insecure that she needed her director to escort her. Maybe she'd be less awful, less needy, if she found a man, got married.

But then, that's what Adria had always said to herself about Jenny too, so she wouldn't hold her breath. There Jenny was, right behind Davina, waving to the crowd. Adria noted that the women in line weren't speaking to each other. Davina, even from a distance, looked slumped and antsy. Jenny was in her own world in her tasteful black gown. No gloves, Adria noted approvingly. There was hope for her.

Jenny was ceaselessly waving at the crowd, taking in coruscating currents of applause and cheers, grinning as if she'd never been to the awards at all. As if this were all new, and so much lay before her, all to be experienced for the first time. That was good too. Adria could admit it. Jenny deserved to feel that.

"We have a little surprise for you," the host said.

They wouldn't. They wouldn't dare bring Jenny into the conversation. Or Davina. The screen was crowded enough, with Adria forced to make room for Delle, to bring her into these feigned inside jokes, into her own narrative. Jenny, Adria could handle. Now. Barely. If she was forced to make conversation on television with Davina, she couldn't be held responsible for what she would say.

"A surprise?" Adria felt herself fill with dread, but she kept her tone light. "I'm—well, I'm intrigued."

"So," the host said. "I want you both to look into that monitor."

All right. Unlikely to involve Davina. A relief. Adria adjusted the glasses she wore—dark-framed, chic enough, certainly expensive enough. Adria had her vanity, but she wanted to be certain that she could read the list of names she held in her purse. This might be her last prize—she doubted they'd give any woman a fifth. So, for number four, she had to be certain to remember, in the heat of the moment and of her pride at her own achievement, to say the names: Bill. Jamey. Willy. Lindy.

"This," the host said, "is what Adria Benedict was doing when she was twenty-eight—the same age Delle Deane is today."

Adria felt blood rise to her face. Felt as if she could cry. It was her. The first time at the awards, standing on the stage. Simple flowered dress. She could remember the day she bought it. She had just found out she was expecting Willy. Got it a size up, to make sure it would drape well, if she was showing.

"Bill," the little Adria on the monitor said, "I love our growing family. Jamey, go to bed!" The Adria within the television laughed at herself, the indulgence and drama of thinking that a three-year-old child would be watching an awards show at all. "Mama and Papa, we did it!"

They hadn't understood, hadn't cared, but this hadn't just been for TV. Adria remembered, back then, feeling as if her parents would be proud she had won, would tell their friends at the union hall or the hairdressers. She made herself believe it.

"Wow," Delle exclaimed. "Adria, don't cry!"

"I'm sorry," Adria said. "It's just—the memories."

The tape kept rolling. A cut to Jenny, in the audience, looking sad. Adria understood that a little better now. Just a month ago, she'd had to clap for Davina. A woman who'd been so unkind. Maybe, if she looked at it a certain way—well, the not-clapping was hard to forgive. But maybe Jenny's downcast eyes, the deep trench in her forehead, were ways of showing just how deeply she felt for Adria, just how much she understood that Adria's growing family was something that was taking her away from her work. That when she did find a way to express herself, she felt a guilt she almost couldn't bear. Maybe she understood that the only thing that Adria had done with her mama and papa was get a continent away from them.

Or maybe she was just sad. If Adria were at home, she'd rewind the tape, over and over, parsing it. Now all she had to go on was a memory. The camera had already cut away from Jenny, and younger Adria was talking about something else entirely now. The tape ended before she was done speaking; the viewers at home had gotten enough nostalgia, or enough of a sense of who this old woman used to be.

"Hoo," Adria said. "It's been a long time. Since I've been in that moment."

"It's incredible," Delle chimed in. She placed her hand delicately on Adria's shoulder. "You must have been so excited."

"I think it's really wonderful," Adria said, "to see Jenny Van Meer in the audience too."

She looked over to the queue. Saw Jenny, still standing there. Still waving. A trick, a conjuring of applause, of which she hadn't yet tired.

Or a gift. Presenting the crowd, whoever it was who'd wait for hours to stand behind a metal fence and stare, with some version of herself for them to carry in memory for the rest of their lives.

"You know . . ." Adria said, looking down for a moment, adjusting the hem of her dress so that it'd sparkle. Gold sequins. She'd impulsively changed her mind about the dresses she'd wear for the rest of the season after seeing Davina's caricature, had picked the couple of colored dresses her stylist had pulled just in case she wanted to break out of her eggshell. She couldn't be outfitted like the woman they'd made her out to be. And this dress matched the trophy she'd be holding—she needed to make sure it caught the light, reflected it out into the audience, into the world beyond.

". . . Jenny and I were both nominated for the first time that night. And it's wonderful—I have to tell you, it's just terrific—to be reunited with an old friend."

Adria looked to the left, to all the people waiting for them. There was Howard, along with Delle's publicist; they'd go up and sit in the theater's wings. Bill, looking as if he'd rather be anywhere else. But he'd shown up. As he always did.

And there she was. It was Lindy's first time at one of these things since college. Even after Adria had blown off the panel, for fear of saying the wrong thing, embarrassing herself in front of her brilliant daughter—the one person she still wanted to impress. The one person she feared she never would. Even after they'd fought, after Adria had gone on to say things she hadn't meant to, over the phone, when Lindy was back in Chicago, studying the way that we are all acting, all of the time. Lindy had watched *Staying Up*. Had seen Davina. And had called Adria Saturday morning. Had bought herself the ticket. With the money Adria sent her, but still. It was something.

It was more than that, Adria thought, looking at her daughter's beautiful face. A mirror of everything she saw in herself. Everything she'd spent a lifetime trying to accept. It wasn't just something. It was the only thing. This, at last, was her life. Her happy, lucky life. This was what it was all for.

Bitty Harbor,
Lyndon and Claudia

BITTY WAS *NOT* RUNNING LATE because she was hungover! Because she wasn't. Not really. It was just that—fuck! Everything took so long to get done. And nobody knew how to do anything!

You'd think that by the very last in a long series of hair and makeup sessions, over months, these people would know how to deal with her face. And, yes, sometimes she woke up a little bloated or tired or impatient. But it couldn't be this hard. God.

She was in her bedroom, taking a minute. Taking a breath. They had to leave in five minutes, and she'd make it happen. She couldn't be yelled at by Leanna again. Last night Leanna had called her, told her that Josh's team had asked that they not be seated next to each other, despite how good Bitty knew they'd look in the shot. The two stars of the movie, the two stars of the night.

Leanna had used that word again. "Sensitivity." Bitty had cried, had screamed. She'd played *Which of Your Children* deep into the night, gotten herself drunk enough to really understand the game, to come so close to figuring something out before she collapsed into bed. But Leanna was being nice today.

Maybe it was that she saw Bitty was trying. She was wearing the dress they'd picked out for her. Her skin was crawling in it. She was being a good little soldier. Her management had, in the past couple of weeks, decided to strike up a deal with a European fashion label. Apparently their deal with Davina had fallen through because they weren't happy with her performance in a perfume ad she'd shot for them. Hard to believe. The deal brought some money in, and it meant that she would get to travel for Fashion Week, and that part would be fun.

Unfortunately, though, this was not the kind of thing that Bitty would ever choose to wear, not even to an awards show. The dresses this designer made were so structured and severe, all in metallic shades with rigid, pointy bodices and skirts that didn't move with your body, didn't flow. They made the women in them look like robots. Sex-bots. And Bitty supposed that's how she looked too, with her hair pulled all the way back in order to complete the look; no reason to do her usual soft, romantic curls if she was playing a silver woman from the future. If only she really could have worn what she'd worn on the Movies Issue cover. But of course she couldn't. That had to be okay.

She checked her phone. They would really have to leave soon. So soon. There were already pictures up online. Contessa, in a peach-colored dress foaming off her in an explosion of tulle. Adria. God, she looked so beautiful in gold. Josh and Rachel. Fuck them.

There was a message from a number she hadn't saved. Aw. It was a picture of Destiny and Sydnee in front of a TV set.

Waiting for our favorite actress to arrive! it said, with the signature Sydnee's mom.

That made her happy. That the kids were watching. And that they wouldn't have the experience of being in the room. All the tension and anxiety floating around. It could be too much for a grown-up.

Too much for her, at least. Anyway. No other texts. She hoped Robby and Brendan would watch, at least. To see what she'd made of herself.

She went into her bathroom, the little one off her bedroom that only she ever used. If she was very lucky . . . yes. There it was. She'd left half a glass of vodka on the rocks there the night before. The rocks had melted into water, but so much the better: This wouldn't be too strong. Just enough to get her through the ride to the awards, and then the wait through all the other categories. What she really wanted was a glass of wine, but she knew Leanna would stop her if she went to the bar cart.

She looked in the mirror, at herself holding the glass. She seemed clear enough, happy enough. She made herself smile, wide, crinkling the corners of her eyes and making herself look just a little less severe, despite the hair, despite the dress, despite the feeling of dread. This would have to do.

She slugged the glass down in one. The melted ice gave it a stale flavor, overlaying the metallic bite of the liquor. She kind of preferred cheap vodka, the kind she bought, to the expensive stuff that'd be behind the bar tonight. You could really taste the alcohol in it. And you understood, as it burned going down, that it would work.

She'd be fine, if she gave a speech tonight. Bitty had moments where it hit her that she probably wouldn't get the chance—she was up against Adria Benedict. And the other three too, but really—who did she think she was? To beat Adria Benedict.

But then why go at all? Why not just stay home? So she had to believe. She believed, too, that she'd be fine for her speech.

There was a knock at the door. Leanna.

"Bitty?" she said. "I think it's now or never. And I'd prefer now."

As Bitty made her way to the front of her little house, where a black limousine sat waiting, she turned the thought over in her mind. There was something electric in the idea. She would probably lose. But she might win. She'd gotten nominated, hadn't she? So had Josh. Maybe they'd both win—they could clink awards, make the trophies kiss, when the winners stood backstage in the press room. Maybe Delle would win too, and it could be all three of them. Getting past all of the weirdness between them. For the next thirty years, forty years, until Bitty and Delle were the last two women standing. Like Adria and Jenny. Bitty would be the Adria.

Bitty felt flushed as she pulled herself into the backseat of the car, carefully fastening her seatbelt so as to avoid bumping the buckle against her dress and ruining the line. She had felt this way back when she and Josh used to get drinks after shooting. Like the world was opening up. She'd felt so hemmed in for so long, trying to play this role, be this person. If they gave her the prize, maybe that would mean she'd played it perfectly, and could move on. Or maybe it would mean they'd seen the girl inside the whole time. That they understood her.

The car was moving.

"Phew, finally!" Leanna said.

Bitty didn't respond. She was okay. She and Leanna were okay. They'd arrive just in time. The show wouldn't need to put a seat-filler in to conceal that Bitty was absent. She'd be there. Front row. She'd laugh at every joke.

Maybe, if she won, if she felt in that perfect moment onstage that they'd understood something about her that she didn't yet understand about herself, she could stop. Not stop working. Never. But . . . stop. Stop searching. For something else, something in the quiet and the darkness and the solitude. Stop asking her mother a question that she would never really hear; accept that some things didn't have answers, and part of the talent that it took to get through life was acting like that could be okay, just to get through a single night without destroying yourself.

Maybe it could be possible. Maybe she could, at nights at home, all by herself, look at the trophy on her bar cart and understand it. She could understand, after an experience that would live forever at the edge of her memory, that she didn't need to erase herself in order to be able to keep on going. Maybe, if she won, it could finally feel like enough.

Contessa Lyle,
The Glass Menagerie

CONTESSA HAD TO CRANE HER head to see Bitty at the other end of the front row. Poor Bitty had missed the whole red carpet. And Contessa knew that wasn't really what mattered about nights like these, but . . . it kind of was. Especially if you were Bitty, and you were apparently debuting a whole new look. She waved, smiled; Bitty smiled back. She looked calm. For her.

There were Josh and Rachel in the middle of the row. Weird they weren't next to Bitty. Or Contessa, for that matter. But they'd all be in the wide shot. Whatever. Then Adria, with her husband and daughter. Her daughter was so pretty! She was in the kind of look Contessa could never pull off, a slightly gothy black dress with a netting effect over it and rich, dark lipstick. But it looked amazing on her. She looked just like Adria. Then Eleanor, with Contessa's mom as a buffer between them. Not a buffer—they'd made up. But still.

It was cool Eleanor was even here. The awards-show producers had really wanted her to attend the show; Jimmy and Contessa were the only Black nominees, which wasn't exactly surprising, but was—you know, it was what it was. So they'd gotten Eleanor to present the top prize, at the end of the night.

They were okay. The studio had made them do an interview together in the final days of voting, had convinced Eleanor to do it even though she wasn't nominated. Flattered her—it'd mean so much for a legend to vouch for Contessa. Things like that. The interview was for a big newsmagazine show, and they'd talked to Contessa's former costars, to her mom, to create what the producers called "a complete picture." Jimmy had outright refused to do it; Josh's schedule, Contessa heard, wouldn't allow it. But after Eleanor and Contessa sat together, in front of a man Contessa later learned had once been a war correspondent, Contessa pulled Eleanor aside, told her that she wanted to get a few things straight.

Eleanor had seemed to appreciate the directness. She asked Contessa to sit with her. Maybe she'd picked up on something in Contessa's fighting with her mom in public. Had seen that Contessa really could stick up for herself. That she wanted, in some part of herself she'd never before had to access, to fight her own battles. But as Contessa finished describing why the set had been so hard for her, Eleanor sucked her teeth for a long moment, looked at Contessa hard. The way her mother had looked at her, all those years ago, when Contessa told her she wanted to move to California to audition for TV shows. Concern, and affection too. Understanding that the person to whom she was speaking had years ahead of her in which she was going to keep getting hurt.

All Eleanor had said was "Wow."

"I know." Contessa looked down at her hands. "I wish I could have talked to you about these things."

"I wish," Eleanor had said, "that I could have heard it." She explained that she'd always known how to talk to directors. That she'd thought this director was something like her husband, who'd died a few years back.

"No," Contessa said. "I wanted to collaborate. He didn't let me."

Maybe, Eleanor had said, she would get there someday. She had to keep trying, keep looking for directors who would let her try. That was better than nothing. There would be other movies. For them both, Contessa thought. Maybe not together—too much had happened. But at least Eleanor got it now.

It was nice to have her here. To have her in the frame. Whatever happened, Contessa knew, at the end of the night she'd be back in her seat, waiting for Eleanor to walk onstage, so that she could leap to her feet. Contessa would vouch for her too. She would be the first one standing for a legend.

♦ ♦ ♦

THERE WERE MAYBE SIX MINUTES TO SHOWTIME. PEOPLE WERE still filing in. From the corner of her eye, Contessa saw Jenny walk to the front row, all by herself. Jenny nodded at Davina, then reacted with a little "Oh!" of amusement as Josh leapt to his feet.

"*Miss* Van Meer," Josh said, as if to make the point that Jenny looked youthful.

All it did, to Contessa, was emphasize that she wasn't married, wasn't young. He could be such a loser. Rachel giggled and clapped. Contessa had read a headline three days ago that said she was going to star in a romantic thriller opposite Josh. That was one way to make sure she had eyes on him.

"I'm going to hit the head one last time," he announced to the air, taking two Josh-sized steps away from his seat, then turning around, appraising the row.

Contessa looked at him. She could sense Bitty looking too, and she strived to make her own gaze less hungry, less urgent. Rachel was right there, after all. Contessa still had some pride.

"My leading ladies," he said. "Jenny. Adria. Bitty. Davina. El. Contessa." Pause, then more syrup ladled over his voice, an LBJ country-boy affect sneaking in. "Contessa's mama." He chuckled. "Let's give 'em a great show, eh? Rooting for you all."

♦ ♦ ♦

"GOD, HE IS AWFUL," MELANIE MUTTERED.

"Sh," Contessa hissed. "Not now."

"At least now I know that you understand what I mean," Melanie said. "Hey. Put that thing away for the show."

"I'm not—" Contessa said. "Look. I'm looking at this." She showed Melanie her phone, where @BestOfContessa had already posted a close-up of Contessa's makeup from tonight.

Our girl doing what she does best, the caption read. Looking ethereal. There was a hashtag, princess, and then an angel emoji, a shooting-star emoji. The commenters were wishing her luck.

"Nice to see," Melanie said. "This is your best look of the whole season. Glad we went with the new stylist."

"Thanks, Mom," Contessa said. "I suppose you can stay."

They exchanged a look. Melanie decided—Contessa could see her gears turning—to laugh, after a minute. They'd deal with their future when this was all over. Once Contessa had her prize.

She was pulling her phone just out of Melanie's eyeline when it vibrated again. A text, from Josh.

hey it read. Then it vibrated again, then again.

Having convinced her mom that she was just reading comments about how beautiful she looked tonight, Contessa felt secure enough in reading as they came in, one after the other, eventually pushing the last text she'd sent, a month ago, can we talk? pls off the screen.

sorry ive been silent Josh wrote.

things have been really crazy with rachel

i really care about her

but i miss having you as a friend

im in the bathroom half tempted to send you a pic like i used to

but i know thats a bad idea

at least when your next to youre mom

right ?

Contessa looked up. Sensed the scope of the room she was in, that she'd entered for the first time in her life. She was only twenty-two years old, and she was here. At the center of the world's attention. Obviously she didn't want to see his dick on her phone.

not a good idea.

k, Josh replied. A winking face. Then:

good luck tonight. i mean it. i really hope you win. you worked really hard.

thx Contessa typed. Josh had better hurry back. There was a countdown graphic on the big screen onstage. Ninety seconds until showtime.

Her phone vibrated one last time.

do u think i will? lol

Contessa knew that her mother wasn't looking at her, because Melanie's hand was skittering blindly across Contessa's lap, seeking hers to hold. They were forgiving each other. Finding their way back. Melanie was watching the countdown clock, which was nearing the thirty-second mark. Josh galloped down the aisle, glanced at Contessa with an open, genial smile, and sat down next to Rachel.

She'd be safe to reply. It was an innocent text, and Melanie was distracted by her hopes for Contessa, her sense that everything they'd been fighting for was all about to happen. Contessa could see that, on her other side, Melanie was holding Eleanor's hand too. Amazing that they had all come so far.

And amazing, too, that soon it would be over. This suddenness, the fact of the show closing in—ten seconds away now—meant that she didn't have the time to type everything she might want to say in that moment. Did she think Josh would win? Wasn't it obvious that, in every way but one, he already had?

Maybe she could leave his text on read, sit through the awards, make her first act at the after-party taking Bitty's hand and leading her to the dance floor. If she found a way to be kind—not just pitying, but kind—to the woman she'd spent months seeing as nothing less than formidable competition and nothing more than an anxious loser, if she could do that . . .

Well. Then maybe that would be Contessa's win too.

Davina Schwartz, *Andronicus*

"I can't believe you're skipping the after-parties. They're really fun." Rory paused. "Even if you didn't win."

"If?" Davina said, staring out the car window.

"Even *as* you didn't win. It's the finish line. You did it—all over. Time to celebrate."

"It's been a long night." Davina exhaled, hard enough to count as a sigh.

"For me too," Rory said, an edge entering her voice. "I lost too, remember?"

"Yes. I'm sorry."

"It's fine." Rory waved her hand. "There'll be a next time. I think."

They weren't moving—every car was trying to escape the gravity of the theater at the same time. Everyone had stayed until the end, to see Eleanor announce that *Enola Gay* had won the top prize. At least it wasn't one of Davina's rivals' films. Davina didn't think it had any women in it at all.

♦ ♦ ♦

IT HADN'T BEEN A FIT; DAVINA COULD SEE THAT NOW. NONE OF it. The dress her stylist had convinced her to wear, with the slits up the sides—it made her skin crawl to think of herself on television wearing it, when just months before she'd agreed that it would be canny and fun to try to show a different side of herself, to be something she'd never thought to be before. Sexy, freewheeling. American, perhaps. She didn't look daring. She looked like she'd been dared.

Her reaction shot must have been just terrible. She knew it as it happened, felt her face, so carefully and tightly controlled as she gazed up at the presenter, sag and hang loose when her name was not called. Humiliating that she'd allowed herself to believe she had a chance.

"I tried really hard," she said into the air.

"I know." Rory sounded apologetic. "Look. These things happen."

She reached for Davina's hand, and Davina allowed it to be clasped. Davina hadn't really been addressing Rory. She didn't need her reassurance. But she could let Rory believe it for a moment. Not every one of Davina's reactions tonight needed to be awful.

She knew that the look on her face had been bad when she checked her phone at the show's final commercial break. She saw an email headlined come home, a second one with a list of flights from LAX into Heathrow. As soon as tomorrow morning.

Beth had seen. She knew how much this had meant. How much Davina, too, had given up for this. All she'd wanted was to meet Adria, at first—that would have made it worthwhile, she had thought. Then she got the chance to try to become her, and had lost whoever it was she'd once been.

It could be easy to find that old Davina—to let this version of herself vanish as she caught an early morning car to the airport. Rory would probably be out late. She and Davina usually just met at one or the other's house, had sex and takeaway, but Davina knew Rory loved a party. She just tamped down that side of herself for her older British . . . well, not girlfriend. Her older British something.

Davina would have to come back in a few months for the final season of *The Screaming at Salem*. They'd asked Jenny Van Meer to play her mother, but who knew if that would come together; it would probably be that other actress Davina had met with, Nancy McCord. Nice enough woman. The work she'd had done made her look strange and ageless, neither a mother nor a daughter, but that was this awful city. That was months away, when Davina would fulfill her final obligation to Los Angeles. Then she could go again. Pull together a production with Beth. It might not be Broadway. It might not be one of the great parts. But there were other roles for her to play.

"I'm hearing that Ceridwen Darby's party is going to be lit, but there's also one farther east where a lot of the nominees are going to turn up later," Rory said. "So let's do Ceridwen first, and we can eat there. There'll be burgers."

"I'm a vegetarian," Davina said. "In case you forgot."

"I meant for me," Rory said. "Don't worry, I didn't forget. I've had a lot of vegan takeout the past few months." Her voice musical on this last sentence, a let's-not-do-this-right-now song.

Davina decided not to start a fight. These would be her final hours with Rory, even if Rory didn't know it.

"I don't think I have it in me to go to a party," she said. "You can drop me off."

"But that takes me way out of my way," Rory whined. "We'll have to double back, in this insane traffic—I'll miss, like, ninety minutes of the party. Two hours, even."

"Well," Davina said. "That's my choice."

Rory sighed, looked out the window.

"Why don't you tell the driver then. Since you're certain that's what you want."

Davina wouldn't need to tell Rory she was leaving, would she. Because that wasn't the kind of thing that had grown between them—it had been simple and fun and had lasted as long as the excitement of the season. Now that season was over. Davina didn't need to mourn, exactly, but it didn't feel like a time to celebrate.

"I guess I was kind of excited," Rory went on, keeping a certain stridence in her voice. "To get to show you off. We sat next to each other tonight, but that was . . . director and star. You wouldn't even let me hold your hand."

"Well," Davina said, "there are many considerations there."

"I know. Different generations. It's just sad to me."

"The more you give the world," Davina said, "the more you lose."

"I just don't agree." Rory shook her head emphatically. "You give love, you get it back."

What?

"Can we just . . ." Davina wanted to get out, walk to the airport. "Please."

"You still haven't told the driver you're going home," Rory said. "Why don't you give him your address now."

The traffic out of the theater had finally, very incrementally, begun to move.

It was Davina's last night in Los Angeles, and maybe it did behoove her to tell Rory that. They'd cared about each other, in their way. Rory had made things seem achievable for a moment. Davina was grateful for that, even as the comedown hurt. It had been good to imagine what things could be like.

Maybe she could try it out. The party. For one last night. She could always catch a car home. This one had been reserved by the studio for Rory and Davina both, so she oughtn't steal it, but a rideshare driver wouldn't recognize her. Not if he'd been driving all night, missing her face falling for the rest of the world to see. She'd just be a woman all made up, aging out of her dress.

"Four-fifths of the room are losers." Rory was gazing at Davina with a puppyish intensity. "Come on."

If she was going to go, she was going to see Adria, surely. The awards were so chaotic that, well, of course she'd *seen* Adria, but only in glimpses, flashes. There hadn't been the remotest expectation that they'd stop and talk. What would she say to her? What could she?

She opened her phone. Maybe she could send an email, apprising Adria that she was headed to the Ceridwen party—no. That was lunacy. She would go and find someone to talk to, someone interesting and new. Someone she'd never meet in London. Be the self she'd never be in London. And that could be the last memory.

Davina had searched Adria's name in her inbox, and now automatically opened the email, the first one Adria had sent her. Maybe this was her trophy. Tarnished though it was by all that had come after. This was what she could hold in the light, to watch what was left of its shine. Her memory of this adventure.

"Your future is very bright," Adria had written. Davina might not ever stand on a stage holding an award. But there were other stages on which she could appear. Other stages of her life to walk through. There was still time.

"All right. Let's carry on. Party on."

She smiled. This was her final penance of the season, the last thing she'd give in order to complete her experience of stardom. She'd text Beth shortly. Tell her to pick one of the flights later in the day tomorrow. Give herself a chance to sleep, if she could. Then the flight home. She could already imagine being up there, aloft, this city receding behind mountains and clouds. Everyone she might see or meet tonight left behind to gobble each other up.

"Let's rage!" Rory said.

Between the roles of Tamora on film and Davina Schwartz in Los Angeles, Davina had raged hard enough for a lifetime this past year. But she was very close to the end of this performance. She could see it through.

"Sure." The car was, finally, picking up speed. She squeezed Rory's hand, a gesture its recipient had to figure was the beginning of a farewell. "Let's do it."

From "Critical Notebook: The Meaning of Jenny Van Meer's Smile," a blog post on a culture news website the week before the awards

Jenny Van Meer has worn something fantastic throughout her current awards-season run. It's not any of her garments (although those have been fabulous too—she's clearly upgraded from the fusty ballgown-and-opera-gloves look that lives in public memory as the much-maligned Jenny Van Meer awards-season look). It's the most distinctive red-carpet accessory this side of the bandages Adria Benedict wore on her right hand back in September and October.

It's her smile.

For decades now, Van Meer has been a go-to cultural archetype: The ultimate example of a worthy person who can't quite put the pieces together to, at any moment, be the very best. And part of that, perhaps, is her own doing. Van Meer has never been one for the safe choice. That's been true since she emerged. The scion of a WASP banking dynasty, Van Meer famously dropped out of Juilliard after two semesters on what she's called "an intuition" in order to bounce around various TV soaps, then reached fame in her early thirties as *The Migrant Mother*. And since then, her choices have seemed, to an outsider, curious. Mercurial, even. (And, with movies like *Kiss the Rink* and the *Chummy Pups* animated franchise, one suspects they've been for money; Van Meer famously supported her late parents after the Van Meers fell on hard times in the 1980s savings-and-loan crisis.)

Unlike her peers, Van Meer doesn't live near the heart of the industry; she relocated to the mountains of Idaho after the death of Charles Van Meer, her father. And that remoteness seems to guide her decisions. For instance, no one who watched *Judith of the Ewes*, which Van Meer fought to make for years and promoted aggressively when it finally came out, would say that was a classic awards-bait role. (If you manage to find it—it's already fallen off of streaming services—watch for the scene where Judith has convinced herself she has learned how to speak the sheeps' language. If there were an award for best original bleat, Van Meer would have a trophy on the shelf.)

Van Meer is driven by her own particular instincts in the awards game too. Those of us who want to see her win have winced along with her as she's suffered loss after loss when it comes time to hand out best actress—with three of those six losses coming at the hands of longtime perceived rival Adria Benedict, early in both women's careers. Her most recent awards runs have had a doomed feeling to them, and, fittingly enough, Van Meer has brought a gritted-teeth energy to the red carpet, a sorrowful and beat-down energy. It hurts to lose. And the safer thing would be to smile through it. But playing it safe is not what Jenny Van Meer does.

Now, in the closest Best Actress race in many years, Van Meer has emerged as a process-of-elimination favorite, with Bitty Harbor, Contessa Lyle, and Davina Schwartz all likely too new to the scene and Adria Benedict possibly too familiar. (Given that they practically nominate her annually, can't they give Benedict her fourth prize another year, when she's actually the lead of her movie?) And she's brought the smile so familiar from her movies, suffused with all the goodness we read into Van Meer, out on red carpets, talk shows, even from the stage of the precursor awards, where she accepted her prize for Best Actress in a Musical or Comedy. It wasn't what she said that mattered. It was how she said it, glowing with a sense of justice finally having been delivered.

Is *The Diva* the movie Van Meer should win an award for? Well, no—and not just because every fan has their favorite. (The standard answer is *The Migrant Mother*, but I'd have given it to Van Meer on her third nomination, for playing the boxing fan who eventually enters the ring herself in *Bantamweight*. Van Meer trained for months, and summoned the intensity of a true competitor determined to prove her mettle and repudiate her opponent.) Even fans of Van Meer can admit that the somewhat silly and more-than-somewhat miscast *The Diva,* with its piped-in Callas arias and the cardboard-looking sets Van Meer devours, is just a vehicle to get this star back into the spotlight.

But what a spotlight it's been! Van Meer has been a delightful presence on late night and a red-carpet scamp, joking with reporters in a way that no one might have imagined even a year ago, let alone in her somewhat self-serious early days. This consummate actress has, for once, committed to the role. Her public persona has, to this point, been one of grave intensity; her smile is a rare gift. (In this, she's like a photo negative of Benedict, who conjures righteous anger or sorrow in every performance but who's such a light and giddy presence when she deigns to give an interview.) Winning looks good on Van Meer—and now that she's celebrating, we get to celebrate with her.

Maybe it's an unfair cultural expectation for women to smile, even when there's no reason to. (Who wouldn't be sad to lose an award?) But that's not a problem that's going to be solved this year! And say this much: happiness looks good on a star whose awards journey has been the inverse of Benedict's. And maybe this, at long last, will make for her path to victory—by campaigning as if she actually enjoys it.

Jenny Van Meer,
The Diva

It was 10:56 in the morning. Three days after the awards. Back home, finally. Jenny had drunk her coffee and taken her walk and checked on the chicken coop. She was as centered as she could be expected to be, and would decide in the moment how much of what she told Fiona would be frank, and how much would be what Fiona wanted to hear.

She sat in a sort of meditative silence, one that she knew she could hold for as long as she had before Fiona came online. Which was four minutes. The totality of her inwardness was interrupted but once, by the thought that a more sustained practice of meditation could replace Fiona entirely. But Jenny banished it. It was comforting to have as much help, from as many sources, as one could get.

Then her screen burst into a muted sort of life: the therapist appeared, monochromatically, in an oatmeal sweater with her shredded-wheat-colored wall behind her. Jenny rushed to cover up that damned little square of her own face.

"So you'll remember it was the awards this past weekend," Jenny said.

"We did talk about that in our last session, yes."

How maddening and grounding, all at once, that Jenny was engaging with someone for whom the awards were not the top priority but merely a thing she only encountered through her work! It might be nice if Fiona acknowledged that the work Jenny did happened in public, if only so that she wouldn't feel quite so vain.

Perhaps it was good, healthy, to be reminded of one's own cosmic significance, or lack thereof.

Jenny knew, at least, not to ask if Fiona had watched.

"Well, I thought that it could be good to talk about how it went," Jenny said.

A pixel or two shifted. The slight crackle suggested that Fiona had leaned forward just barely, as if to encourage conversation.

"Where should I begin?"

Jenny was deciding whether to deliver an early catharsis, to unburden herself right now of exactly how she felt about the outcome of her race, or to walk herself there. While it would feel better to lean right into it, she might be a better therapy patient if she made it more of a narrative.

That damn word. Her narrative had been "It's her time." And it hadn't been.

"I imagine you're feeling disappointed right now," Fiona said. "Forgive me for jumping ahead. But even as I try to avoid learning beyond what you tell me, your case presents unusual situations."

"Yes," Jenny allowed herself to admit. "Yes, I am feeling disappointed."

"That's very understandable."

"It's just," Jenny said, "I'm disappointed in myself. I think about the women I met over the course of these months."

She recalled Davina, standing on the stage to present the award for best film editing. As the orchestra rose and Davina stood there, waiting for her cue to speak, she gazed out at the audience with what looked to Jenny like the most painful loneliness she could imagine.

"They have these burdens they carry," Jenny went on. "They do. And they were all suffering—we were all suffering. For this trophy."

She thought about how, at the commercial break as Davina returned from presenting the award, Rory had tapped her on the shoulder. The director had asked Jenny, in a whisper, if she could arrange a moment at the after-party for Davina and Adria to speak.

"Davina is more important to me than you understand," Rory had said. "And she's hurting."

Jenny had begged off, told her that some things were beyond her power, and congratulated her on being a strong female filmmaker. "We need more women like you!" she'd said, pumping her fist in the air, trying to exit the conversation. Jenny only saw Davina briefly at the after-party, kissing Rory furiously in a corner, looking like she wanted to devour her, or to be devoured. Jenny understood how she felt.

This was too much to explain cogently. Jenny knew the process of therapy was about finding the order within the disordered, but she still liked to have a script. To feel like there was an arc.

"I've had a good life," she went on. "But . . ."

"You sound like you have mixed feelings, as you say that," Fiona said.

"Oh, profoundly mixed!" Jenny felt herself laugh, as she often did when she grew expansive. Professor Jenny, Pup used to call her, when she got grandiose. "Profoundly," she repeated.

Time to reel it back in, to focus on what was true. She remembered a concept she'd learned when she was first looking into meditation—to focus on what was in front of her. Not on Fiona, that blur of beige pixels gathered to look inquisitively at her, and not the Post-it note blocking her own face, a face she suddenly badly wanted to see emoting. The tissue box. Simple, tidy, store-brand from the Albertsons in town. She'd bought it herself on a store run before the campaign even started, before she'd asked Ned from down the road to check on the house and the chickens while she was away. When she could, she did things for herself up here.

"It's hard, isn't it." Jenny knew that Fiona was at least pretending to come to understand this for the very first time. "They take you all over, tell you that you're going to be honored. And that it would mean something. You do know this. How much I've given up, to do this work. The things I haven't experienced."

She waited for Fiona to nod before going on; extracting this much from their shared work gave her a bit of confidence.

"They convince you that you can win. I knew in my heart that it wasn't my best work—I didn't actually sing the songs, did I? And I could have learned to sing them. Probably. I knew that if history books said I won for *The Diva*, it wouldn't be right—it should have been for so many other things. But—"

"But you'd be in the history books."

"Yes," Jenny said. "So there's a justice in it. In having lost. But there were so many moments when I just thought how good it would have felt, despite it all, to—you know. To win."

Fiona gave her a moment to collect herself.

"If you don't think you really deserved to win," she asked, "who did?"

"Well, goodness," she said. "I'm sorry." She dabbed at her eye—thank you, Albertsons. "Oh, perhaps Contessa. Or Eleanor, who wasn't even nominated. Or, really, Delle Deane. My little buddy. I was glad she won supporting, at least."

Jenny felt the warmth of watching Delle win—in the wrong category, but still—fill her.

"Not Bitty? You have talked a fair amount about her," Fiona said.

Bitty had cornered Jenny at the after-party, asked her in too loud a voice if she'd gotten the chance to hold Josh's best actor trophy—he'd been passing it around, which, Bitty burbled, was *so* funny! Her eye had a manic gleam in it. That poor woman. This business was not easy for the sensitive. And only a truly sensitive actress could have done what Bitty did onscreen.

"Anyway, do you want to find a script to work on together?" Bitty had asked, again too loudly, the rhythm of the sentence creaking against Bitty's state of mind.

It hadn't been the right moment. But Jenny tried to put herself in Bitty's shoes. Who knew when she'd have another one?

"She's an incredible performer," Jenny said. "But I don't think she's ready. For what winning entails."

"You were, though. You'd waited your entire career for this honor. And I think it'll take some weeks to work through that."

Jenny nodded in agreement. "I am, though, a bit embarrassed over—oh, how maudlin I was at the after-party."

"Were you?"

Jenny recalled walking up to the table where Eleanor, Contessa, and Melanie sat. She'd shaken off her publicist, was just doing a tour of the room before she got in the car and headed home. Her flight to Idaho was booked for the next morning. After that, she was beginning to realize, she would never be in a room like this again.

"Two losers and one ex-winner." Eleanor had put a touch of lilt in her voice to let Jenny know she was kidding. But still. It hurt a bit. Did Eleanor always have to be so tough? "It's the hottest seat in town," she went on.

"Eleanor," Contessa said, "you know this, but I wish you'd been nominated. I mean it."

"You're just saying that because you're young, and you'll get more chances," Eleanor said. "But you worked harder than I knew on that set. I see that now. Thank goodness you set me straight." She looked Jenny in the eye, unnervingly. "It's been a long season. And we're finally talking. Would you believe how little time we get to do that?"

"I know, don't I ever." Jenny was being too folksy. "Why, just over there is Delle—"

"They set it up this way," Eleanor continued, "so that we don't talk. So that we can't help each other." She stared right into Jenny. "So that we *compete*."

"Yes." Jenny was unsure of what offense she'd committed. "I do . . . I struggle with that."

"I know," Eleanor said. "If anyone has had to struggle with that, it's you." She patted Jenny on the hand, smiled. "Come sit with us. Help me bore our friend Contessa with old war stories."

Jenny shifted, touched her ear as if worried her earring was missing, or as if she were trying to adjust the receiver that would give her instructions on how to behave. She didn't know what to do with her hands. They were supposed to be holding a trophy.

"It's really good to see you, now that it's over," Contessa said. "It's kind of a relief, isn't it? Not having to worry about your speech? Mine would have been: 'Thanks, Mom!' And then Eleanor too. That's it, probably, I think. Fuck everyone else."

She stuck out her tongue and buzzed it between her lips. Her mother laughed, began to speak, to correct her.

"Oh, Mom, don't." Contessa's voice had a surprising sharpness, one Jenny had not expected the girl could summon.

Melanie's smile deflated slightly, and she let out a small exhalation as she shook her head.

"I don't know. I feel . . . I feel a bit like a prop." Jenny struggled to get the words out. "Like a piece of scenery. Art direction. Like I'm here to let my reactions show how people are supposed to feel about the . . . I don't know, the protagonists. Like I never had a chance from the start."

Contessa blinked, looked back at her mother, who touched her lightly on the shoulder. Eleanor held eye contact with Jenny, patted the seat next to her. Jenny took a moment to decide whether to sit. This was a tragic ending—joining the other losers, toasting their bad luck. She was about to walk away from the table, she was sure of it, when Eleanor cracked a smirk.

"Well, look who it is."

Jenny didn't need to look—Ceridwen Darby's whoop, somewhere in the distance, said it all. Adria Benedict had arrived.

♦ ♦ ♦

SHE'D TOLD ALL OF THIS TO FIONA, IN AS PLAIN A MANNER AS SHE could.

"How did it feel?" Fiona asked. "Seeing Adria. I know you two recently had a bit of a breakthrough."

"It was funny. It was as if we didn't need to say anything. Or neither of us wanted to. But I feel, now, this understanding. We've been through life together, in this odd way. Closer than sisters."

"Really?" Fiona asked.

"Well, there I go," Jenny said. "No, not that. But just in the sense that—so few people even know what it's like to be in that room once. We have been there, again and again. One of us always wins. . . ."

"Take your time," Fiona said.

"And, you know," Jenny went on. "There's me. So." She exhaled. "It was somewhat perfect."

Jenny had looked over at Adria, there in her golden dress. Across the room, Adria met her eyes, raised her hands and applauded. Applauded Jenny. Both women smiled, feeling something shift between them, something fall away.

Thank you, Adria mouthed.

That was all they needed to communicate that night. Jenny was ready to head home.

"Contessa," Jenny said, "you looked wonderful tonight. That's the prize. One of them."

The young woman looked at her, shook her head slightly as if trying to figure Jenny out.

"Thanks, Jenny! You're the best." She gave up on her study of Jenny, and simply smiled. "I should probably go say hi to Bitty."

Jenny considered warning her to tread lightly. But let Contessa see what nights like these could do. If she didn't guard some part of herself, learn how not to give all of herself to the race. She pivoted to the other actress at the table instead.

"Eleanor . . . what can I say?"

"Let's not let it be this long next time," Eleanor told Jenny.

She reached her arms out for an embrace, and Jenny had the horrifying thought, gratifying in its proof of her capacity to surprise herself, that she hoped one of the photographers captured the moment. Saw this legendary, challenging woman enclosing Jenny in the long-ago history she'd made.

♦ ♦ ♦

"OUR TIME TOGETHER IS COMING TO A CLOSE SOON," FIONA SAID, "and I'd like to zero in on something, if you don't mind. On how you felt right when the award was announced. Certainly, there's disappointment. But I'd like to dig in a bit."

"Oh, shoot. I'm sorry. I guess I thought I'd have more time to get there, and I wanted to tell the story in a way that . . ."

"That what, Jenny?"

"That would impress you," Jenny said. "I know you don't know me or my work—well, I'm proud of my work, that's just it! But, if you don't know this . . . people think of me as . . ."

"Let's focus on what we can do together, in this room—this virtual room."

Jenny knew that Fiona hadn't meant this to be a joke, that she'd really slipped. She felt a strange sort of pride that her pain was real enough to Fiona to make it feel as though they were physically together.

"What is it you see, when you see me?" Jenny asked.

"I don't think it'd be helpful for me to answer that," said Fiona. "Not as helpful as my asking what you see when you see yourself."

It all came out of Jenny, guided less by any remaining desire to be a good patient than by the sudden knowledge that *this*—a torrent of words, to be sorted through—was all that Fiona had wanted.

"I think I'm a good daughter," she began. "I was proud of how I took care of Pup—of my father. I missed some years with him, and with my mom, God knows. But when work began to slow down, I got to be there. And I hope he knew that I was proud of him too, despite . . ." She trailed off, felt her throat get tight.

She powered on.

"I knew it was hard for him to accept my help, and I tried to make it easier. And I haven't had luck in love, but I'm a good friend. To people I haven't seen in months, but they know . . . they know I'm there. I think I am great at what I do. I work—" She shuddered and let out a sound she couldn't imagine conjuring on a set, great though she was. "I work so hard."

Fiona nodded.

"But the only thing people will remember of me in fifty years, when I'm dead, is that I was a loser. That I never won. Born in the wrong time, under the wrong star."

"I don't know this world," Fiona said. "But do you think any of your performances will stand on their own? That people will watch them?"

Jenny sensed for the first time that Fiona knew slightly more than she was admitting—she was no cineaste, sure. Fine. But somewhere in the question was the suggestion that maybe, just maybe, Fiona had a friend or a daughter or a mom with a favorite Jenny Van Meer movie. Maybe she had one too.

That scrap wasn't enough right now, and Jenny attempted to go back to the evidence, to find something that she could hold on to that bore the weight of fact. She always, always did her research.

She wasn't, in the end, proud of *The Diva*, if she ever had been. And the things she loved, like *Judith of the Ewes*, people seemed not to understand, seemed to find stranger and more off-putting the more she expressed her passion. Her older performances seemed, in this moment, so tied up in the memory of loss—the collaborators she hadn't been able to thank from the stage, the message to Pup she couldn't give to millions watching—that they weren't even real to her. There had been so many losses that blotted out the parts of her life that really were gold.

She had been paid well, her entire life, to pursue her passion. She had made her decisions, and she didn't regret where they'd brought her. But she had never been the best.

Something came to her then, and she wondered how she could

explain it to Fiona. She began by, as imperceptibly as she was able, removing the Post-it from her computer screen: she didn't want to have to explain to the therapist why it was important to see herself describing this, but she knew it was. She couldn't restrain herself from touching her cheekbone gently. There it was, even with her expression slack; she still had that.

She needed to get Fiona to understand that there was a performance she was proud of, and it had already been more widely viewed than *The Diva* would ever be; it would live online for any amateur historian more interested in awards than in art to find and dissect.

Jenny had gone into the evening believing that she had as good a chance as anyone, a better one, that she might win, that she would: Hadn't she finally made the kind of movie that they wanted an older actress to humble herself with? Hadn't she done enough—allowed them to make her use another voice, not her own? Hadn't she subjected herself to the press, given appropriate and tasteful speeches, saved one essential piece of herself to give them at the final pageant?

She knew somewhere inside herself, somewhere that she could be honest about the things that were real and the things that were rivalrous, that Contessa wouldn't win, she wasn't ready. And Davina . . . it just wasn't plausible, though she certainly was known now for things beyond being the witch from TV. And, even before she saw her falling over herself at the after-party, she had hoped, for the girl's sake, that Bitty wouldn't get it: a thing like this could be wonderful, could make a career, or could be the moment that things turned. Jenny was willing to admit that she'd gotten a share of public sympathy by being personally winning as she lost, and that seemed a clearer path for Bitty than burning any brighter, any faster, than she already was.

But as the envelope was opened, even before the presenter's sharp intake of breath, Jenny knew, knew from a place somewhere past reason and a place that she had learned to trust, that it was Adria's prize. That Adria would get to thank her daughter, the woman who would later hold her trophy as Adria walked into the after-party—who had to carry that weight for her mother. Knew that this would mean something Jenny could never understand.

And she had known, beyond knowing, what she needed to do, for Adria and for herself. Jenny would never be in this audience again—she had come begging, and they hadn't found it enough. It hadn't fit. It wasn't the way she wanted to see herself, the way that she had earned the right to be, after so many years of trying, sometimes failing, to applaud others. She would find a new way to work.

That new way would begin tonight, she thought. Begin with the six syllables Jenny had been expecting for two and a half seconds of utter electric connection to the moment. Her reaction would be on tape forever, and Jenny would give them a show. Her plan going into the evening had been to win, to say all the words she'd wanted to for so long about what art meant to her, the stories that cherished collaborators had allowed her to tell, but in a flash she worked up a different kind of narrative.

At the "A" that began the winner's first name, as soon as the record broke, Jenny would burst into the gladdest smile, for the history being made and the woman being rewarded, and the fact of Jenny's ability to raise other women in their triumphs, and in so doing getting to share in it, have a piece of it to take with her. That would be enough for the weeks afterward when the phone wouldn't ring, after she'd told her neighbor that she could handle things herself, so that it could once again just be her and Fiona and the chickens.

And at the second "a" of "Adria," the tricky turn when the audience was processing exactly who had come from behind and taken Bitty's emergence, or Contessa's coronation, or Davina's breakthrough, or Jenny's own long-awaited victory, Jenny would be the first to stand. They might call it performative, or silly, or dramatic, but it was what it would take to force herself, for the evening and for a moment, beyond today, when her feelings had settled, to believe that this was the way things were meant to be. That there was a beauty in it. Jenny knew that then.

"There's something I really am proud of," Jenny said, dabbing her eye, overcoming, beginning to. "It's the role I got to play. For her. For Adria."

She began to describe to Fiona, in whatever time she had before the window closed and she was left to contemplate what art she would make with the rest of her life, that she had done it. Jenny had known, as soon as she realized Adria would win, that she would need to be the champion of her own private battle.

And in the moments before the cameras turned elsewhere, the moments when all the masses wanted was something at the farthest boundary of her capacity to give, she would shine. For a corner of this night that belonged to another, she would be something more than Jenny Van Meer, something better. Something transcendent. She would find it: a way to be joyful, as radiant as the sun. A star.

Acknowledgments

Jessica Spitz at Janklow & Nesbit, a creative, curious, and thoughtful agent, is the reason this book exists; thank you, JJ. Taylor Rondestvedt at Gallery Books and Scout Press refined and clarified my manuscript into a book, with a canny sensibility and an astute sense of how these women would be perceived in the public eye; thank you, Taylor.

At Gallery, this book and its author were ably supported by Jennifer Bergstrom, Aimée Bell, Alison Callahan, Caroline Pallotta, John Paul Jones, Kate Kenney-Peterson, Sydney Morris, and Sophie Normil; Lisa Litwack designed the striking cover. Thank you to Beowulf Sheehan, who captured the portrait on the book jacket, for seeing me, and to Jeska Sand for invaluable assistance on the shoot.

Orly Greenberg and Mirabel Michelson at UTA believed in this story, and Lee Daniels and Ken Segna at Lee Daniels Entertainment and 20th Television showed inspiring and enthusiastic support. All have my sincere gratitude.

This book was written in large part in various locations of the Work Heights coworking space in central Brooklyn. Thanks to Sam Strauss-Malcolm and to the community there for providing a calm, consistent place to write. I am also appreciative of the workers at businesses where this book continued to take shape: the Crown Inn (with a glass raised in particular to Zhenya Kampanets) and Anything Bar in Brooklyn; the Mondrian Los Angeles; and the West Hollywood location of SoulCycle.

I have been shaped by colleagues past and present. Thank you to Kelly Conniff, Radhika Jones, Sam Lansky, Elizabeth Spiers, Kat Stoeffel, and Matt Vella for teaching me to think like a journalist. And thanks to the team at *Variety*—including Jay Penske, Dea Lawrence, Michelle Sobrino-Stearns, Donna Pennestri, Cynthia Littleton, Brent Lang, Trish Deitch, Rachel Seo, and my trusted and painstaking editor Kate Aurthur—for providing a home for my work and for your trust in the stories I can tell. Special thanks is owed to Ramin Setoodeh for his encouragement and belief in my work.

Many friends provided encouragement, counsel, and cheer as I wrote. Bobby Finger, Nash Jenkins, Richard Lawson, Andrew Lipstein, Patrick Sullivan, Lucy Tang, and Ed Wasserman gave crucial early support. Thanks to Rumaan Alam, John Blair, Sarah Blakley-Cartwright, Brian Burns, Hillary Busis, Marisa Carroll, George Civeris, Ellen Cushing, Amanda Dobbins, Daniel Drake, Leah Finnegan, Kate Flynn, Michael Goldsmith, Selome Hailu, Alison Herman, Fran Hoepfner, Jamie Johns, Christian Kamongi, Peter Kispert, Zack Knoll, Daniel Lefferts, Lindsay Long-Waldor, Liam Lowery, Bennett Madison, Frances McGrath, Brian Montopoli, Nicholas and Molly O'Brien, Julia Phillips, Steven Phillips-Horst, Noam Prywes, Jordan Richmond, John Ross, Roko Rumora, Lindsay Griffith Shapiro, Julie Slotnick, Alexandria Symonds, Myles Tanzer, Jeremy Todd, Mike Vilensky, Lindsey Weber, and Daniel Wenger. I am especially grateful to Paul Danilack—over busy, challenging, and productive years, you have helped me to stay creative and to stay focused.

Thank you to my parents, Peter and Susan D'Addario, for everything. And love to my daughters, Cleo and Iris, for still more—not least the hope both of you provide by performing only as your brilliant selves. (Now go to bed!)

Finally, the greatest portion of my gratitude goes to Jacob Schneider, for creating the conditions under which this book could be written, and for diving, dauntless—and often sleepless—into the astonishing experience of our lives together. I reserve my highest possible praise for you: What we share is better than any movie.

About the Author

Daniel D'Addario is chief correspondent at *Variety*. He has won awards from the Los Angeles Press Club for profile writing and for political commentary and is among the moderators of *Variety*'s Actors on Actors video series. He was previously the television critic for *Variety* and for *Time*. A graduate of Columbia University, he lives with his husband and two daughters in Brooklyn.